An award-winning novelist and film writer/producer, Andrew J. Fenady has received critical acclaim for a wide variety of work. He has written and produced dozens of movies, including *Chisum* starring John Wayne and *The Sea Wolf* starring Charles Bronson. For television, he created the classic series *The Rebel* and *Hondo*. He received an Edgar Award from the Mystery Writers of America and the Golden Boot Award for career achievement in Western movies. His novels include *Runaways*; *The Man With Bogart's Face*; *The Secrets of Sam Marlow*; *Mulligan*; and *Claws of the Eagle*, a fictional account of Tom Horn and the Apache Kid, which was praised by *Bookmarks* as "notably superior . . . a powerful story." Fenady lives in Los Angeles, California, with his family.

THE REBEL
JOHNNY YUMA

Andrew J. Fenady

BERKLEY BOOKS, NEW YORK

THE REBEL: JOHNNY YUMA

A Berkley Book / published by arrangement with
the author

PRINTING HISTORY
Berkley edition / October 1998

The Penguin Putnam Inc. World Wide Web site address is
http://www.penguinputnam.com

ISBN: 0-425-16579-5

PRINTED IN THE UNITED STATES OF AMERICA

10 9 8 7 6 5 4 3 2 1

for NICK ADAMS
    A Rebel
    who heard the cry of Angels
    too soon

and MARY FRANCES
    A Lady
    who only hears the Angels
    sing

ONE

This probably will be the last entry. I am writing by first light—Saturday, April 8, 1865. We have been ordered to attack, secure, and hold the bridge at Three Forks. If this journal is found, please try to get it to my father, Sheriff Ned Yuma, in Mason City. I am with . . .

Sniper fire. Two rapid shots. Then a third and fourth whipped by, inches above the Confederate contingent dug in near the southern bank of the Little Dirty.

"Keep your heads down!" Lieutenant Cane snapped.

"If that's an order, sir, I am happy to obey and oblige." The voice belonged to Private Danny Reese of General Robert E. Lee's Army of Northern Virginia.

Danny smiled from out of the receding darkness and winked at the Reb next to him, Corporal Johnny Yuma.

Yuma almost smiled back and tucked the diary into his tunic. Johnny Yuma and Danny Reese had met a little less than two years ago in the Yankee prison at Rock Island.

If Andersonville was the hell of the Confederacy, then Rock Island was the purgatory of the North. For months

Yuma and Reese shared meager rations of bread, beans, and tobacco. Johnny Yuma had never smoked before, but he smoked at Rock Island. The tobacco dulled his appetite. And Yuma, like the other prisoners, was always hungry and, unlike Danny Reese, always serious. Yuma was most serious about escape, and finally they did, the two of them, surviving the icy waters near Sault Sainte Marie.

Together, Yuma and Reese made their way south as far as Freeport, Illinois, then separated, figuring they had twice the chance split up as they had together.

Danny Reese, who wore a perpetual smile, even in the purgatory of Rock Island, grinned as they separated.

"Johnny, if you get to heaven before I do, just bore a hole and pull me through." He slapped Yuma on the shoulder and disappeared through the bramble, heading southeast.

Johnny Yuma made his way due south along the course of the Mississippi to Vicksburg, where he intended to rejoin his brigade, the Third Texas. But there was no longer a Third Texas. After suffering overwhelming losses inflicted by U. S. Grant's Army of the Tennessee, the Third was broken up and survivors, few as they were, were attached to other regiments.

Yuma had managed to stay ahead of Sherman's blue bellies on their march toward the sea. In late summer of '64, Johnny Yuma hooked up with General Jubal A. Early at Cold Harbor.

Jubal Anderson Early, a Virginian, graduate of West Point, Indian fighter against the Seminoles in Florida, and veteran of the Mexican Campaign, had voted against secession at the Virginia Convention in April 1861. But when war broke out, he accepted a commission as a colonel in the Virginia troops. He won victories and promotions at

Salem Church in the Wilderness Campaign and defeated Lew Wallace in the Battle of Monacy.

Johnny Yuma was with General Early at Cedar Creek, where what was left of Early's small force was overwhelmed and broken by General George Custer of Sheridan's Army.

After that, Corporal Johnny Yuma became an infantryman in a battalion of General Robert E. Lee's Army of Northern Virginia. As casualties mounted and survivors dwindled, the battalion was reduced to a company, then little more than a platoon under the command of Lieutenant Clayton Cane, with orders this Saturday dawn of April 8, 1865, to attack, secure, and hold the bridge across the Little Dirty at Three Forks, Virginia.

The last months had held mostly defeats for the ragged Confederates, and Johnny Yuma suffered those defeats along with his comrades, but he had survived in spite of twice inflicted wounds, once from a sniper and again in hand-to-hand combat at Falls Church. The wounds had healed. He was lucky to be alive, and he was lucky in two other respects.

First, he had met up again with Danny Reese, who was beside him now, and he had met Douglas Baines, who was also dug in next to him on the other side. Baines had saved Johnny Yuma's life at Falls Church, when a Yankee sergeant was about to squeeze the trigger as Yuma, disarmed, wrestled the enemy on the ground. Baines's bayonet struck the sergeant, who died while Johnny Yuma went on living. Until now.

Baines, a farmer from bleeding Kansas, was only a few years older than Yuma and Reese, but he became almost a father to both young Rebels in the fading cause of the Confederacy. Every night when there was light to see by, Douglas Baines would read softly from his Bible while Johnny,

Danny, and the rest listened. When there was no light, Baines would recite a passage or two from memory. Last night, there was no light. No campfires were allowed. Baines spoke softly. Words from Psalm 91:

> *He shall cover thee . . . and under his wings shalt*
> *thou trust; his torch will be thy shield and buckler,*
> *Thou shalt not be afraid for the terror by night;*
> *nor for the arrow that flieth by day,*
> *A thousand shall fall at thy side, and ten thousand*
> *at thy right hand; but it shall not come nigh thee.*
> *He shall raise you up on eagle's wings.*

"Amen, brother," Danny Reese had added.

And now, the three of them together, along with the others, waited for the order from Lieutenant Cane. The certain outcome, no matter which side took the bridge, would be more casualties.

The only uncertainty was who would live and who would die.

Night's sorry blue faded into a yellowish dawn creased by the crack, crack of intermittent sniper fire.

The Rebels looked toward Lieutenant Cane and waited for his command. Cane had no resemblance to a fighting officer; his appearance was more like the bookish schoolteacher he had been.

Tall and thin, with an overlarge brow, an unsoldierly stoop, still, he had proved to his men that he was a soldier and a leader. Twice in the last month he had led them against superior forces. They had followed him into hell and victory.

Cane had taught high school English and literature until there was no one left to teach, and then he finally prevailed upon the Confederacy to accept him in spite of his diseased lung. He knew from the beginning that the Confederacy was doomed but that there would be one last stand, a remembered battle, and most probably, Robert E. Lee would be there. Clayton Cane wanted to be there, too, despite the fact that he abhorred slavery. He loved Virginia.

Now, he realized that no one would remember the battle for this bridge. And Robert E. Lee was nowhere in sight.

But Lieutenant Cane had his orders. He would follow them—and his men would follow him, the ones who were still alive, who were once so skeptical of Cane. The rope-thin schoolteacher had replaced Dion O'Brien, a barrel-chested, heavy shouldered, hard-hitting Irishman who could lick any man in the regiment but not a six-ounce minié ball that went through his heart.

After that first charge led by Lieutenant Cane, one of the men asked why the frail officer seemed so unafraid. Cane quoted a few lines from one of Shakespeare's plays:

> *It seems to me most strange that men should fear,*
> *Knowing that death, a necessary end, will come when it will*
>   *come.*
> *A coward dies many times.*
> *The valiant never taste of death but once.*

Yes, they would follow him, even though they knew that many of them would taste of death that April morning.

The Little Dirty was barely more than a creek, less than thirty yards across and no more than waist deep. Trying to wade across, the Rebels would be easy targets. The only chance, slight at best, was a charge onto and across the wooden bridge to the other side.

And now from the other side came the Yankee taunts, along with sporadic rifle shots.

"Hey, you Rebs. You gonna have no more breakfasts!"

"Rebs! You want this bridge? Come and get it!"

"You're finished, Rebs!"

"We're gonna hang Lee!"

"And Jefferson Crowface Davis!"

"We're gonna hang 'em both from the same tree!"

Shots.

And more taunts.

"You're gonna have to pick your own cotton!"

"If you live!"

"But you ain't gonna!"

"We'll play taps over you, Rebs! All of you!"

Shots.

"What're you waiting for, Lieutenant?" One of the Rebs said. "Give the order. Let's get it over with!"

"Quiet! The order is to wait a half hour after dawn. Wait for reinforcements. If they don't come by then, I'll give the order, all right."

"How much longer?" the same man asked.

"Ten minutes."

More bullets whistled among the branches and nipped the trees. The Little Dirty became amber-tinted with sunlight. The Rebs tried to keep hidden from everything but sky.

"Hey, Rebs! This is Bart Vogan! Come ahead! I'll take you on. Just me and my little ol' Yankee slingshot. Lookee here! I'm standing tall! All in blue!"

Danny Reese raised his rifle and his head just enough to take a shot.

He took it. Simultaneously, another shot rang out.

Danny Reese fell on his back in the mud. Johnny Yuma bent down and grabbed Danny by both shoulders.

He was being looked at by a dead man, eyes still open, a black hole in his brow, and for the first time, there was no smile on Danny Reese's face.

Johnny Yuma looked into the vacant eyes for only a second, but for that second, he, too, was dead, drained of mortality, suspended in eternity, without future, without purpose, without feeling—but for only a second. Johnny Yuma had seen other men die, friends and foes—and women, too: nurses in the field blown apart by the bursting blossom of cannon. And he had waited and watched as his mother died in the bed of his father and mother while he was too young to really understand and while his father, wearing a badge and gun, was away killing someone who had killed someone else.

But seeing, touching, and realizing the death of Danny Reese was like nothing that had ever happened before. Nobody wants to die. Every living thing wants to go on living. Nobody was better suited to go on living than Danny Reese. When Johnny Yuma's despair had reached its lowest depth at Rock Island, it was Danny Reese's unconquerable spirit, eternal optimism, and sunny face that kept Yuma going. And now the sun had set on that face. There would be no more smile—except for the grave's eternal smile which creases every skull.

All this in one suspended second, and then every fiber and feeling in the body and soul of Johnny Yuma was consumed by a single emotion.

Hate.

The voice came again across the sun-splattered stream.

"Hey, you, Rebs! There's one less of you now! Vogan! Bart Vogan's the name, Sharpshootin's my game! Ohio Volunteers! Who's next?"

Hate: a wild, chaotic hate. A black hate for a man whose face he had never seen. A name he would never forget. Vogan. Bart Vogan. Yankee. Sharpshooter. Killer. And war or no war, murderer.

In that instant, the barking sound of cannon, or so

thought Johnny Yuma and the other Rebs, but only for an instant.

The dawning sun suddenly seemed covered by a purple sheet. Lightning, then thunder, tore that sheet and an April storm exploded out of the sky, pouring into the stream and onto the soldiers now lying in muddy rivulets.

"Follow me!" Cane cried.

Johnny Yuma looked up from the corpse of Danny Reese to the face of Douglas Baines, whose lips were moving. Curse or prayer, Yuma could not hear, but they all heard Cane's command.

"Charge! Follow me, you valiant Rebs! Valiant Rebels, follow me!"

The rain poured down, as if to wash away the blood that would be shed. A crooked sword of lightning struck the sky, and thunder reverberated like a hundred drums.

And then—the Rebel yell!

It erupted from the throat of a single soldier, and then became a screaming whirlwind, a challenging chorus, searing screams, each outscreaming the other. A terrifying torrent—ghostly, ghastly—a rebellion against reality, reason; a call to annihilation.

Johnny Yuma tore through his comrades. He would be the first to cross the bridge—or die. Consumed with burning hate. Propelled by rage for revenge. His brain echoing the rasping voice, *"Bart Vogan's the name... Bart Vogan's the name... Bart Vogan's the name... Bart Vogan's the name..."* Like the screeching whistle of a speeding train... Yuma charged, elbowed and stumbled past the churning gray tide.

"Bart Vogan, you bastard! Where are you?" He yelled with all his fury, but his yell was buried in the ringing rifle fire, the clash of wet steel, the screams of zeal, and the tumult of agony and dying.

The bridge over the Little Dirty became Hell's own

bridge across the Styx. Wet with rain and blood, blood bursting from tunics of blue and gray. Rifles and swords, pistols and bayonets, hand to hammering hand.

The Yanks had risen out of the brush and mud of the northern bank, their dirty blue uniforms steaming from the sun and rain. The Billy Yanks clashed against the screaming, rampaging, valiant Johnny Rebs, fighting and clawing for every yard and foot and inch of a nameless bridge, as if the war and their lives depended on it.

The war did not, but their lives did.

As hard as Johnny Yuma fought through his own ranks and tried to be the first to reach the enemy, he failed.

Lieutenant Clayton Cane was first, and he was among the first to fall. The shot tore into his throat. He spun with a final grunt and slammed into Johnny Yuma, who held him dead for just a moment, then let him drop.

"Bart Vogan, you craven bastard! Here I am!"

But the challenge went unheeded and unheard. It was impossible to distinguish any single voice out of the thunder and gunfire, the turn and tangle of bodies: bent, broken, and bleeding, cursing and screaming their frenzy and fury through the morning nightmare from which many would not wake.

Johnny Yuma let his empty rifle drop and drew his side arm, firing into the chest of a Yankee corporal, a lad his own age and rank. Yuma hoped the name was Vogan, Bart Vogan. They were all Bart Vogans, and he fired again and again. Yuma caught a glimpse of Doug Baines and thought he saw him fall.

And then, above the din of battle, a slight rending sound—a bugle, bugles. The Rebels caught sight of a mounted column splashing through the stream, men in soaked gray uniforms, firing. But something was wrong. The guns and rifles were pointed in the air, and it was not a single line but twin columns. The other column was wearing blue and the bugles were sounding "Recall."

Battle guidons slanting forward, field trumpets now closer and louder—

"Recall"

And the voices of both captains leading the columns, advancing side by side.

"Cease fire! Cease fire!" Came the command again.

Those who had fallen and were able, rose slowly, carefully, still dazed and bleeding, but alive. One of those who rose with blood leaking into his eyes was Baines. He made his way toward Yuma. Instinctively, the Yankees slowly gravitated together, just a little closer to the northern section of the bridge and the Rebels closer to the south, as both captains shouted, "Regroup, men! Regroup!"

"Armistice!" The Yankee captain shrieked as he reined his animal to a stop a few feet from the bridge.

"Truce!" The Rebel captain confirmed and reined up next to the Yank.

"Men," the Yankee captain went on, "Generals Grant and Lee are meeting tomorrow. Until then, all activities, all hostilities are suspended!"

Soldiers on the bridge, soldiers on both sides, looked at each other and murmured. The reality still had not sunk into most of them.

"You men of the Ohio Volunteers are to fall back and follow me to Three Forks," the Yankee captain ordered.

"What do we do, Captain?" One of the Rebs shouted.

"Your orders are to return with me to Appomattox Court House and wait."

"For what?" The voice was Johnny Yuma's.

"For Lee and Grant," the Confederate captain replied.

The rain abated. There was no more lightning or thunder. What remained of the Confederate infantry regrouped with the Confederate cavalry column on the south bank of the bridge.

Johnny Yuma approached the captain, who had not dismounted.

"Sir."

"What is it, Corporal?"

"May I have permission to look after a friend of mine who was hit?"

"Wounded?"

"Killed."

"He'll be looked after, Corporal. By a burial detail."

"But . . ."

"That's all, Corporal. Your orders are to return to Appomattox Court House with us, now."

"Sir, General Lee's not going to surrender, is he?" Johnny Yuma asked.

"Corporal, General Lee does not confide in captains. And captains do not confer with corporals."

"Yes, sir."

Johnny Yuma did not move.

"Is there something else, Corporal?"

"Just one thing, sir."

"What?"

"We would have taken that bridge."

"I know that, Corporal." The captain turned his mount and moved south.

Doug Baines's hand touched Johnny Yuma's shoulder. "Johnny, you all right?"

"Yeah. What about you?"

"Just a knock on the head. Nothin' to speak of."

Yuma turned and faced the opposite bank of the Little Dirty, where the Yankee forces were retreating.

"I hope he got his," Johnny Yuma said.

"Who?"

"Bart Vogan."

TWO

Palm Sunday. April 9. A nation divided and bleeding. A nation less than a hundred years old. A nation whose sixteenth president, a man who wanted peace, but who led his country into a bloodbath of battle after battle, burying thousands upon thousands of sons and fathers and brothers. And there were thousands more whose limbs were torn and maimed, survivors who would never be the same in body, mind, or spirit.

The battles on land and sea, in fields and streams, in cities and swamps—conquests and defeats—on horseback and foot, all the dynamite and destruction, fire and devastation—all led to the inevitable end:

Appomattox.

Wilmer McLean had been forced to move twice. First from Manassas Junction where the war's first fierce battle had occurred in 1861, then again during the Second Battle of Bull Run. He settled in the quiet little community of Appomattox Court House, and that is where the conflict would be settled.

Appomattox.

An unreal quiet prevailed outside McLean's house that fateful Sunday. The sky remained melancholy from the recent rain, the ground still April soft.

April. The time of rebirth. Of aspiring life. With spring rain bathing newborn birds and chasing the chill winds of winter. April. The time of seedling hope. Of budding promise.

April at Appomattox. The time for burying yesterday's casualties. The time to pause. The time to listen to the silence of the machinery of war—and wait for the rebirth of a nation.

Outside of McLean's house they waited, some of the remnants of General Robert E. Lee's Army of Northern Virginia.

One Confederate soldier stood in front of the steps leading to the porch of McLean's house. The soldier's uniform was dirty and worn, and in the area of the left shoulder there was a wound, slight, but with a crusted crimson. With his right hand, the soldier held the reins of a magnificent white steed.

Most of the rest stood with a weary rigidness, looking toward the north. But there were two others in the nearby barn: Johnny Yuma and Douglas Baines. Baines sat on a stool, rubbing his forehead. Yuma paced and spoke with a hushed nervousness.

"Doug, we can't let it happen. . . ."

"Let what happen?"

"The surrender."

"Johnny . . ."

"It's got to be stopped."

"Johnny, your saddle's slippin'. You're off your feed. . . ."

"I'm telling you . . ."

"You think you, a little ol' nubbin' of a corporal, is

going to tell General Robert E. Lee what to do? It's all over, son!"

"Not yet, it's not."

Baines rose from the stool and faced Yuma.

"Well, it will be and, thank God, in a matter of minutes. No more fear and death every morning. Pretty soon, old fuzzy face Grant and his staff'll ride up to McLean's house outside, and Lee'll sign a piece of paper and give him a tin sword and we can go home, son."

"To what?"

"I'll tell you . . ."

"No, I'll tell you. To boot lickin' shame and sufferin'."

"To life! To my Cora and little Jimmy."

"Not me."

"Well, then," Baines turned away and walked two steps, "you stay and keep playing soljer."

Yuma advanced, grabbed the man, and whirled him so they were face-to-face. "Don't you fun me, paperback! I fought every day you fought. . . ."

"Did you fight as much as Stone Jackson and Jeb Stuart? Hill and Pender? And Rhodes? They're all dead . . . and most of their soljer boys with 'em!"

"Sure they are, all dead. And if we give up now, what'd they all die for? What?"

"Sometimes you lose."

"Well, not yet."

"Yes, yet! Now! Lost! Listen to me. I ain't no general, but I know somethin'. Two weeks ago, Gordon had seventy-five hundred men. Now there's less than two thousand, all starved. You listenin'?"

"I'm listening," Johnny Yuma answered.

"Field's got more men absent than present! All that's left of Pickett's whole army is sixty bone-beaten men! Now, what do you expect to fight with?"

"So long as I got a gun, I fight!"

"Johnny . . ."

"If I didn't, I'd be untrue to those screamin' Rebs I charged with at Cedar Creek and Cold Harbor. We vowed together that we'd fight until we were all dead if we had to—and then our ghosts 'ud go right on fighting!"

"Yeah, well that's about all we got left is a phantom army. And as far as I'm concerned, Grant's welcome to the leavin's."

"Grant!" Yuma grunted out the name. "Grant! That hogback blisterface! That craven drunk, no good blue belly! I can see him strutting up to General Lee trying to make him grovel—humiliating a saint—beating him over the head with the bones of the Confederacy!"

"There's nothin' to be done about it, son, so you'd just better be content to witness some history this here Palm Sunday."

"Witness?" Johnny Yuma drew the side arm from its holster. "Witness? I'm gonna make it—and alone if you're not a mind to help. . . ."

"Johnny . . . What you nurturin' in that hot Texas head of yours?"

Johnny Yuma took a couple of steps toward the door of the barn, then turned back, still gripping the gun in his hand.

"I've been in McLean's house this morning."

"So?"

"So right now General Lee's sitting in the parlor. I'm climbing around back to a room right over that parlor. A room with a vent. It's there, all right. I've laid it all out, and when Grant walks in that room, he's going to run straight into a head full of lead."

"You're fevered!"

"I sure am. If a Southerner kills Grant, there'll be no

peace. We'll have to keep fighting. And you'll see, we'll win."

Doug Baines leaped at Yuma, grabbed him, and tried to get the gun away.

"No, I won't see, you young owl head. Give me that . . ."

Yuma smashed his left fist into Baines's jaw, and as Baines started to fall, lifted the gun to hit him with the barrel but realized that it would not be necessary. Baines was unconscious as he fell to the floor.

Johnny Yuma looked around. He spotted a length of rope across one of the stalls. He walked over, holstered the gun, took the rope, and started to tie up the unconscious soldier lying on the floor.

"I'm sorry ol' Doug. But now you know, and I got to make sure you don't spoil it. Four years is nothing. We'll fight forty. And we'll win without them having Grant."

THREE

General Ulysses Simpson Grant, mounted on his black stallion Cincinnati and accompanied by several of his general officers, rode into the clearing where another detachment was mounted and waiting.

Grant's face and uniform were used up and dirty. His eyes told of tired victory and inconsolable sadness. The stub of an unlit cigar stemmed from his thin, creased lips.

"Sheridan!" Grant waved and rode closer. General Philip Henry Sheridan nodded and faintly smiled as Grant approached. Sheridan's uniform was not in much better shape than Grant's. He was a man with penetrating dark eyes, the largest part of his head forward of his ears. A combative man, restless of spirit, not politic in language. His Black-Irish bloodlines were evident in his long, mobile face. He had the reputation of being sharp and peppery, a self-reliant man of courage and decision.

Sheridan was born in Albany, New York, graduated from West Point in 1853, ranked as captain at the outbreak of the Civil War, and by this day, as he waited for Grant, held the rank of major general. He had fought at Chickamauga, commanded cavalry of the Army of the Potomac, campaigned at the Wilderness, Spotsylvania, and Cold Harbor, destroyed Confederate communication lines at Richmond, commanded the Army of the Shenandoah, and laid waste to that great valley. He made rubble of the principal towns: Winchester, Front Royal, Laury, Staunton, Waynesboro, and Lexington.

In his report, Sheridan had stated, "Even a crow flying over the Shenandoah would have to bring his rations with him." General Philip Henry Sheridan was not prone to exaggeration.

"Phil, you made good time. But then," Grant added, "you have right along. How are you?"

"First rate, sir."

"Been waiting long?" Grant's voice was raspy and dry.

"Not too long . . . not for this."

"Lynchburg?" Grant inquired.

"All gone our way."

"Good. I wanted you along for this."

"Thank you. I hear you've been feeling poorly."

"Phil, I had the damnedest headache . . . for near a week now." He looked at the butt of the cigar he had taken from his mouth. "Pain so fierce it hurt to open my eyes. Hurt worse to close them. No sleep. Couldn't eat. But after I got Lee's letter . . . there was no more pain."

"Was a long time coming. Don't know how they held out this long."

"I do. Lee . . . Where is he?"

"At the McLean House, just down the way."

"Well, then." Grant nodded. "Let's go over and see him."

The road to Appomattox was less than a mile away and level all the way. But the road that Ulysses Simpson Grant had traveled to get this far was uphill: twisted and strewn with disappointment, danger, drink, disillusionment, depression, and death.

But no road was traveled by a man with more determination, guts, and endeavor.

After putting his faith in nearly a dozen generals, including McDowell, McClellan, Lyon, Scott, Fremont, Halleck, Hooker, and Meade, President and Commander in Chief Abraham Lincoln had to discard or demote them all.

Lincoln finally found his general in chief, a man who just a few years before had been tossed on the ash heap of life and was considered by friends and even family a flat-out failure by the age of forty.

Born in Point Pleasant, Ohio, on April 27, 1822, as Hiram Ulysses Grant, he grew to be a strong, healthy, go-ahead little fellow with a great regard for the outdoors and horses and a disinclination toward study and schools. Still, he was accepted at West Point where his congressman had entered him as Ulysses Simpson Grant. He liked the ring of it—U. S. Grant—and kept it for the rest of his military and civilian life.

He was once quoted as saying that he "graduated at the top of my class—if you turned the class upside down," which was not quite true but close. One achievement few could dispute: U. S. Grant was the best horseman in his or any other class at West Point, with the possible exception of George Armstrong Custer a few years later.

Lieutenant Grant served with distinction and valor in the Mexican War in 1846 under the command of General Zachary Taylor. He was at the front of the charge at Buena Vista, led by a colonel named Jefferson Davis, along with other comrades, including young West Point graduates such as Robert E. Lee and George McClellen. Grant fought at Monterrey and at the fall of Vera Cruz and marched with General Winfield Scott into Mexico City.

After the Mexican Campaign, Captain Grant married Julia Dent. Never before or since had Grant been with another woman. But he was sent to a remote outpost in California without her. That was the beginning of his heavy drinking and led to the end of his military career—until a few years later.

Meanwhile, though Julia stuck with him, he failed in every business endeavor he could lay his hands on, including farming a piece of land he appropriately named Hard Scrabble, real estate, and even store keeping.

Grant reentered military service at the outbreak of the Civil War as a colonel of an Illinois volunteer regiment. In August 1861, he was appointed brigadier general and found his destiny—or destiny found him.

There was no more tenacious, aggressive, defiant, and determined officer in the history of warfare. He never hesitated or faltered, no matter the cost—and the cost was terrible to the North but worse to the enemy. He never shied from personal danger, and his men loved him because, inevitably, he led them to victory—at Fort Henry, Fort Donaldson, at Shiloh, and at the siege of Vicksburg where he divided the Confederacy in two. Grant stormed Lookout Mountain, Missionary Ridge, and Chattanooga. He took command of the Army of the Potomac and dogged Robert E. Lee's Army of Northern Virginia, culminating in the Battle of the Wilderness. Lee's Army never recovered, and finally, Richmond fell. The U. S. in Grant came to stand for Unconditional Surrender on the part of the enemy.

Sheridan, Grant's right arm, routed the Confederate defenders at Five Forks and wiped out Pickett's column, capturing more than five thousand Rebels. On April 8, Sheridan reached Appomattox Station, cutting off Lee's retreat.

Lee's men, hungry and worn out, stayed with the colors

only because of their unshakable confidence and love for Lee himself. But Lee realized that confidence and love were not enough, no match for the overwhelming numbers, strength, and power of Grant's army. And so Lee had sent, out of his thin lines, a Confederate horseman with white flag fluttering.

And now, U. S. Grant was on the road to Appomattox, where Lee waited.

But at Appomattox someone else was waiting. Waiting with a loaded revolver for Ulysses Simpson Grant.

Someone named Johnny Yuma.

FOUR

Johnny Yuma had bound Douglas Baines and dragged him out of sight into one of the stalls. For extra good measure, Yuma had piled straw on top of his unconscious friend and comrade. The young corporal could barely keep his hands from trembling.

At first, it had been a wild notion he had thrown out at Baines without even thinking, something said in a mad moment, something so unlikely, so impossible, so daring as to be dismissed with the passing of that moment of madness.

But Johnny Yuma would not let it pass. He would not dismiss it or let it be dismissed. He, a lowly corporal, would change the course of history, even though the odds were that he would not live to see the change. The odds were that he would be dead. But he had faced death many times before for lesser reasons: for a hill, a barn, a bridge; for no good reason except that he was a soldier and a soldier followed orders.

This time he would not follow.

This time he would lead—lead the Confederacy to a new day, a new chapter, a new beginning. He had felt hate for the enemy—all the enemies who took the lives of the men who fought beside him, the lives of his fellow Texans, the sons of the South, from Mississippi, Alabama, Georgia, South Carolina, Virginia and all the rest who followed the stars and bars.

Still, if he had met those young enemies at other times and at other places, without uniforms, without weapons, the chances were that they would work and laugh, play cards and drink together. They would stand together and fight a foreign enemy as did their fathers and grandfathers before them.

But war had come. A war he never really understood, but a war that had torn him away from Texas, across the Red River and the Mississippi, him and thousands of other young men like him. A war that drained the life out of Texas and drained the blood out of thousands of other Texans. A war that was being waged and won under the leadership of a great general. A general who outfought and outmaneuvered everyone and everything the enemy could throw against him.

Until—

Until U.S. Grant, who was not just interested in taking Confederate territory, but more interested in taking Confederate lives. Grant knew he could sacrifice more soldiers than could the South. And sacrifice he did. The capture of strategic points and occupation of Southern territory were secondary. Grant's primary objective was the destruction of the Southern army. The only way to destroy that army was to kill. And kill he did.

And now Johnny Yuma would kill Grant, even if he had to sacrifice his own life in the killing.

Maybe that sacrifice would spark a new flame, a new fire for those comrades he would leave behind, and maybe the South would reap a second glory.

But no matter what else happened, General Ulysses Simpson Grant would not live to see it.

Grant would be dead.

Yuma took a long, deep breath. He looked at both his hands and silently commanded them to stop shaking. They ignored the command.

He took another deep breath, opened the barn door, went out, and closed the door behind him.

Yuma tried not to look at any of the other soldiers, not to meet their eyes. Few were talking to each other. Most stood silently waiting. The few who said anything to the other men spoke in whispers.

Yuma did not want to be whispered to or even noticed. He would not be one of those who waited.

He made his way from the area of the barn toward the side and then the rear of the McLean house. It was a two story redbrick structure fronted by a porch with four square columns. The porch also had a second story; both stories were bordered by wooden railings painted white. Cedar and maple trees, April green, rimmed the house on all sides. Soldiers stood under the shade of the trees and in front of the porch. Their uniforms bespoke of time, travel, and defeat. There were no smiles; the faces were grim, and there were tears.

Yuma barely glanced at the soldier holding the reins of the white horse, then moved on. There was no one at the rear of the house. Johnny Yuma went to a trellis, took a final look around, and began to climb.

The latticework was covered with vines, slippery, and not meant to support human weight. Slowly he made his way upward, step by tentative step. Four feet upward. Five, six. He reached the second story, then stopped, frozen by a sound.

A bell tolled in the village. A church bell. Of course. It

was Sunday. Palm Sunday, at that. Church bells were
sounding in all the villages. In all Virginia. In all the cities
in all the states. North and South. In all the country. In all
the countries all over the world. Bells were tolling.

On the grounds below, a dog barked. For a terrifying
second, Johnny Yuma thought the dog was barking at him.
But no, the dog was not in sight. Still, in Johnny Yuma's
mind, every sound was magnified. The dog barked again.
Dogs don't know it's Sunday, thought Johnny Yuma.
Sometimes soldiers don't know either. There were times in
the past years when he didn't know what day it was, or
care. Calendars didn't count. The machinery of war went
on seven days a week, day and night.

There had been no time out from war. No time out from
killing.

Wherever Grant was at this time, and he must have been
near, he, too, could hear the church bell peal.

The poet was right:

. . . Never send to know for whom the bell tolls.
It tolls for thee.

*That's right, General Ulysses Simpson Grant, you hog-
face Yankee bastard,* Johnny Yuma thought, *it tolls for
thee—and maybe it tolls for me. Sunday's as good a day
as any to die. Everybody dies.* Not everybody can die for
a cause and be remembered for the dying. Yuma was ready
to die; not willing—but ready.

He had already done and experienced more than his share
of almost everything, of sorrow and pain.

Sorrow at the death of his mother and of all the young
men who had fought and died alongside him, most recently
at the bridge without a name: Danny Reese and Lieutenant
Cane and all the rest.

Pain. Pain at Rock Island and from the wounds of battle.

He, too, had inflicted wounds, often fatal wounds. He would inflict one more and make sure it was fatal.

All this he thought in less than a second. That's all it took to clear his mind. It seemed that another set of reflexes had taken over: reflexes honed for revenge and retribution.

He felt a surge of readiness and confidence. His body was prepared. His mind was clearer than it had ever been.

Johnny Yuma started to climb again.

The church bell fell silent and there was a different sound.

Hoofbeats.

Generals Grant and Sheridan, Ord, Parker, and Williams, along with the staff that would see to the details of the surrender.

Reflexively, the soldiers of the South stood at attention and clenched their fists.

They were trying to neither look at nor avoid looking at Grant, who was the first to dismount.

One of the Yankee soldiers hurried over to take the reins of Cincinnati's bridle. Grant, followed by his staff, approached the nine steps that slanted up to the porch, but he paused as he noticed the Confederate soldier standing with his hands on the reins of the majestic white animal.

Grant turned and took a step closer. He gently touched the horse's head. The officers stood by.

Johnny Yuma moved quickly and quietly across the upstairs room toward the vent that faced the parlor below.

"His name's Traveler, isn't it?" Grant asked.

"Yes, sir," the soldier replied with a soft, Southern meter.

"You been tending him long?"

"About a year, sir."

"Looks like a good animal. Where you from, soldier?"

"Chattanooga, sir."

"Chattanooga." The campaigns flashed across Grant's mind. Lookout Mountain, the Tennessee River, Moccasin Point, the assault on Missionary Ridge: stunning victories for Grant. Shattering defeats for the Confederacy.

Grant took note of the Confederate soldier's wound.

"When did you get creased?"

"Yesterday, sir."

"Doctor see it?"

"I guess . . ." The soldier shook his head. "I guess they're all up at the front lines, sir."

"The front lines . . ." Grant removed a handkerchief from an inside pocket of his tunic and awkwardly pressed it to the soldier's wound. The soldier took hold of the handkerchief and Grant touched the soldier's hand.

"You take care," said Grant, "and take care of old Traveler there."

"Yes, sir. Thank you, sir."

Grant turned and walked to the porch steps where Sheridan and the others were waiting.

"You know, Phil," Grant spoke just above a whisper, "I met General Lee during the Mexican campaign when we were both in the same army. I was just a captain then. I wonder if he will remember me.

"After today, he'll remember you."

"Yes, I s'pose . . ."

Grant hesitated. Sheridan looked at him as if to say, "There's no putting it off." Grant threw down the butt of his cigar and moved forward.

Johnny Yuma knelt by the vent. He had his gun in hand and was checking the cylinder.

FIVE

Doug Baines rose out of a murky, black pit into consciousness, but his body lay prone. At first his brain could not tell him where he was. He knew he had been hit, hard but not fatally. He was alive. That much he knew.

For a fleeting moment he thought he was on that nameless bridge near Three Forks. But the only battle that was raging was the battle in his brain.

And he was dry. Then he realized something else. He was bound. Hand and foot. Hog-tied. He could barely move, and the gag in his mouth prevented him from crying out.

His eyes were shrouded in darkness. Hay. His face and body were covered with hay. He managed to move, then turn, dislodging the hay that covered his face.

Then it struck him. What had happened. No, he was not on the bridge. That was yesterday. A lifetime ago. He was at Appomattox. In a barn. Bound and gagged. Alone. And Yuma, Johnny Yuma, where was he? What was he doing? Or about to do? Was it too late? How long had Baines been unconscious? He strained to listen, for what he was not sure.

A gunshot? Or gunshots? Footsteps? Voices? Anything that would tell him it was not too late.

Even if it weren't too late, it soon could be. He remembered the words of Johnny Yuma; "... We can't let it happen ... It's got to be stopped ... If we give up now, what'd they all die for ... so long as I got a gun, I fight ... Grant! That hog back, blisterface ... craven drunk, no good blue belly ... a room right over that parlor ... I've laid it all out ... when Grant walks in that room, he's going to run straight into a head full of lead."

Was it possible? Could one lone man with a gun do what the great generals of the South—Lee, Stuart, Beauregard, Jackson, Bragg, Early, Johnston, Longstreet, and the rest, with all their armies could not do—stop Grant? Not just stop him, but kill him?

Douglas Baines tried to remain calm and think. It could not have happened yet. If it had, there would not be this silence at Appomattox. There would be noise, activity and, very likely, hostility.

If Grant had been shot, there would be more shooting. First, at Johnny Yuma; then, God only knew. The whole village might erupt in gunfire. Neither side had laid down its arms.

So, no, it hadn't happened yet.

There was still time, but how long? And for what? What could he do, gagged and tied in a barn, while in a house only yards away, the great generals of a nation's worst war would meet to make peace, a rendezvous with history?

SIX

Johnny Yuma looked through the vent into the room. There were several Southern officers, but Yuma was looking at only one man: The imposing figure of General Robert Edward Lee, commander in chief of the Confederate Armies, the heart and soul of the South.

Lee was the son of Henry "Light Horse Harry" Lee. The name Lee went back as far as Virginia itself—and before.

Robert E. Lee had been the most distinguished officer in the United States Army. He had graduated from West Point at the head of his class in 1829. He had served with honor and glory in the Mexican War at Vera Cruz, Churubusco, and Chapultepec. He became the superintendent at West Point, then saw frontier duty in Texas.

It was he who commanded the detachment that suppressed the uprising led by John Brown at Harper's Ferry.

And it was Robert E. Lee who first was offered command of the U.S. Army at the outbreak of the Civil War. Declining, after a monumental struggle within himself, he wrote almost apologetically to his beloved sister who lived in the North:

> ... now we are in a state of war which will yield to nothing. The whole South is in a state of revolution, into which Virginia, after a long struggle, has been drawn ... and I have had to meet the question whether I should take part against my native state.
>
> With all my devotion to the Union and the feeling of loyalty and duty of an American citizen, I have not been able to make up my mind, to raise my hand against my relatives, my children, my home.
>
> I have therefore resigned my commission in the Army, and save in defense of my native State, with the sincere hope that my poor services may never be needed, I hope I may never be called on to draw my sword. I know you will blame me; but you must think as kindly of me as you can, and believe that I have endeavored to do what I thought right.

But, of course, Lee was called upon to draw his sword. He did so reluctantly but effectively. And with him in command, the South seemed invincible, winning battle after battle: Fort Sumter, Lexington, Belmont, Shiloh, Fort Royal, Bull Run.

No one expected a long war. No one expected half a million casualties. The South had superior tacticians, but the North had superior everything else. It took more than four years, but the culmination was predestined.

There was some slight noise from the hall. Lee did not move, but two of the officers, Babcock and Marshall, reacted. Babcock went to the door and opened it. Framed there was Grant, dressed for the field in tunic, breeches, and mud-spattered boots.

Johnny Yuma started to bring the gun up to aiming position.

Grant stepped inside and offered his hand. The other Northern officers entered. Lee rose. He and Colonel Charles Marshall moved to meet Grant. Johnny Yuma's aim was spoiled. He decided to wait for a clean shot.

He knew he would have only one chance.

Below in the room there was some awkward hesitation. By now, Lee was seated. Grant moved to the table and sat across from the Southern commander.

Johnny Yuma started to take aim again, but Sheridan leaned down and whispered something to Grant, obscuring Yuma's target. Sheridan, for the time, remained between Grant and Yuma. Grant cleared his throat and smiled toward the elegant man on the other side of the table.

"I met you once before, General Lee . . . while you were serving in Mexico . . . when you came over from General Scott's headquarters to visit Garland's brigade. I have always remembered your appearance and think I would have recognized you anywhere."

"Yes," Lee replied softly. "I know I met you on that occasion . . . and I have often thought of it and tried to recollect how you looked, but . . ."

"I know," Grant smiled slightly, "you probably couldn't recall a single feature."

"I'm sorry."

The fingers of Lee's right hand touched the edge of the table. His voice tried to disguise what must have been unmeasurable anguish.

"I . . . I suppose, General Grant, that the object of our present meeting is fully understood."

Grant nodded.

Johnny Yuma could feel and almost hear his heart pounding.

"I asked to see you," Lee continued, "to ascertain on what terms you would receive the surrender of my army."

Yuma's gun was ready, his hand unsteady as he braced himself to squeeze the trigger. Only then did the full import of what he was about to do strike him . . . but he would do it.

General Grant put his hand to his forehead and tried not to look directly at Lee, tried to make the moment easier.

"The terms I propose, General Lee, are those stated in my letter of yesterday. That is, the officers and men surrendered, to be pardoned and properly exchanged . . . and all arms, ammunition, and supplies to be delivered up as captured property."

Lee nodded, not displeased.

"Those are about the conditions I hoped would be proposed."

"And I hope," Grant added, "this will lead to a general suspension of hostilities, sir. And be the means of preventing any further loss of life."

Johnny Yuma shuddered at the words "further loss of life."

"May I suggest, General," Lee said, "that you commit to writing the terms you have proposed so they may be formally acted upon."

"Very well," Grant replied as easily as he could. "I will write them out." He pointed to his manifold order book and addressed one of the officers, Colonel Ord. "Can I have that book and something to write with, please?"

This was not what Johnny Yuma had anticipated. No strutting, commanding, or disrespect. Still, his gun was ready. His clear opportunity had not yet presented itself, so he told himself.

Douglas Baines struggled fiercely against the bindings. He rubbed the rope against the sharp hook of a screw attached to the worn and splintery side of the stall. The rope was starting to fray. His wrists were bleeding.

Grant wrote rapidly. Sheridan leaned over beside him, impeding Yuma's aim. When Grant was finished, he rose and slowly took the few steps to Lee and handed him the paper.

"I have written that what is to be turned over will not include the side arms of officers nor their private horses or baggage."

There were reactions from the Union officers, Sheridan, Ord, Parker, and Williams. And from the Confederates, Marshall and Babcock, and from General Lee.

"This will have a very happy effect on my army." Lee looked at the paper in his hand.

"Unless you have some suggestions in regard to the form of the terms as stated, I will have a copy made in ink and sign it." Grant took a couple of steps back toward Sheridan as General Lee began to read.

Baines could feel the blood leaking onto his hands and sleeves, but he could also feel the rope loosening.

Johnny Yuma now thought of shooting Sheridan, who stood in front of Grant, then quickly firing again at Grant, but it was too risky. Grant would instinctively react and become a moving target. There was still time.

Lee had finished reading. He hesitated, as if embarrassed to speak, but did.

"There is one thing, General. The cavalry men and artillerists own their own horses in our army. I know this differs from the United States Army."

Grant nodded.

"I would like to understand," Lee went on, "whether these men will be permitted to retain their horses."

There was a stilted moment.

"The terms do not allow this, General. Only the officers are allowed their private property."

Yuma's face was grim. He placed the barrel of the gun between the vents.

There was a regretful nod from the commanding general of the South.

"No." Lee looked back at the paper. "I see the terms do not allow it. That is clear. . . ."

General Grant could not fail to recognize Lee's wish and with the consideration that prevailed throughout the meeting, would not humiliate the great general by forcing him to make a direct plea for modification of the already generous terms. Grant spoke as gently and respectfully as possible.

"Well, the subject is quite new to me. Of course, I didn't know that any private soldiers owned their own horses." Grant paused for just a beat. "I take it that most of your men are small farmers. I know they'll need their horses to put in a crop to carry their families through next winter. I'll instruct my officers to allow all men who own a horse or mule to take the animals home to work their little farms."

Lee's face was filled with manifest relief and gratitude. He looked directly into the eyes of the man who had defeated him.

"This will have the best possible effect on the men. It will do much toward conciliating our people."

As he watched and listened, a shadow of confusion fell upon the face of Johnny Yuma, but his finger was still on the trigger.

The other copies of the terms were being written by

Grant's staff. Lee wished in some way to reciprocate for the kindness shown to him and his army by the victorious general.

"General Grant, I have about a thousand of your men as prisoners. I shall be glad to send them to your lines as soon as possible, for I have no provisions for them. I have, indeed, nothing for my own men."

"Of course." Grant smiled warmly. "I should like to have our men within our lines as soon as possible."

"I've telegraphed to Lynchburg," Lee said, "directing several trainloads of rations to be sent by rail. I should be glad to have the present wants of the men supplied from them."

The Union officers reacted uneasily to this. There was a slightly perceptible movement in their shoulders. Their eyes shifted toward Philip Sheridan.

"I'm sorry." Grant did his best not to embarrass General Lee. "Those supplies won't be coming, General. Phil . . . I mean, General Sheridan here, captured the train from Lynchburg last night."

"I . . . I see . . ." There was a dignified but final resignation in the voice of General Robert E. Lee.

Doug Baines was free. He made his way to the barn door, opened it, and looked out. The officers and men of both sides were standing near McLean's house, silent and waiting, some for victory, others defeat, but all silent.

Grant wanted to divert Lee's mind from Lynchburg. It was not easy for him to think of anything to say, but after a brief hesitation, he spoke. "Of how many men does your present force consist, sir?"

"I'm not able to say," Lee replied. "My losses in killed and wounded have been exceedingly heavy." He paused.

"Many of our companies are without officers. I have no means of ascertaining our present strength."

Yuma's finger started to squeeze the trigger as Grant looked to Sheridan, but something made him pause and listen.

"Suppose I send over twenty-five thousand rations," Grant said. "Do you think that would be a sufficient supply?"

"I think it will be more than enough," Lee replied softly, a soldier doing his best to hold back emotion. "And it will be a great relief, I assure you . . ."

Doug Baines was climbing the lattice and leaving blood on the vines as he climbed.

Marshall had finished and blotted the inked letter from Lee to Grant, accepting the terms. Lee was reading it aloud and preparing to sign.

Grant and the others in the room waited and listened. So did Johnny Yuma.

Lee read aloud in his soft, Southern voice. He neither rushed, nor lingered over the words:

Lieutenant General U. S. Grant,
Commanding Armies of the United States,

General: I have received your letter of this date containing the terms of surrender of the Army of Northern Virginia. They are accepted by me and I will proceed to designate the proper officers to carry the stipulations into effect.

Very respectfully,
Your obedient servant,
Robert E. Lee

He signed.

For Grant and the other Union officers, the long, bitter-sweet victory had finally come. Still, their faces were not those of brute conquerors, but of compassionate comrades.

Then Lee stepped closer to Grant, readying himself for the final gesture of defeat. He spoke as he moved slightly in anticipation of giving up his sword.

"Thirty-nine years of devotion to military duty has come to this . . . and this, too, is my duty . . ."

But Grant gently placed a restraining hand toward General Lee's gesture.

"General," said Grant, "the war is over. You are all our countrymen again." And Grant extended his hand.

Lee did not hesitate. He withdrew his hand from the hilt of the sword; then he, too, extended his hand in a gesture of reconciliation and friendship. Grant took it warmly.

Doug Baines burst through the door of the upstairs room, ready for anything . . . except for what he saw . . .

Johnny Yuma, with the unfired gun in his hand and in his eyes, unashamed tears. Both Lee and Grant had shown Johnny Yuma the ways of defeat and victory, of endurance and honor.

Johnny Yuma had wanted to make history. But now he was thankful to be alive and to have watched it. To have seen two of the greatest men one nation had ever produced . . . and, like both of them, to be a part of that nation again.

The war was over. There would be a new beginning for the country . . . and for Johnny Yuma.

SEVEN

Johnny Yuma and Doug Baines were now outside, waiting
with the remnants of the Army of Northern Virginia.

Grant and his contingent had gone. A newspaper corre-
spondent who was there later wrote:

As Lee left the house, he found his men waiting outside. . . .
It was a stark, tragic moment for the tired officers and soldiers who had fought so long and hard. . . . As Lee appeared, a shout of welcome instinctively went up from the
army. But instantly recollecting the occasion that brought
him before them, their shouts sank into silence, every hat
was raised, and the bronzed faces of grim warriors were
bathed in tears.

As he rode slowly along the lines, his devoted veterans
pressed around the noble chief, trying to take his hand, touch
his person, or even lay their hands upon his horse, thus ex-
hibiting for him their great affection.

The general then, with head bare and tears flowing down
his manly cheeks, bade adieu to the army.

Douglas Baines turned to Johnny Yuma. Neither thought he'd live to see this day, whether in victory or defeat.

"Well, Johnny, I always said the shortest farewells are the best."

"Yeah, it's best to go easy on the good-byes."

"But this good-bye's not easy."

"Doug, I'm sorry for what I did back there. . . ."

"I'm happy for what you *didn't* do."

"There was a crazy man in that barn. I just hope that he's not crazy anymore."

"He's not. I learned that in that room up there. Johnny, what're you gonna do?"

"Do?"

"I mean, you're going home, aren't you?"

"Home? Where's that?"

"Mason City, isn't it? That's what you said."

"It was, home, but I don't know anymore."

"Why's that?"

"Well, Doug . . . you been like a father to me, almost. What I mean is, well, I didn't leave my father under the best of circumstances. I guess you could say it was under the worst. I'm not sure I'd be welcome."

"Didn't you ever write him? Seems like you were always writing something to somebody."

"Yeah, to myself mostly. I figured I'd get killed and never see him again . . . so I wrote a lot of things . . . to him . . . and to a man named Elmer Dodson . . . and to . . ."

"A girl?"

"Her name's Rosemary. I should've written to her, but I didn't."

"Well, since as far as I can tell, you didn't get killed, why don't you go back and . . ."

"And what?" Johnny Yuma asked.

"I don't know, maybe straighten things out."

"Maybe there's something else I got to straighten out first."

"What's that?"

"Myself."

"Look, Johnny, we been pretty close for some time now, haven't we?"

"Yeah, I guess we have."

"Well, I don't see much wrong with you, if anything . . . anymore."

"Maybe you been too close, Doug. And that goes for me, myself, too. You know, the forest for the trees. Maybe I've got to step back and get some perspective or maybe even climb a mountain and get a good look at everything . . . including myself . . . get something done, before I go home. Hell, this was supposed to be a short farewell. I haven't talked so much in years."

"Sometimes . . . sometimes it's good to talk. Johnny, you go ahead and climb that mountain. You'll know when it's time to go home. I do. And the time for me is now, right now, and the place is . . ."

"Kansas." They said it at the same time and laughed.

"Lawrence." Baines still smiled. "Easy to find and not much out of your way to Texas. Come visit a contented old farmer and his family. Cora'll cook you up the best beef stew you ever sat down to."

"I just might do that, Doug. And I just might go visit another friend's family."

"Danny's?"

Yuma nodded.

"Sure, Johnny, that'ud be good. Oh, when you do come see us, don't be surprised at something else."

"What's that?"

"Well, before I left, our little community was in need of

a pastor. If the job's still open, I just might take it . . . along with farmin'."

"That doesn't surprise me. Well . . . take care of yourself . . . Reverend."

"So long . . . Reb."

They shook hands. The two former Confederates.

EIGHT

It has been almost a week since Appomattox. This night I made camp alone. A strange thing happened. . . .

Johnny Yuma had been mustered out. For days he had drifted aimlessly, not far from what had been battlefields and before that, villages and farms. He wanted to be away from everyone and everything.

He was tired. For the first time in a long while, he realized just how tired he was. Of taking orders. Of being on the alert for an enemy who might have broken through the lines. But now there were no lines. And there was no enemy. He told himself he could relax. He had not prevailed, but he had survived, unlike so many who fought on either side, more than half a million casualties.

It seemed that there was not enough land to bury them all, but buried they were. There was land enough for all the dead and for all who lived. But the living had a choice. The dead would stay forever in their little plot of land.

The night was cool and becoming cooler. Johnny Yuma built a small fire even before unsaddling his horse. For a long time, he had been carrying five twenty dollar gold coins. Double eagles. He no longer carried them. Four of the double eagles went for the horse and saddle, most of the fifth for supplies, food that would have to last until . . . until something happened.

It did. Yuma had relaxed too much. In trying to wipe away too many memories too soon, too hard, while looking into the yellow flames of the little fire, he was unaware until the man on horseback was too close.

Another time, in another place, if the man on horseback had worn a blue uniform, Johnny Yuma might already have been dead. But the man wore no uniform. He was dressed in civilian clothes, fine, expensive clothes but now dirty from what had to have been a long, hard ride. The horse, a buckskin, was lathered and seemed barely able to stand.

Against the firelight, the man looked ghostly. His garments and face were spattered with mud and dirt, but a face still handsome and finely chiseled, though thoroughly exhausted from the ride. The eyes were like living jewels, black and weary. Hatless, his long, dark hair curled down and across his formidable forehead.

Reflexively, Johnny Yuma's hand went toward his side arm but stopped short as the man spoke. His voice was deep and cultured.

"Good evening, Reb."

"Evening." Yuma still wore his uniform and Confederate cap.

"Alone?" The man looked around.

"Not anymore."

The man smiled, a warm, charming smile.

"That animal looks beat." Yuma pointed to the buckskin.

"It is."

"So do you."

"I'm not," the man replied. "No, I am not." He said the words slowly, emphatically.

"Well, would you like to step down off that horse and have something to eat?"

"I would," the man said and began to dismount. But it wasn't easy. It took great effort. He strained and grimaced. Yuma started to move toward him as if to help, but the man smiled and waved him away.

"I would," the man repeated, "I would like to stay and enjoy your generous Southern hospitality, but I'm afraid it was not meant to be."

"Why not?"

"Because of this." The man removed a six-inch brass derringer from the pocket of his coat and pointed it at Yuma. "And because I need a fresh horse and need it now."

"You don't look like a horse thief."

"I'm not."

"I paid eighty dollars in gold for that animal as it stands. Four double eagles."

The man's left hand dug into another pocket. He held the contents in his fist for a moment, then let them fall to the ground. They glinted by the firelight.

"Five double eagles and the buckskin in the bargain." He pointed toward his horse. "He'll be fit to ride by morning."

The man limped as he moved toward Yuma's horse, but he kept the derringer aimed at the Rebel.

"And now, I have an appointment to keep."

"I don't think you'll make it, but I won't try to stop you."

"I'll make it."

Yuma watched as the man struggled, then finally boarded Yuma's horse.

"I'm sure," the man said, "that you were a good soldier."

"Most of the good soldiers are dead."

"But not all, and believe me, I am sympathetic to your cause."

"Sympathetic enough to've fought in the war?"

"We all have different roles to play. Godspeed, Reb."

The man wheeled Johnny Yuma's horse and rode into the night, south.

NINE

The following day, Johnny Yuma sat at a table in the Willows Tavern in Narrows, Virginia. He had ordered, paid for, and consumed most of the soup, bread, and tankard of beer that remained on the table where he was writing in his journal.

Outside, the buckskin was hitched to a post. The animal still suffered somewhat from the effects of the stranger's reckless ride. It had been Yuma's intention to have the animal cared for at the local livery, but there was none. It had been closed due to the war and had yet to open again for business, due to the death of August Gork, former proprietor and former infantryman.

Yuma finished the entry in his journal describing the stranger on horseback and what had happened. He then finished the last swallow of beer from the tankard and the last spoonful of soup from the bowl.

Gunshots!

Gunshots sounded outside the Willows Tavern, and voices, footsteps, and attendant excitement. There were half a dozen customers in the tavern, all Southerners, most of them veterans, some still in uniform as was Johnny Yuma. The owner-bartender had a peg leg and had introduced himself as Mac when he served Yuma the soup and suds.

Ten or twelve men poured through the tavern door, led by a tall, middle-aged, overweight man waving a newspaper, and a younger man who had the same girth, features, and red hair as the man with the paper.

"Mac, listen! Everybody, listen to this! He's dead! Been shot dead! That no good Yankee son of a bitch's been killed!"

"What no good Yankee son of a bitch you talkin' about, Kinkaid?" Mac took a peg step toward the man with the paper.

"Lincoln!" Kinkaid exclaimed.

"What? Are you sure?"

"Sure, I'm sure! Randy here just rode back with the paper from Charlottesville!" Randy, still standing next to his father, beamed with delight. "Yes-sir-ee-bob," Kinkaid went on, "deader than a can of corn beef!"

"Who did it? How'd it happen?"

"Well, according to this," Kinkaid held up the newspaper, "a fellow named Booth, some actor, split the ol' railsplitter's head with a derringer at a place called Ford's Theatre . . ."

At the mention of a derringer, Johnny Yuma stiffened. He thought of the stranger with the derringer pointed at him last night.

"Did they catch him doing it?" Mac asked.

"Hell, no! This fella jumped right onto the stage, said somethin' in Latin, then yelled, 'The South is avenged!' Got away clean, even though he broke his leg or ankle in the jump. Hot damn! 'The South is avenged,' he said, and he was right! I'd admire to buy him a drink! Matter of fact, I'm buying everybody a drink! Mac, set 'em up on Tom

Kinkaid and son! Yes-sir-ee-bob, we're all gonna drink to
. . . lemmee see," Kinkaid referred to the newspaper again,
"Booth. John Wilkes Booth! The man who laid Abe Lincoln in his grave and avenged the South! And, by God, if
he hadn't done it, I mighta done it myself!"

Mac started to draw beers. The reaction of the others in
the room was not as exuberant. In fact, some were subdued,
even stunned.

But none as subdued or stunned as Johnny Yuma. He
was certain that the man last night was John Wilkes Booth.
He certainly had the carriage and voice of an actor. And
the limp from the broken bone as he jumped onto the stage.
The juiced-out horse and the fatal derringer. Yuma remembered the actor's words just before Booth rode south.

"We all have different roles to play."

At Ford's Theatre, Booth had played the real-life role of
an assassin and had rewritten history with a cartridge of
lead.

And now Booth had Johnny Yuma's horse and was being
hunted like no man had ever been hunted before. His fate
was sealed, along with the fate of anyone else who could
be implicated in helping him escape. Booth would be found
and hanged or shot. There could be no doubt about that.

Booth had Yuma's horse, and Johnny Yuma still had the
double eagles. It was unlikely that the double eagles could
be traced to Booth, but could the horse be traced to Johnny
Yuma? How far could Booth ride on that horse? Would he
ride it into the ground and get another? If Booth were captured alive . . . What then? Would anyone believe that he,
a Rebel, did not know about the assassination? He who had
come so close to assassinating Grant?

Yuma's only chance was to get away, as far away from
Washington and Virginia as he could. And as soon as he
could.

All this flashed across his mind as he sat at the table in Willows Tavern. How long he sat there, stunned, he did not know, but he did know that now a lot of the others were drinking and thinking about what had happened.

The ones who were celebrating the most were the Kinkaids, drinking down beer after beer with relish and laughter.

Yuma looked at the journal still on the table. If anyone ever read what he had just written, they would know about his encounter with Booth. But would they believe that was how it happened?

He had to get out of the tavern, out of the town, and take the journal with him. Destroy those pages that mentioned the incident last night. He had to get out of there unnoticed.

But it was too late. He already had been noticed by the Kinkaids. Tom Kinkaid was approaching with an extra tankard of beer in hand, accompanied by his son.

"Here you are, Johnny Reb." He set the beer on the table just as Yuma rose. "Looks like everybody's had a drink except you."

Johnny Yuma just stood there for a moment.

"Looks like you did some fightin'." Kinkaid grinned.

Yuma was silent.

"I said, looks like you did some fightin'."

"Some."

"Where?"

"What difference does it make?"

Kinkaid paused and looked around as the room fell silent.

"I just wanted to know. You *did* do some fightin', didn't you?"

"Did you?" Yuma regretted the words even before he finished speaking them. That hot Texas temper had erupted again. Even as he spoke, he knew he should have restrained himself. He should have been respectful to Mr. Kinkaid, answered the question politely, drunk the beer, thanked Mr. Kinkaid, taken his journal, and left quietly.

But there was something about the man that grated on Yuma. No, not something. Everything. His attitude. The smirking smugness. The vilification. The bravado and boasting. Yuma had learned to read men, friends and foes, soldiers and civilians. He did not like what he read in Kinkaid. There was deceit and weakness in the man's eyes despite his size and bluster.

"What did you mean by that remark?" Kinkaid was not going to let it pass. Not in a room full of people he knew and lived among. Not from a stranger. And not after too many drinks.

"Nothing," Yuma said it, but without much conviction.

"Nothin'? You musta meant somethin'..."

"No." Yuma made one more attempt at conciliation. "I'm sure that you," he glanced at Kinkaid's towering son who stood nearby, "and your son did more than your share of fighting. But it's over, so I'd just admire to get out of here and go about my business, Mr. Kinkaid."

Yuma did not know it, but he had said the wrong thing. Neither Kinkaid nor his son had served the Southern cause, at least not in the military, and everybody in the room knew it.

"And I'd admire to let you go about your business, whatever it is . . . just as soon as you," Kinkaid pointed to the tankard, "pick that up and have a drink on me, to John Wilkes Booth, the man who avenged the South."

Johnny Yuma stood motionless. He knew the wise thing to do was what Kinkaid said. His good sense told him to do it. His common sense told him to do it.

But there was something uncommon about Johnny Yuma, and something unacceptable about the way Kinkaid put it. It sounded too much like an order, a command. And something in Johnny Yuma rebelled when it came to taking a command from someone like Kinkaid.

Still, he had decided he would. But it took too long for him to decide, or so thought Tom Kinkaid.

"What's the matter with you, boy? Where do you stand? What are you, some sort of Yankee-lickin' turncoat?"

Yuma said nothing. Did nothing.

"Pick that up and drink to Booth!"

Nothing.

"All right, then . . . I'll pick it up."

Kinkaid reached down, picked up the tankard, held it for a moment, looked around the room, then flung the contents into Johnny Yuma's face.

Yuma's left fist smashed into Kinkaid's jaw, knocking him over a chair onto the floor. Randy Kinkaid leaped at Yuma, swinging a looping right. Yuma caught it on his left forearm and threw a straight right that sent the younger Kinkaid crashing against the table, then down.

Tom Kinkaid rushed in again, but met a backhand by Yuma that whirled the man into a wall. From the floor, Randy Kinkaid drew his gun and thumbed the hammer, but Yuma's gun fired first.

The slug hit bone in Randy Kinkaid's right shoulder, and he dropped the pistol.

Another shot went off and hit the ceiling. It had been fired by a man standing at the door. A man with one arm, holding the gun now aimed at Yuma. The man wore a badge.

"All right, that's enough."

"You saw it, Pete!" Tom Kinkaid rose from the floor. "This Yankee-licker shot Randy."

"Yeah, I saw it."

"He tried to kill my boy."

"I said I saw it."

"I want him arrested."

"You do, huh?"

"That's right, attempted murder . . . I . . ."

"You better get your boy over to Doc Reeves."

"But . . ."

"Never mind the buts. I'll handle this. Now get moving, Mr. Kinkaid." The sheriff looked toward Yuma. "You. Place that weapon on the table. Slow and gentle."

Yuma did. Kinkaid escorted his son toward the door and growled at the sheriff, "You do your duty, Pete."

"I intend to." The sheriff walked to the table where Yuma stood. He holstered his gun, lifted Yuma's revolver, and motioned toward the entrance. "Let's go."

Johnny Yuma picked up the journal from the table and walked toward the door as the sheriff followed.

"All right," the sheriff said to the patrons, "go back to your drinkin'."

It was noon bright as Johnny Yuma and the sheriff, still holding Yuma's gun, walked outside.

"Stop right here," said the sheriff. "Is that your animal?"

Yuma nodded.

"Sheriff, all I did in there was . . ."

"I said I saw what happened, most of it."

"Then why am I being arrested? I just . . ."

"Who said you're arrested?"

"Well, Kinkaid . . ."

"Kinkaid is a blowhard bastard, never fought a lick. Him and his fat-ass son stayed home and profited from the likes of you and me. Feed and grain . . . for gold, not Confederate currency. What was your outfit?"

"Third Texas . . . Rock Island, then with Jubal Early."

"Gettysburg." Using Yuma's gun, the sheriff pointed

toward his empty sleeve. "What's that?" He nodded toward the journal Yuma had in his hand.

"Just some things I wrote down . . . nothing important."

"Going back to Texas?"

"I don't know. Maybe . . . someday."

"Well, that's up to you, I guess, but I'm going to give you some advice, not as a lawman. Soldier to soldier."

"Yes, sir."

"Don't sir me, Corporal. I was no officer, just a Johnny Reb like you. What's your name?"

"Johnny, Johnny Yuma, s . . . Sheriff."

"Well Johnny Yuma, get on that buckskin and ride out . . . to Texas, or someplace . . . and don't ever pass this way again. Will you do that?"

"I will."

The sheriff handed the gun to Yuma. He took it and slipped it into the holster.

"Thank you . . . Sheriff."

"Good luck, Johnny."

And, so far, Yuma's luck had held. Through the fighting with the Third Texas, at Rock Island, with Early, and at Appomattox. Then with Booth and at Narrows, thanks to a sheriff who had lost an arm at Gettysburg.

But how long would Johnny Yuma's luck hold? Booth was still at large, and his trail might lead back to Yuma, who would have a lot of explaining to do to people who might not be as sympathetic as the sheriff in Narrows.

He would make tracks—trying not to leave any—out of Virginia. He would read the newspapers and listen, wherever and whenever possible, for the fate of John Wilkes Booth and maybe of himself.

TEN

As he rode west, Johnny Yuma saw hundreds of them. On trees, barns, poles . . . on the sides of buildings, on boards at public squares—the posters:

WAR DEPARTMENT, WASHINGTON, APRIL 20, 1865

$100,000 REWARD!

THE MURDERER
OF OUR LATE BELOVED PRESIDENT,
ABRAHAM LINCOLN
IS STILL AT LARGE.

ALL GOOD CITIZENS EXHORTED TO
AID PUBLIC JUSTICE ON THIS OCCASION.

EDWIN M. STANTON, *SECRETARY OF WAR*

On April 26, twelve days after he killed the president, the end came for John Wilkes Booth in a tobacco shed in Port Royal, Virginia. More than a hundred miles to the west, Johnny Yuma read the accounts in newspapers.

After a frantic two-week search by the army and secret

service forces, during which time he had received medical aid from a Dr. Mudd, Booth had been discovered hiding in a barn owned by a man named Garrett. The barn was set afire, and Booth was either shot by his pursuers or shot himself rather than surrender.

That ended it as far as Johnny Yuma was concerned. There was no mention of any assistance by or encounter with anyone except Dr. Mudd. Near South Fulton, Tennessee, Yuma traded the buckskin for a sorrel, gave the farmer twenty dollars to boot, and continued to move west. The sorrel had a good mouth and responded to the slightest pressure on the bit.

Johnny Yuma had already destroyed the pages in his journal referring to the stranger on horseback, but first he memorized them in case he ever wanted to write about the incident again.

There were thousands like him in the South, tens of thousands, who had served and survived and lost. Johnny Rebs. But like snowflakes and cinders, no two were exactly alike.

They had buried and left their brethren behind in fields, on hillsides, near streams and forests, north and south of the Mason-Dixon Line. Eternally asleep by one another. Countrymen again forever.

They had come from the streets of the cities, from the fields of farms, rich and poor, from plantations and backwoods shacks, across the flowing waters of the Mississippi, the Missouri, the Red, and the Shenandoah to heed the call of the Confederacy—at first to the trumpets of victory, and finally, to the dirge of defeat.

For those who returned, the journey was bittersweet. The men could never be the same, and neither could the places from where they came and now returned. Most were anxious to get back. Some traveled day and night. Home, no matter how much it had changed, had to be better than where they had been.

Some of the survivors, by choice, would never go home. They were the ones who had fallen in love with other places and other people, who had been looking for a way to escape and found it in a lost war.

Johnny Yuma fell into neither category. He knew that he would go home someday, and he was heading in that general direction, west. But for the first time since he left Mason City, which wasn't a city, not really much more than a village, he was not being ordered, told in which direction to go, or where and when.

There were things and people in Mason City that he was in no hurry to face: his father, Rosemary, Mr. Dodson.

Even as a young boy, Johnny Yuma had run away from home more than once. And always his father had come after him, and like the lawman that Ned Yuma was, tracked him down and brought him back. This time, Johnny Yuma would go back when he was ready. When he was somebody or something. Money would make a big difference, at least in people's eyes, and Johnny Yuma at this time didn't have much. He'd see to it that he had more, a lot more, before he went home.

Then there was Rosemary, Rosemary Cutler. Red hair aflame, eyes green as jade, the prettiest girl in town, who grew into the most beautiful lady anywhere.

And Elmer Dodson, owner, publisher, editor, and staff of the *Mason City Bulletin*, except when Johnny Yuma worked there with him. It was what Dodson wrote and the way he wrote it that started Johnny reading and wondering about a lot of things.

When he had left Mason City, he was in a hurry to get to the war. Like so many others who had left in a hurry from so many other places, he didn't want to miss out on it. Everyone said the fighting would be over in six months or less. They all wanted to come back with tales of glory and victory. But the six months or less had turned into four years and more. And the garlands of glory and victory had turned into the bitter taste of ashes and defeat. There would be no brass bands and celebrations for the returning Rebels.

They knew that they had done the best they could. Better than the best. But better was not good enough. Not good enough to beat or even withstand the overwhelming war machine of the North. A machine that produced an unending supply of men and matériel; a naval wall that blocked the harbors and ports of the agrarian South, the South that produced cotton and tobacco, sugar and grain, not guns and ammunition.

Still, they had reaped more than a measure of glory, even in defeat. But glory in victory rang loud and strong; glory in defeat was silent and subdued.

Yes, Johnny Yuma would go back. He knew that. In that respect he was one of the lucky ones. Not like Danny Reese and so many other Rebs, now silent, subdued—and buried. That was just one of the things Yuma would do before going home. He would visit Danny's mother and sister.

Yes, Johnny Yuma would go back, but in his own time and on his own terms.

ELEVEN

Halleluiah! The war is over,
Reconstruction has begun!
Lincoln's gone to heaven
to get a bit of rest.
Carpetbaggers are a-commin',
Me, I'm movin west.

Johnny Yuma saw the lines scrawled on what was left of a barn near Clarksdale, Missouri. The farmhouse had been burned down, maybe by Yankees, maybe by the owner himself who had decided to follow the sun. Other owners who had also abandoned property knew that they could not prevent those who would take over from bene-fiting off lost land, but the carpetbaggers and bankers would have to build their own houses to live in or sell.

The former owners usually did not scorch the land, but many of them scorched everything on it. Yuma decided to sleep in the ruins of the barn. He wrote a few lines in his journal, wondering about who had lived there and where the family was now, if they were still a family.

While there was light enough, Johnny Yuma read an article from a newspaper he had found earlier that day on a street in Clarksdale. The article was about the new president, Andrew Johnson. Yuma knew very little about Johnson. Always eager to read, Yuma learned more about Lincoln's successor before dark.

Born in a shack in Raleigh, North Carolina, Johnson was three when his father died. After a desolate childhood, Johnson, at age fourteen, became apprentice to a tailor. At eighteen, he moved to a poor mountain village in Tennessee where he married Eliza McCardle, who encouraged him to pursue his studies as well as the tailoring trade. In 1843, he was elected as a Democrat to the United States House of Representatives.

On that floor, Jefferson Davis had done his best to insult Johnson with reference to "the common tailor from Tennessee." Johnson did not reply directly, but in his next speech on the same floor, he referred to the "son of a common carpenter from Nazareth."

When Tennessee seceded, Johnson stuck with the Union, and after Grant invaded and reclaimed the state, Lincoln appointed Johnson military governor. Even though Johnson was a Democrat, Lincoln chose him as his running mate in 1864. On April 15, 1865, grief-stricken like most everybody else, but unlike anybody else, Andrew Johnson took an oath and became the seventeenth president of the United States.

He resisted those who urged a harsh, vindictive reprisal on the South and chose to follow the path of Lincoln, "to bind the nation's wounds," but it would not be an untroubled path, not for Johnson and not for the South.

Johnny Yuma, the Rebel, learned more about that the next day. The carpetbaggers were coming south, and many of the freed slaves were moving north—but not all of the former slaves who left moved north.

Late in the afternoon, Johnny Yuma, astride the sorrel, was crossing a shallow stream. He had already spotted the wagon in distress that had not quite made it to the other side.

He continued the crossing, moving closer to the wagon and to the people who had occupied it. A woman and a young boy, about eight, stood on the bank at the edge of the stream. A man was in the water, up to his thighs, working where a wheel had broken off.

They were a family—a black family.

"Howdy," Yuma said as he reined the horse to a stop in the stream a few feet from the wagon.

The man looked up at the horseman, still in the uniform of the Confederacy.

The man's clothes were wet. He was huge, even in the water, a dark brown, handsome face, power-laden shoulders and arms, narrow waist, coal black eyes glistening out of an unsmiling face.

Silence.

Yuma's look went to the woman and little boy. She was a comely woman in her late twenties, and the boy next to her appeared to be a miniature replica of his father.

"Ma'am." Yuma smiled. "Hi, young fella."

Silence still. The woman nodded slightly, but the boy just stood, looking at his father.

"Name's Yuma, Johnny Yuma." He headed the sorrel a little closer to the man. "Looks like you could use a hand."

The man went back to work.

"I'd be glad to be of some help."

The man kept at his work. Johnny did not move.

"Ben," the woman said, but the man did not look up.

"Quite a load on that wagon." Yuma rose in the saddle and pointed. "That looks like an anvil."

"It is," the woman said. "Ben's a blacksmith."

"That so?"

"Listen, mister . . ." The man spoke with a deep, strong voice, but he didn't look up. "Are we botherin' you?"

"No." Yuma smiled.

"Then why don't you leave us be?"

"All right, I will."

But Yuma did not move.

"Well?" the man finally said.

"Well, what?"

"Why don't you move on?"

"I will, but first I need some help."

"You?"

"Yeah, me," Johnny said.

"What kind of help?"

"Horse's got a loose shoe. Must've knocked it on a rock some ways back."

"That so?"

"Yep. Hate to keep on riding him like this. Might get crippled. He's a good horse. Don't you think?"

The man looked at the sorrel and nodded.

"Say, Ben . . . That your name? Ben? I got an idea." Yuma glanced at the woman, then back to the man. "Maybe we could help each other out . . . me with the wagon, you with the shoe. I'm sure this horse would be mighty grateful. What do you say?"

"Ben," the woman repeated.

The man looked at the woman, then the boy. He rubbed the massive palm of his wet hand across his face.

"All right."

"Good," Yuma said. "We'd better go to it before it gets dark."

They worked until after dark, but the wagon was repaired. Not many words passed between them, only the words needed in the repairing. Yuma didn't press for conversation. He knew that the sight of his uniform was not a pleasant reminder to the man and his family. But the wagon now stood near the campfire, ready to roll in the morning.

The woman had asked Yuma to stay and eat what she had prepared while they worked. There was little conversation while they ate. Later, Yuma spread his bedroll some distance from the others and was about to lie down and get some sleep. Fixing the wagon had been hard work, but Ben had gone about it almost without conversation or effort.

"Mister Yuma." The woman stepped out of the darkness and spoke softly. "My name's Louise."

"Well, I'm pleased to know you. My name's Johnny."

"I just wanted to . . . well . . ."

"What is it, Louise?"

"To thank you for helping . . ."

"Nothing to thank me for. Like I told Ben, my horse . . ."

"Yes, I know. About Ben . . ."

"What about him?"

"Well, I know he appears to be kind of . . . starchy."

"Starchy? I wouldn't blame him for being downright resentful. I don't expect that gray is his favorite color."

"And I wouldn't blame you for . . ."

"For what?"

"Well, you know that we were slaves, and you fought for . . ."

"Louise, I wasn't fighting for slavery, I was fighting for Texas, or I thought I was. There weren't any slaves where I come from, out West."

"There weren't?"

"No, ma'am."

"That's where we're going you know, west."

"That's a good idea. I'm going back myself, someday. Where'd you come from?"

"Georgia," Louise replied.

"Georgia, huh?"

"Ever been there?"

"One step ahead of Sherman." Yuma smiled.

"Ben's awful good with his hands, can do most anything, and he's got a gentle touch for such a powerful man."

"He's powerful, all right. You're a lucky woman."

"I know that."

"And so's the boy. What's his name?"

"Benjie."

"Lucky to have such a father . . . and mother."

"Thank you for saying that, and for what you did this afternoon. Now, I'd better get back," she said.

"Good night."

"Good night."

"And Louise . . . all of us . . . we've got to get used to all colors . . . including gray . . . white and black."

The next morning, Ben was examining a hoof on the sorrel as Yuma approached.

"Morning, Ben."

Ben only nodded.

"Did you get a good night's sleep?" Johnny Yuma inquired.

"I did, but there's something I want to talk to you about."

"Sure."

Before Ben could say anything else, both of them noticed

the three riders splashing through the stream toward the camp.

Ben let go of the sorrel's leg.

The three men were big and dirty. Yuma saw that the biggest man wore an army hat. Union army. Neither Johnny Yuma nor Ben said anything as the men reined up.

"Well, what we got here?" said the man with the Union hat. He looked at Yuma and Ben, then at Louise and Benjie, who now were standing nearby. "Joe, Charlie, what do you make of this?"

"I don't know, Sam. What do *you* think?"

"I think we ought to get down and find out."

All three dismounted with hands never too far from their weapons.

"What's your name, boy?" Sam was looking at Ben.

Ben didn't answer.

"I said, what's your name?"

Ben said nothing.

"Well, it don't matter. What else we got here?" He took a step away from Yuma and Ben toward Louise and her son. "Oh, yeah, a fine lookin' negro woman and her child. That is your child, isn't it?"

She didn't answer.

"Hell, fellas, looks like we come across a band of dummies. Nobody here can talk." He turned to Yuma. "What about you, Reb? Can you talk?"

Johnny Yuma didn't answer.

Sam's fist slammed into Yuma's midsection. Joe pulled out his gun, and all three laughed.

"We all know you can't fight," Sam said. "We found that out, all right. Didn't we, boys?"

The men laughed harder.

"Say, I think I know what's goin' on," Sam said after he quit laughing.

"You do, Sam?" Joe's gun was pointed at Yuma.

"Sure I do. You want to hear?"

"Tell us," Charlie nodded.

"All right. This here Reb, why he's trying to run away with his slaves. That's what's goin' on."

"Could be," Joe agreed.

"Could be, hell! That's what it is! Plain as a piggin' string. We got to do something about that."

There were tears in Benjie's eyes.

"Don't you cry, little boy. We're here to help you people." Sam turned toward Ben. "What's the matter with you? Ain't you heard you're free? You don't have to tend to his kind anymore. We done whipped their ass clear across the South, didn't we, Reb? I said, didn't we, Reb?" His fist rammed into Yuma's stomach again.

"Stop, please!" Louise cried out.

"I'll stop when I please . . . *ma'am*."

"You want to fight?" Yuma said. "Put away those guns. I'll fight all of you."

"All of us?" Sam grinned.

"All of you."

"Three to one? Them's unfavorable odds, Reb."

"We're used to it."

"You hear that, fellas? He's used to it. Well, you're gonna get used to something else, and I don't need no odds against the likes of you. Watch this, boys!"

Sam swung at Yuma's jaw. This time Yuma blocked the punch and landed a hard left, followed by blows to Sam's face and body. Sam fought back as the other two watched and cursed and urged Sam on. He was bigger than Yuma and maybe stronger, but Yuma was faster, and he knew how to use his speed.

Sam managed to grab Johnny and wrestle him to the

ground, but Yuma broke free and clubbed Sam with both fists.

"Joe!" Sam yelled as he dropped.

Joe leveled his gun at Yuma, but Ben slapped it away and smashed a boulder fist into his face, then backhanded Charlie before he could draw.

Yuma sprang up, panther quick. The two of them, Ben and Yuma, back to back, with exploding blows. Still on the ground, Sam went for his gun, but Yuma kicked it out of his hand, lifted him to his feet, and dropped him with a right as Ben collected the artillery and set it in a pile on the ground.

"Three to *two*." Ben grinned.

"Thanks," said Johnny Yuma.

"You're welcome," Ben nodded.

"All right, get up!" Yuma motioned to the fallen men. "Get up, get on your animals, and get out."

All three staggered to their feet. There was blood on their faces, and broken cartilage, but they managed to climb on their mounts.

"We'll keep these," Yuma pointed to the ground, "as mementos. This is one fight you Yanks didn't win, but I got to admit our side had some help." He smiled at Ben.

The three rode away without looking back.

Louise ran to Ben and kissed him. Benjie was not crying anymore.

"Are you all right, Johnny?" she asked.

"Like I said, Benjie's lucky to have a mother and father like you two."

"Johnny." Ben stopped smiling. "I said there was something I wanted to talk to you about."

"Sure, Ben, what is it?"

"About your horse. There's nothing wrong with those shoes."

"There isn't?"

"No, there isn't." Ben smiled again.

"Well, I'm sure glad to hear that. I must've been mistaken. Oh, one more thing, Ben . . ."

"What's that?"

"Those guns." He pointed at the guns the three men left behind.

"What about them?"

"You might as well keep them. You being a blacksmith, maybe you can make something useful out of 'em."

TWELVE

July 4, 1866

Today I won a rifle shooting contest in St. Louis. It cost twenty dollars to enter. That's about a month's wages for just about any job. Trouble is, for just about any job, there are about twenty job seekers.

I was down to my last thirty, so I risked two-thirds of my fortune and won by a dog hair—finally. The prize was worth well over a hundred. A new model Henry rifle—.44 caliber, fifteen-shot, weight nine and a half pounds, with the breech made of shiny, golden brass . . .

The entries Johnny Yuma had written into his journal through and shortly after the war had always been grim. Times were grim, and his entries reflected those times. Things were still grim, but the grimness was not as stark. There no longer was death and danger in every living minute of every day and night.

And while Johnny Yuma still was a serious young man, more serious than most, a touch of humor had begun to

seep into his aspect and into at least some of the notations
he made in his journal.

That night of July 4, the celebration was still in full
swing on the streets of St. Louis and in the saloons. Johnny
Yuma was in one of the saloons, the Lady Luck, and his
luck was running good.

The Henry leaned against one arm of the Douglas chair
he sat in, and near the rim of the table in front of him were
three stacks of chips worth ten dollars a stack. He felt flush,
what with a brand-new shiny, golden, brass-breech Henry
at his side, thirty dollars in front of him, and a red flush in
his hand. Yuma pushed one of the stacks toward the center
of the table.

"I'll raise," he said, looking at the well-dressed gentleman opposite him.

The three other players in the game had dropped out of
the hand. The well-dressed gentleman had only one stack
of chips in front of him. He studied Yuma, then the lone
stack. His eyes went back to Yuma.

"Too bad. I got you beat, son. But I only got enough to
call, so I call . . . with a straight to the nine."

"All red." Yuma turned up the cards.

"Damn!" said the gentleman. "Well, son, this is your
lucky day; first the rifle, and now the biggest pot of the
night. Well, I'm busted. Good night, gentlemen!" He rose
and moved away from the table, broke, but still with dig-
nity.

Johnny Yuma liked to play cards. He had played with
Danny Reese and other prisoners at Rock Island. But here
in Saint Louis, it was a far different game, with whiskey
drinks, candled chandeliers, loud music, and a new deck of
cards. And if a player lost, he could get up and go out the
door.

At Rock Island, they were lucky if there was enough

water to drink. It was always too dark. The only music came from a harmonica played by a near-blind young prisoner named Ralph. The cards in their only deck were bent and dirty and soggy from the sweat of the prisoners. And, win or lose, nobody could leave the compound.

Yuma gathered the chips from the center of the table.

"You boys mind if I sit in?"

Yuma looked up. It was the man who had come in a close second in the rifle contest. Nobody minded. The man removed his hat and sat.

"They call me Red," he said as he settled.

"How come?" one of the players inquired. "You ain't got no red hair."

"Red for danger." The man smiled. "And I've just got a feeling that your lucky streak has come to a finish, Mr. . . . sorry," he looked at Yuma, "didn't catch your name earlier today."

"Yuma. Johnny Yuma."

"I guess it's your deal, Mr. Yuma." Red called for chips. He was in his late twenties, a tall, handsome man, not as handsome as he would have been without the telltale effects of a long-ago bout with smallpox.

Johnny knew that Red was a good shot. The truth was that Yuma wasn't all that anxious to find out how good a poker player Red was. He would have been content to leave the game with his winnings and his rifle, but he dealt the cards.

Half an hour later, Yuma hadn't won or lost much, but the rest of the players had. They had lost to Red, who sat with close to two hundred dollars worth of chips in front of him. He won the next hand, too. Three of the other players said they'd had enough.

"How about you, Mr. Yuma? How about one more

hand? Just you and me, five card draw, to make the night worthwhile?''

"Thanks, I don't think so."

But the spectators urged Johnny on. One of the saloon ladies, the prettiest of the lot, leaned down and kissed Yuma on the cheek.

"That's for luck," she said. "Go ahead and play, Johnny."

Everybody laughed and clapped, and Johnny Yuma didn't have much choice. All he really stood to lose was the ten dollars he started with. The rest he had won. And there was always the chance that he could win some more.

Yuma nodded at Red. Everybody clapped again.

"Cut for the deal," Red said.

Yuma drew a jack. Red turned up a queen, then dealt.

Johnny looked at a pair of kings, a pair of deuces, and a six.

He opened for ten dollars.

Red saw the ten and raised twenty.

Yuma saw the raise. That left him with twenty. Yuma discarded the six and took one card.

Yuma didn't know it, but Red held three aces, a six, and a seven. He discarded the two numbers and drew two cards.

Neither player looked at his new cards.

Johnny bet the twenty.

There was a pause. A long pause.

"See it," Red said. "And raise a hundred and fifty."

There was an audible reaction from the spectators, then silence, dead silence.

"Table stakes," Johnny reminded the man across from him.

"I know that," Red smiled. "As far as I'm concerned, that rifle's on the table, and it covers the difference. You drew one card, I took two. Haven't looked at my hand and

won't. Two hundred dollars against the pot and the Henry.
What do you say, Johnny?''

There was a murmur from the watchers, but this time,
nobody laughed or clapped.

"Well?" Red goaded.

The same saloon girl leaned down again and kissed
Johnny Yuma again, this time full on the mouth, sweet as
larrup.

"I'll call," Yuma said. He turned up the first four cards:
two kings, two deuces. Then he turned over the fifth card.
He had caught another deuce. Full house.

Red did not change expression. He showed the three
aces, then, one at a time, the two other cards. First, a nine.
He looked across at Yuma and turned the final card. A king.

Now everybody did laugh and clap and cheer. Everybody
except Red, who rose, put on his hat, and left without a
word.

Yuma cashed in. He had never had so much money in
his life. He had never even seen as much. He was rich.
Over two hundred fifty dollars in legal tender and a brand-
new Henry rifle to boot. He thought it best to get away
from the Lady Luck before somebody else suggested a
game.

Somebody did. A different kind of game.

"My name's Cherry," the pretty saloon girl said. "Don't
you think I deserve a drink?"

"Uh, yes, ma'am."

"Don't call me ma'am. I'm not as old as you. Jake!"
She called to the bartender. "Johnny Reb here is buying
me a drink, aren't you, Johnny?"

"Yes, uh . . . yes."

It didn't take long for Jake to pour the drink.

"What about you?" Cherry looked at Yuma. "Don't you
want a drink?"

"No, thanks."

"Is there anything else you do want?"

Johnny Yuma hadn't much experience with saloons or saloon girls, and Cherry was attractive—more than attractive. Her face was beautiful, and it didn't need all the paint and powder she laid on it. And her body was enough to stop a stampede. But Johnny Yuma was not about to expose himself to the likely consequences of what Miss Cherry had suggested. He had heard stories from some of the older soldiers about big city saloons and some saloons in not such big cities. Especially stories about big winners in card games. The upstairs rooms, the painted ladies, the drinks called Mickey Finns—and waking up in some alley with a turbulent head and empty pockets. Not for him, not for Johnny Yuma.

"I said, is there anything else you want?"

"Uh, look, ma'am . . . uh, Miss Cherry, please don't take offense . . ."

"Oh, oh, I think I know what's coming." She smiled.

"No, what I mean is . . . I appreciate your rooting for me, and bringing me luck, and . . ."

"And?"

"And all . . . but . . ."

"But what?"

"Well . . ."

"Is it because you've never been with a woman?"

"No, ma'am."

"What does that mean? You have? You haven't? Because the time comes . . ."

"Cherry, listen . . ."

"No, Johnny, you don't have to explain. That's not what I'm here for, to listen to explanations. But you listen to me. I like you. I really do. And I'm sorry we met like this. So, thanks for the drink. You take care of that poke you won, and the rifle. See you sometime. I got to get back to work.''

She turned and walked away.

Johnny Yuma felt embarrassed and ashamed. Ashamed of the way he had treated her. He thought of going after her. But what would he say? ''Excuse me, but I've changed my mind. Let's have a drink and go upstairs. Let's . . .''

No, he would do the smart thing and get out of the Lady Luck and out of St. Louis while the getting was good and while he was still lucky.

The sorrel was tied out back of the saloon. He'd take it over to the livery, get a room for the night, and sleep with his money under his pillow and the Henry by his side. In the morning he would buy some clothes and supplies and head for other parts. Johnny Yuma knew those other parts eventually would lead to home, and on the way he would make sure that he stopped by to visit Danny Reese's mother and sister. That's what he would do, and he would start now.

Yuma walked down the dark alley alongside the Lady Luck toward the hitching posts in the rear. He held the Henry in his right hand and thought about Cherry at work upstairs. She said she was younger than he was. She didn't look it, but it was hard to tell with all that rouge and talcum on her face. He wondered what her face looked like without all that war paint. He would never find out.

He loosed the sorrel's reins from the hitching post. First, he heard the hammer click back. Then the voice of the man who stepped out from around the corner behind him. The man tried to change his voice, but still, it was familiar.

''Drop the rifle and put your hands out front.''

Yuma did both.

He could hear the man's footsteps come closer.

''Take the money out of your pocket and drop it next to the rifle. Don't turn around.''

Yuma thought about going for his side arm, but he knew he had no chance.

"The money," the man said. "On the ground. Now!"

"Okay." Yuma slowly started to remove the roll of bills as he mapped out his strategy. He would make sure the bills scattered out as they fell so they would spread all over the ground. He might have a chance to make his play as the man went to pick up the scattered currency, if the man didn't knock him out or shoot him first.

But the man seemed to have read Yuma's mind.

"Hold it!" he said. "Don't drop it. Just hold it out back of you."

"Okay," Yuma repeated. Slowly, he moved his hand close behind him with the money in it.

"Out further."

"Right."

He could hear the man take another step forward. Then Yuma heard something else.

A hard, dull thud.

Johnny Yuma whirled, with the gun in his hand as the man fell forward on the ground and lay unconscious where he dropped.

Cherry stood over the man with a bung hammer gripped in both hands.

"I said I'd see you sometime." She smiled.

She was the loveliest sight he could remember seeing in a long, long time, war paint and all.

The unconscious man on the ground wore a bandanna across his face. Even so, his identity was apparent. Yuma reached down and pulled the kerchief from Red's pock-marked face.

"I had a feeling," Cherry said. "He's a poor loser."

Yuma put the money back in his pocket, then picked up Red's gun as Red groaned and began to stir.

"All right," Yuma said. "Up."

Red struggled to his feet, wiping his left hand over the lump behind his ear.

"I . . . I'm sorry. I . . . I just wanted that rifle . . ."

"And my money," Yuma added.

"Yeah . . . I guess so."

"Well, you're gonna get neither."

"I know. All right, let's go see the sheriff."

"Red, you want to make a deal?"

"What're you talking about?"

"I was lucky today. At the contest and at cards. You weren't. Let's let it go at that."

"You mean it?" Red asked.

"I do, but if I ever see you again, or she does . . ."

"You won't, neither of you."

"Here's your gun. Good-bye and good luck."

"Thanks, Reb."

"You're welcome, 'Red for danger.' "

Red disappeared in a hurry around the corner of the Lady Luck.

Johnny Yuma picked up the Henry and brushed the dirt from the shiny, golden brass. He looked at Cherry.

"Say, you're pretty handy with that bung hammer."

"A girl in my business has to be. Well, so long, Johnny." She started to turn.

"Cherry."

"Yes." She looked back.

"Could I . . . buy you a drink?"

"Are you sure you want to?"

"I'm sure."

THIRTEEN

Someday I know I'll go back home to Mason City, maybe to stay and maybe not, but before that, there's one thing that I've got to do. I've got to stop and see Danny's mother and his sister, Cynthia . . .

Johnny Yuma had written that on the day he left St. Louis, with all the events that had preceded his departure fresh in his memory: the rifle contest, the card game, the encounter out back of the Lady Luck with Red . . . and later with Cherry.

He knew that they would never see each other again, and she knew it, too. Before he left her, she said some lines from a poem.

> *Abashed the devil stood,*
> *And felt how awful goodness is, and saw*
> *Virtue in her shape how lovely . . .*

She said it was from Milton's *Paradise Lost*.
Johnny Yuma wrote the words down so he wouldn't for-

get them. He knew he would not forget her, a saloon girl called Cherry, in St. Louis. It occurred to him later that he didn't even know her last name. It didn't matter. Cherry probably wasn't her first name, either.

He stopped in at a dry goods store. It had been over four years since he had bought anything to wear. In the meantime, his entire wardrobe had been provided by the Confederacy, except for the outfit issued by the Yankees at Rock Island. The uniform he wore into St. Louis was mostly worn through, patched, and worn through again. It was frayed and reeked of desolation and defeat. It had done its duty and then some.

Still, out of defiance, or pride or maybe in silent tribute, he didn't want to discard it entirely.

He bought a new buckskin shirt, two pairs of gray wool trousers, some socks, and a pair of boots. But he kept the tunic with the corporal's stripes, the belt with the buckle engraved with CSA, and the confederate cap. He also kept the Colt side arm and bought cartridges for the Colt and the Henry.

Johnny Yuma was content to drift for a time. Waking each morning with the glow from the east, he felt vital, lean, and alive. He would ride until the sun aimed from the middle of the sky, fix a noon meal, sometimes lie near a stream, even drop off to sleep and sometimes wake with a violent jerk until he realized again in that same instant that the war was over. He would drift some more until sundown, make supper, and sleep under the star-studded dark of night.

The long, hot, shimmering summer days cooled down into autumn. The velvet greens turned into burnished browns.

In Jonesboro, Johnny Yuma went to the post office. He mailed a brief letter to his father, saying not much more

than that he was alive and would be home someday. To
Elmer Dodson he sent a stack of pages from the journal he
had written, asking the newspaperman to read them and
keep them until he got back to Mason City.

He thought of writing to Rosemary but decided not to.
He knew that she would hear from his father or Mr. Dodson
that he had survived.

But he wasn't sure that she even cared. No, that wasn't
true. Johnny knew that she wouldn't want to see him dead,
but it was also probably true that she didn't want to see
him at all.

He decided that it was time to quit drifting for awhile.
It was time to go and see Danny Reese's mother and sister.

FOURTEEN

Tomorrow I will be in Natchez. Danny spoke so often about his mother and sister that I feel I already know them. I know he mentioned me in his letters to them. Maybe I can be of some comfort . . .

In April of 1862, Rear Admiral David G. Farragut of the United States Navy, with a strong squadron of warships and nineteen mortar schooners, their masts camouflaged with branches of trees, had headed for New Orleans, the South's greatest seaport.

An observer remarked, ''The ensuing cannonade seemed like all the earthquakes in the world, and all the thunder and lightning going off at once.'' Farragut's flagship was grounded and set ablaze by a fire raft, but Rebel ships ultimately were wrecked or scattered. New Orleans surrendered, then Baton Rouge and Natchez. By the middle of summer, the South's grip on the Mississippi was limited to Vicksburg. Then came U. S. Grant.

Johnny Yuma walked past the horse and buggy, onto a porch that fronted the large colonnaded house a few miles from Natchez. The place needed attention: paint, caulking, roofing. Not only was the house in disrepair, but most everything on the property: outbuildings, the barn, fences. And the land that surrounded the property had not been tended.

Johnny took a long breath and reached for the brass knocker on the wide, arched door. Once, twice, three times, metal sounded against metal. Yuma waited a reasonable time and used the knocker again. Almost immediately, he heard the voice from inside, a woman's voice.

"Yes, yes. I'm coming, for heaven's sake! Have a little mercy on that door, it's older than I am."

The door opened, framing a gray-haired woman in her late sixties. Eyes, magnified by a set of thick-lensed spectacles, peered out of a pale, wrinkled face. Over her black dress, her bony shoulders were covered by a faded shawl, the pattern no longer completely discernible.

"Well," the woman said in a surprisingly strong voice, "what is it?"

"Excuse me, ma'am . . ."

"What for?"

"Huh?" Johnny didn't expect that.

"What do you need to be excused for? When I was teaching, it was because the students had to go to the toilet, heh, heh . . ." She seemed very pleased by her own humor. "Do you?"

"Well, no, ma'am."

"What is it then? Do I know you? I don't see as good as I used to, or do anything else as good, for that matter. Were you a student of mine?"

"No, ma'am."

"What's your name?"

"Yuma. Johnny Yuma."

"Never heard of you . . . Did I?"

"No, ma'am."

"Who is it, Miss Morrison?" The voice came from inside, a woman's voice, but not as strong.

"Somebody calling himself . . . What was that name again?" Miss Morrison moved her face a couple of inches closer, either to see or hear better, or both.

"Yuma, ma'am. Johnny Yuma."

"Says his name is Johnny Yuma." Miss Morrison turned her face toward the room on the right when she said it.

There was a pause.

"Tell him . . . please tell him to come in."

"She says to come in," Miss Morrison repeated as though he hadn't heard.

"Thank you, ma'am." Johnny Yuma stepped over the threshold.

"At least you were on the right side," Miss Morrison remarked as Yuma removed his Confederate cap.

Now a man stood at the entrance of the parlor door, a man even older than Miss Morrison. Gray hair, hawk face, a pince-nez on the bridge of his aquiline nose, and a stethoscope hooked around his neck. For some reason, he appeared very glad to see Yuma and spoke almost as if he knew him.

"Come in, Johnny, come in." The man extended his hand. "My name's Pickard. Dr. Miles Pickard. We're glad you're here, my boy. Very glad."

"Thank you, sir." Johnny shook the man's hand. It was a large hand with an unexpectedly strong grip. "This will be very good medicine for Amanda. Very good. Please come in."

Yuma followed Dr. Pickard into the parlor. But it was no longer only a parlor. A large bed had been brought down from an upstairs bedroom, and propped up on that bed was

Danny Reese's mother. She extended both arms, her face smiling and crying.

"Johnny! Come here, son, and let me kiss you."

Johnny Yuma went to her. She kissed him and held him tight, with all the strength she had in her.

"Johnny! Johnny!"

His face was wet from her tears.

"Oh, look at what I've gone and done! I'm sorry. Forgive me, Johnny, but it's so good to see you. Have you got a handkerchief?"

"I'm all right."

"Miss Morrison." The old teacher now stood inside the parlor door. "Would you please get Johnny something for his face?"

"No thanks, I'm fine."

"Probably needs something for his innards," Miss Morrison said. "How about some tea? Or better yet, some bourbon? Damn Yankees didn't get away with everything, you know!"

"No, thanks."

"Sit down, Johnny. You've met Dr. Pickard and Miss Morrison . . ."

"Yes, ma'am." Yuma nodded and sat in the straight-backed chair near the bed.

"I don't really have to stay in bed all the time, but I prefer to, even though Miles objects. He thinks I should get up and plow the fields and plant the crops, don't you, Miles?"

"Yes, Amanda. You see, Johnny, it's easier to just agree with her . . . about everything."

"Hush, Miles. Now, Johnny, tell me about what you've been doing since . . . since Appomattox. You were there, weren't you?"

"Yes, ma'am. I was."

"You saw General Lee?"

"Yes, ma'am."

"That must've been sad. Very sad."

Johnny Yuma just nodded slightly.

"And Grant?" Her voice grew darker. "Did you see him, too?"

Yuma nodded again.

"They say that he'll be president, someday. . . . But tell me, Johnny, what have you been doing? You know Danny wrote so much about you. You know that, don't you?"

"Yes."

"Have you been home yet?"

"Not yet."

"Don't wait too long, Johnny. Anything . . . anything can happen. Don't wait too long."

"No, I won't."

"Where have you been? What have you been doing?"

"Just sort of drifting, but I wanted to . . . well, I'm sorry I don't have anything of his to bring you, but . . ."

"The sight of you is enough. Just to know that you were his friend. Johnny, were you with him when . . . when he was . . . when he died?"

"Yes."

"How many times have I looked out that window, hoping against hope that there had been some mistake . . . that Danny would run across that field, through that door, and into my arms. So many plans for when he came back, Johnny. But finally, I knew that it would never happen . . . that he would never come back. And so I don't look out the window anymore. I just stay in this room and . . . Johnny, please, I want to know. You were there . . . please tell me how it happened. Did he suffer? Please . . . we, all of us here, loved him. Will you tell us . . . did he die a hero?"

"Yes, ma'am. It was the day before Appomattox. We had been ordered to take a bridge, a very strategic, important bridge. All our officers had been killed. Even the sergeant. That left me in command of what was left of us. At dawn the time came for me to order the charge, but . . . well, to tell the truth, I froze. I knew it was hopeless, and I just lay there waiting for . . . I don't know what. Danny was right next to me, like he always was. 'Come on, Johnny,' he said, 'we're waiting. Give the order.' But I didn't. For some reason, I couldn't. He grabbed and pulled me over practically on top of him. 'Come on, Johnny,' he said, 'we've got to take that bridge. We've got to!' And he shook me till I snapped out of it. I gave the order, and we charged toward the bridge. But I didn't lead the charge; Danny did. He was ahead of all of us, screaming the Rebel yell and waving for all of us to follow him. We did. He had guns blazing out of both hands. He was the first across, and one of the last to get hit. One shot, clean and fast. He didn't suffer, Mrs. Reese, and we took that bridge because of him. That's how it happened."

"Thank you, Johnny." She was wiping the tears from her eyes, but smiling. "If he had to die, I hoped that it would be something like that. Thank you."

Nobody in the room spoke for what seemed like a long time. Then Miss Morrison wiped at her eyes and nose, cleared her throat, and walked toward the sideboard.

"Well, I don't know about the rest of you, but I'm going to have a shot of bourbon. Anybody care to join me?"

"I think we all should," said Dr. Pickard. "And you, too, Amanda. Doctor's orders. A drink to Danny."

"Well," smiled Mrs. Reese, "I always follow doctor's orders."

"The hell you do," Dr. Pickard snorted.

"What did you say, Miles?"

"I said, 'Yes, you do.' "

"The hell you did," she replied and smiled at Johnny.

"Can I help you with those drinks, Miss Morrison?" Yuma rose from the straight-backed chair.

"All right." She handed him two glasses. "Here's yours and Amanda's. And these are for Dr. Pickard and me. Guess which one is mine." She gave Dr. Pickard the glass with the least whiskey.

"Miss Morrison's come to help me ever since she retired." Mrs. Reese took the glass from Johnny.

"Retired, my foot! They booted me out! Said I was too old, too deaf, and too blind. But I'll fool them. I'll bury every man on that school board and spit on their tombstones."

"Sit down, Johnny." Mrs. Reese held the glass in her hand. "Now, you are going to stay with us for a while aren't you?"

"Well, yes, ma'am, for a while."

"Good." She raised the glass. "To Danny."

"To Danny," they all said, and drank.

"Johnny, I can't tell you how much better seeing you has made me feel."

"Good enough to get you out of that damn bed?" asked Dr. Pickard.

"I'm thinking about it. Now, Johnny, when I said stay with us, I meant here in this house. You understand that, don't you?"

"Well, I . . ."

"Nonsense, there are plenty of empty rooms upstairs. You can take . . . Danny's room."

"Say." Johnny Yuma looked around and smiled. "I've been so busy talking, I didn't even ask about Cynthia. Where is she?"

The room fell silent.

Johnny Yuma realized that there was something wrong.
He knew that Cynthia had been a nurse and had served in
hospitals near the front lines, that she had been injured and
sent home almost a year before the war ended, but Danny
had never said anything more than that, and maybe that's
all Danny ever knew. But Johnny could sense by the reaction of everyone in the room, especially that of Mrs.
Reese, that something had happened.

After too long a silence, he realized that nobody was
going to say anything more.

"Mrs. Reese," Yuma asked quietly, "what is it? What
happened to your daughter?"

"Who?"

"Danny's sister. Your daughter."

"I don't have a daughter."

"Cynthia isn't your daughter?"

"No," said Mrs. Reese. "She's a whore."

FIFTEEN

"She's a whore . . . She's a whore . . . She's a whore . . ."
Johnny Yuma could not erase the sound of those words
from his mind.

What happened and what was said in the Reese parlor
after Amanda Reese spoke those three words became a blur.
It seemed impossible. Yuma remembered the warmth and
pride and affection in Danny's voice whenever he mentioned his sister Cynthia. No, not affection. Affection was
too shallow a word. Love. Devotion. Adoration. They all
came closer, but still not close enough to completely con-
vey what was in Danny's voice and heart when he spoke
of his sister. Danny would have laid down his life for his
sister.

Yuma remembered all those hours at Rock Island and
later when he and Danny were together again with Lee's
army, how Danny, who always looked on the bright side,
would brighten even more when he spoke of his sweet sister. She was only a couple of years older than Danny but
so much more mature. Gentle and strong. Patient and encouraging. Wise and genial. Beautiful and without vanity.

From the time their father died when he was thrown from a horse, while they were both children, and their mother had to assume responsibility for the farm, a time that Danny barely remembered, it was his sister who raised him to the strapping young soldier who left Mississippi to serve the South.

Cynthia became his mother, father, brother, teacher, and playmate, as well as his sister. Young Danny would play with the other boys and he was as rough and ready as the rest, but even as with the roughest and readiest of boys, there came the times when Danny needed comforting and encouragement.

During those times in Danny's young life, Cynthia was always there. When Danny was eight years old, an epidemic of deadly fever hit Natchez, felling young and old alike. Doctors, nurses, and medication were in short supply. Dr. Miles Pickard did what little he could for Danny, then left to attend to the countless other stricken patients, most of whom did not survive. But Danny did survive, and Dr. Pickard was the first to credit Danny's survival to the boy's sister, Cynthia.

Danny's mother suffered from a milder case and was not in mortal danger, but she was too weak to minister to her son. It was Cynthia who stayed with him, hour after hour, day and night after day and night, spoon-feeding him what little medicine Dr. Pickard had been able to spare, changing cool, damp compresses, holding his fevered hand, bathing him, encouraging him—never allowing his spirit to shrivel—her voice rallying him, exhorting, challenging, mustering, entreating, pressing, praying, demanding—*willing* him to live.

And live he did.

Danny never forgot his sister's dedication and care, and he swore that someday, somehow, he would find a way to repay her for saving his life. But for Cynthia, the fact that Danny was alive was payment enough. More than enough. She had prayed to God for his survival and swore that if God would save Danny's life, she would devote her life to saving other lives. She would become a nurse.

Cynthia kept her promise. She was the first woman to leave Natchez and volunteer as a battlefield nurse. How many lives she helped to save was impossible to determine, but she was there, ministering to the battered, broken bodies, those who were dying among the dead, and those who did not die because of Cynthia Reese and the other nurses and doctors who imperiled themselves to save the brave young soldiers who fought and fell on both sides of the struggle.

Johnny Yuma could still hear Danny's voice: *"My sister Cynthia . . . my sister, Cynthia . . . my sister, Cynthia . . ."* and then through the blur of what happened that afternoon, the voice of Amanda Reese, *"I don't have a daughter . . . I don't have a daughter . . . I don't have a daughter . . . She's a whore . . . She's a whore . . . She's a whore . . ."*

Dr. Pickard and Johnny Yuma had left Amanda Reese in the parlor with Miss Morrison. Yuma pressed the doctor for any and all information about Cynthia. What had happened to her during the war and after? How seriously was she wounded? Did she come back to Natchez? Where was she now?

Johnny Yuma wanted to know. He wanted to see her, to help her. He wanted Dr. Pickard to tell him everything. There must be something he could do, for Danny's sake and more important now, for Cynthia's.

"Johnny," Dr. Pickard spoke softly as he and Yuma drank coffee in the Reese kitchen at twilight, "Cynthia is a casualty of war, just as surely as if she had been a soldier at Gettysburg. A casualty like the hundreds of soldiers she tended in the operating rooms and hospitals at the front lines. And sometimes there were no lines. You know that. Yesterday's victory turned into today's defeat. Emergency hospitals were set up too close to the battlefields. An enemy bomb exploded near one of those hospitals. A piece of shrapnel tore into Cynthia's back, but she stood by the doctor's side for hours while he operated on who knows how many patients.

"Finally, she collapsed, weak from loss of blood and the infection of the wound. The doctor removed the shrapnel and gave her something to relieve the pain . . . something called morphine."

"Yeah," Johnny nodded. "The doctors gave it to us, too, for everything from amputations to dysentery."

"Unfortunately," Dr. Pickard said, "it seemed like a quick and easy solution, and it was, in some cases. But unfortunately, in many others, too many others, the solution was worse than the affliction. And that's what happened to Cynthia."

"Morphine?"

"Morphine. At first, the doctor gave her shots to ease the pain. For hours and days and weeks, she refused to leave the sick and dying, while she, herself, required more and more morphine to erase her own pain. In the beginning, it was the doctor who injected her and then . . ."

"And then what?"

"She began to inject herself."

"Damn."

"Yes, she was damned. Addicted. The doctors knew it, and she knew it, but she couldn't help it. Even after the pain subsided, the craving was still there and stronger. The doctors thought it best to send her home, away from the strain of warfare and away from the ready supply of morphine available at the hospitals and battlefields. And that's when she came home to her mother and me.''

"Danny said that she had been engaged to a man named . . . was it Renfield?''

"Yes, Hurd Renfield, a good man, Captain Hurd Renfield, but he was away fighting for the cause, and by the time he came back, it was too late.''

"What do you mean, 'too late'?''

"When Cynthia came back, she told me about her wound, and I examined it. The wound had healed, but she said she needed something for the pain that was still there. Of course, she didn't tell me about her addiction. But it didn't take long to find out. I had given her several injections, then refused to give her more. Her condition became obvious, at first to me, then to her mother, and then, well . . .''

"Well, what?''

"She began to take things from the house, jewelry, other valuables to sell in order to support her . . . habit.''

"God!''

"And then she met . . . him: Cameron.''

"Who?''

"Will Cameron. A very attractive man. And, Johnny, in spite of her addiction, Cynthia was still attractive and desirable, very desirable to Mr. Cameron.''

"What does he do, this Mr. Cameron?''

"Oh, among other things, he owns the Emporium. It's an establishment just inside the Slot. Gambling. Easy money. Easy virtue. He pursued Cynthia, although I must say it didn't take that much pursuit, because he provided her with what had become a necessity.''

"And what did she provide him with?''

"Unfortunately, you know the answer to that. To put it politely, she became his mistress.''

"Cynthia," Johnny whispered.

"Yes. But Amanda didn't put it politely. You heard her."

"I heard."

"Johnny, I brought them both into this world, Cynthia and Danny. Amanda's gone through hell, more hell than anybody should have to suffer. First her husband, then Danny, and now . . . Well, as I said, more hell than anybody should . . ."

"What about Cynthia? What about her hell?"

"Johnny . . ."

"What about helping her, *Doctor* Pickard?"

"Johnny, you've got to understand. Nobody can help her unless she wants to help herself, and it's probably too late. The odds . . ."

"Probably? Odds?" Johnny flared. "What the hell do I care about probablys and odds! Damn it Doctor, as long as there's a chance, any chance, she's got to be helped to help herself. What about this Hurd Renfield? Captain Hurd Renfield? Did he get killed?"

"No. Wounded."

"Did he come back?"

"Yes."

"Well, what about him?"

"He tried . . ."

"How hard?"

"As hard as he could, but she refuses to see him after . . ."

"After what? After Will Cameron?"

Doctor Pickard nodded.

"Well, I'm going to see her *and* Will Cameron. I'm going to . . ."

"Johnny . . ."

"What?"

"I'm afraid it gets even worse."

"What do you mean?"

"Cynthia, from what I've heard, is no longer just Will Cameron's mistress." There was a moment of ominous silence. "Mr. Cameron has found someone else for his exclusive . . . pleasure, and Cynthia, I've heard that . . ."

"That what? What've you heard?"

"I'm afraid that what Amanda said is true."

SIXTEEN

Johnny Yuma was on his way to the Emporium, just inside the Slot. This was the designated area of Natchez for gambling, prostitution, and any of the other vices the city's citizens and pilgrims passing through could indulge themselves in, so long as their conduct conformed to the acknowledged precepts of gambling, prostitution and any of the other vices citizens and pilgrims had indulged in ever since individuals banded together into tribes, villages and societal intercourse.

Some of these vices were known to occur in other sections of the city, but more discreetly. There was little or no need to heed discretion inside the Slot—short of murder. The Slot was wide open and open wide. The city elders felt it was better to contain immorality and look the other way than to allow it to proliferate throughout the community and try to keep an eye and a hand on such goings on.

Yuma was ready for trouble, and he knew trouble would be ready for him at the Emporium. And unlike war, this trouble he would have to face alone. Not as part of an army, a division, a brigade, a company, a platoon, or a squad. It would be just Johnny Yuma. Not even Corporal Johnny Yuma. The only thing that counted in the Slot was money, and the things that money could buy. And in the Slot, money could buy anything.

Dr. Pickard had said that Cynthia Reese was a casualty of war, as much a casualty as those who fell at Gettysburg. And there were thousands upon thousands like her on both sides, North and South. Victims of the army disease. Drugs. But almost all of them were men. Cynthia Reese was a woman. And she was Danny's sister.

Johnny Yuma had heard about and had even seen first-hand some of those casualties who had survived the bullet and the blade only to be devastated by another weapon, the needle.

Soluble morphine had been isolated by a chemist in Germany in 1804. The hypodermic syringe was developed in 1853 by a physician in England. But it was during the Civil War in the United States that the two elements were combined and put to widespread use.

Injectable morphine, the most effective antidote for the wounds and trauma of war, was the readiest of remedies in the field and in hospitals and sanitariums. And the doctors were ready and eager to administer the anodyne. Injecting morphine was the quickest and most effective method of alleviating the pain of soldiers writhing in agony and begging for relief. And it worked.

Instead of suffering, there was sedation. Instead of pain, there was placidity. Instead of despair, there was enchantment. But after a while, there was something else.

Addiction.

The price of peace carried a mortgage, payable in regular installments. The penalty for missing a payment was immediate and heavy: agony of mind and spirit and body—

relentless, racking, wretched prostration—the torment of
purgatorial fires.

Morphine was a derivative of opium, offspring of the
poppy imported from the Orient. When the Confederates
suffered the effects of the Yankee naval blockade, they cul-
tivated the anodyne poppy in Virginia, Tennessee, Georgia
and South Carolina.

Besides being used for the wounded, morphine was ad-
ministered for every disease that had been given a name
and for some that had no nomenclature. The presence of
dysentery alone in the Army of Northern Virginia was 740
cases per 1,000 men.

In addition to the vast numbers of soldiers treated for
dysentery and fever, the wounded numbered 265,000 Confederates and 318,000 Yankees, most all of whom were
dosed with morphine during prolonged and painful recov-
ery periods.

A Dr. C. M. Campbell wrote in a medical journal, "The
daily rounds of some physicians consisted largely of going
about with syringe and hypodermic needles and indiscrim-
inately giving sedatives to patients standing in line with
sleeves rolled up ready to receive their daily dose of chem-
ical restraint."

No wonder that in many cases survival was tantamount
to addiction.

And Cynthia was one of those cases. But no, Cynthia
wasn't a "case"—not to Johnny Yuma—not a "patient"—
not a "victim."

She was Cynthia Reese, Danny's sister, the sister whom
Danny loved, who had saved Danny's life and the lives of
countless other men. And whether the old woman was willing to acknowledge it or not, she was Amanda Reese's

daughter—even if she was a whore at the Emporium. She needed help.

And Johnny Yuma was going to the Emporium to help her—no matter what the odds.

SEVENTEEN

The Emporium was the first and biggest and liveliest saloon that anybody crossing into the Slot came across.

Johnny Yuma tied the sorrel to the hitching post and entered through the batwings. It was about what he expected from what he had heard. A little more ornate, dark wood and velvet drapes. An oak bar with round tables and Douglas chairs. A stage, and a stairway leading to auxiliary services on the second floor.

A little more pretentious than most saloons in the Slot, with higher prices, better whiskey, cleaner glasses, higher-class clientele, and laudable ladies in costlier costumes, catering to the cravings of customers with cash in hand or pocket or wallet.

Whiskey and women, both to make the customer shudder and shake, forget and remember—the best hope this side of the grave—illusions by night to face the demands of day.

It was still early in the night, and only about half the regulars had arrived, along with those passing through Natchez who had heard about the pleasures of the Emporium one way or another.

But Johnny Yuma wasn't there for pleasure. Still, it wouldn't be smart to appear too concerned. He would be as casual as a Confederate corporal could be, having survived the lost cause and managing to keep enough cash for a night's pleasure at the Emporium.

He ordered a beer and had barely turned his back to the bar when she approached. Young, ripe, yellow hair piled high above her smooth, too-white forehead, with just enough body showing so that any warm-blooded male would want to see more.

"Evening, Reb. My name's Mary."

"Hello, Mary."

"Congratulations." Mary smiled.

"For what?" Yuma smiled back.

"For being alive."

"Yeah, I guess you're right."

"And that's not all."

"No?"

"No. For being all together. Doesn't appear like there's anything missing." Mary looked him up and down, her gaze pausing near the Confederate buckle. "Both arms, both legs . . . everything appears to be in working order. That right?"

"Guess so."

"Guess? Don't you know? We could find out and have some fun in the bargain. What do you say, Reb?"

"I say thanks." Yuma took a swallow of beer.

"Good, I'll make . . ."

"Thanks, but . . ."

"But what?"

"I'm here to see . . . somebody else."

"Yeah? Who?"

"Somebody named Cynthia."

"You, too, huh? Say, what's that drowsy daffodil got?"

"I don't know, but I'm here to see her," Johnny said.

"You are, huh?"

"Yep."

"Well, you'll have to make . . . arrangements."

"How do I do that?"

"You see that . . . lady over there?" Mary pointed to a middle-aged woman sitting alone, playing solitaire at a table near the foot of the stairway.

"I see her."

"Name's Stella. You go talk to Stella."

"I will. Thanks." Yuma finished the beer and set the glass on the bar.

"And remember, my name's Mary. Maybe next time, huh, Reb?" She looked him directly in the eyes and pinched his cheek, close, very close to Yuma's lips. "You won't regret it. I'm not the least bit drowsy."

Yuma made his way across the room, past the men playing poker, past others who were at the roulette table, and the ones drinking with the female employees of the Emporium.

Stella was a handsome woman, who had been beautiful at an earlier age, an age without the added poundage and lines about her eyes and mouth, lines she made no attempt to conceal with makeup. In fact, they appeared to be lines of defiance and even pride, lines that announced she had nothing to hide. She was what she was and not what she used to be: no pretense, no nonsense.

"Miss Stella?"

"Just Stella." She looked up from the queen she had placed on a king. "Just Stella, Reb. You new in town?"

"Yes, ma'am."

"Don't call me ma'am. Stella."

Yuma smiled and nodded.

"You got a nice smile, Reb. What can I do for you?"

"Mary said I'd have to make . . . arrangements with you."

"About what?"

"About seeing . . . Cynthia."

"Cynthia, huh?"

"Yes, ma . . . yes, Stella. Cynthia."

"Well, that can be arranged. But Cynthia's busy right now." Stella looked at the locket watch on a gold chain between her breasts. "Will be for another . . . oh, fifteen minutes."

"I'll wait."

"Sure you will, you . . . Oh, Reb, meet the boss."

A man was now standing near Yuma, a big man, dressed all in black except for the starched white shirt and the pearl-handled revolver gleaming out of the vent in his suit coat. His deep-set eyes and slicked hair were as black as the suit and boots he wore.

"Hello, Reb."

"You Will Cameron?"

"No."

"I thought . . ."

"Will Cameron's the *big* boss." Stella grinned. "This is Al Rattigan. He runs the Emporium for Mr. Cameron. The Reb's new in town, Al. He's here to see Cynthia."

"That so?" Rattigan's voice was as dry as his dusty, deep-set eyes. "Where'd you hear about Cynthia?"

"I . . . just heard."

"Sure. Word gets around."

"That's right. Word gets around."

"Well, I'll see you later, Stella. You, too, Reb."

"Yeah," said Yuma, looking directly into the black, dry eyes of Al Rattigan, "I'll see you later."

Johnny Yuma knocked softly at the door in the hallway of the second floor.

"Come in," said the voice inside the room.

Yuma entered and closed the door behind him. He took off his cap and held it in his left hand.

"Oh," she said, "a gentleman."

She was pale, almost white as flour, and a little too thin, but still beautiful—large, blue eyes full of despair; auburn hair spilling over the curves of her shoulders; alabaster shoulders outlined against the dimly lit room—an ethereal portrait that might have been in a museum.

Yuma took a step forward.

"My name's . . ."

"It doesn't matter."

"Maybe it does."

"I don't want to know your name." She rose from the straight-backed chair in front of the mirror. "Or anything about you. I know what you're here for."

"Do you?"

"You're just another customer and you're wasting time."

"What're you wasting?"

"Look, mister . . ."

"Yuma. Johnny Yuma."

She sat, almost fell, back into the chair. She covered her face with the palms of both her hands. She trembled, and Yuma knew that there were tears in her eyes.

"Johnny . . . Johnny . . ." she sobbed.

"It's all right, Cynthia." Yuma moved even closer, touched her shoulder. "Go ahead and cry. Wash it all away."

"I can't, Johnny. It's too late . . . and I don't care anymore. There's nothing left."

"Sure there is, Cynthia. Sure there is." Gently, he lifted

her out of the chair. "Look into that mirror, Cynthia. Go ahead, look."

Slowly, she lifted her head and through the tears looked at both their images in the mirror.

"It's not too late, not yet, and you've got to care . . . for Danny's sake, for your mother, for Hurd Renfield, for me . . . and most important, for yourself."

"No."

"Yes! I'm here to help you, Cynthia. We'll all help. But you've got to care. You've got to care. You've got to want to beat this. You can do it. Other people have done it. People not as strong and as good as you . . ."

"I'm, I'm not strong, Johnny, not anymore . . . and not good. I'm just a wh . . ."

"Shut up, Cynthia! I don't want to hear that! And you're not going to say it! Not ever again!"

"Oh, Johnny . . ."

"Listen to me. We're going to help you, Dr. Pickard and me . . . and I'll bet Hurd Renfield, too."

"No, he doesn't want to see me."

"It was you who didn't want to see him. I'll talk to him. We'll come and get you. Will you leave with us if he and I come back together?"

"I don't want him to see me here."

"Why not? He knows. Everybody knows. If we come back, the two of us, will you come with us? Will you let us help you?"

"I don't know . . ."

"Sure you do, Cynthia. Danny told me about you. Sure you do. Say you'll come with us. Say it!"

"They won't let me."

"Who's they?"

"Cameron . . . Rattigan . . . *Rattigan.*"

"You let me worry about that. Just tell me you'll come

with us if we come back tomorrow. We'll walk out that door together, Cynthia, into the daylight. You be ready. Don't take anything with you. Not anything. Do you hear?''

"I hear.''

"Will you do it? Will you?''

"Yes.'' She was still sobbing.

"Where is it?''

"What?''

"You know what, Cynthia. Where do you keep it?''

She pointed to the top bureau drawer under the mirror. Yuma walked to the bureau, pulled open the drawer, and lifted the needle and syringe. He smashed the metal casing and glass tube of the syringe against the side of the drawer, let the pieces fall back into the drawer, then slammed it shut.

Cynthia Reese cringed at the sound of the slam.

"It's done, Cynthia.'' He walked to her and put his arms around her trembling body. "It's broken, smashed. That's the first step. We'll be with you the rest of the way. We'll come and get you tomorrow, and we'll stay with you until you're cured. You won't be alone, Cynthia, not for a minute.'' He lifted her chin with the tip of his finger. "We'll be with you, and so will Danny.''

Johnny Yuma adjusted the Confederate cap as he walked down the stairs from the second floor. The Emporium was busier and noisier than before. What passed for an orchestra, made up of a piano player, a fiddler, a banjoist, and a drummer, were making music in the pit preparatory to the evening's stage entertainment, which would begin in a few minutes.

Stella still sat at her table, looking up and talking to the boss, Al Rattigan. But now, standing beside and slightly in front of the boss, was a man who obviously was the *big* boss, Will Cameron.

Will Cameron looked, dressed, and even smelled of success and confidence. His suit, shirt, cravat, and boots were more elegant and expensive than Rattigan's, and he knew how to wear them. He was clean-shaven and well-groomed with the trace of a superior smile curved across an aristocratic face.

A small, eager man passed Yuma, taking the stairs two at a time as he hurried upward to his rendezvous.

"Well, Reb," Stella smiled, "everything come off all right?"

"I think so."

"What does that mean?" Stella remarked. "Never heard that answer before."

"It means I'll be back."

"Good. Reb, this is Mr. Cameron, he owns the Emporium."

"And all the people in it?"

"What is that supposed to imply, Mr. . . ."

"Yuma," Johnny answered. "Johnny Yuma. And I wasn't implying anything, just asking. Those ladies upstairs, for instance. Do you own them, Mr. Cameron?"

"You might not have heard, Mr. Yuma, but before he died, Lincoln freed even the slaves. Nobody owns anybody anymore."

"Good."

"I'm glad you approve."

"Because tomorrow I'm coming back in the morning."

"To see the lady you saw this evening? We don't open until . . ."

"This isn't business, it's personal. I'm coming back to take Cynthia Reese with me. Any objections?"

"No, of course not. They're all free to come and go as

they please. But you'll have to speak to Mr. Rattigan. He's in charge of . . . the operation.''

"That right, Mr. Rattigan?"

"That's right," Rattigan sneered.

"Any objections?" Yuma repeated.

"You heard what Mr. Cameron said. They're all free to come and go as they please."

"Including Cynthia Reese?"

"Including anybody. All she has to do is walk past me . . . and so do you."

"Fine. We'll do just that."

EIGHTEEN

It was close to midnight. Yuma had been talking to Hurd Renfield for more than an hour.

Johnny Yuma had first talked to Dr. Miles Pickard, told him of his meeting with Cynthia and that she had agreed to leave the Emporium if he returned with her former fiancé and if the former captain would see her through the ordeal of withdrawal, along with Yuma and Dr. Pickard.

If Yuma could get her past Cameron and Rattigan.

"That's a mountain range of ifs," Pickard replied, but he said he would do what he could to help. The first help Yuma needed from Pickard was directions to Hurd Renfield's place.

Renfield was a handsome man in his early thirties, a six-footer, with a saber scar on his left cheek. He walked with a noticeable limp and with the need of a cane. He had been wounded while with General William J. Hardee when Savannah fell to Sherman just before Christmas of '64.

Yuma began by talking about Danny and their friendship. When Renfield asked about Danny's death, Yuma told him the same story he had told Danny's mother, and then

Johnny Yuma began to speak about Cynthia.

The captain's eyes welled when Yuma told him he had seen her that night.

"At the Emporium?"

"That's right, Captain."

"Is she . . ."

"Is she all right?"

Renfield nodded.

"No. She's not all right. She's all wrong. She's addicted to morphine."

"Yes, I know . . ."

"Then you know the rest."

"Yes."

"But, Captain, that's not Cynthia up there. Not Danny's sister. Not the Cynthia Reese you knew and loved. That's not your Cynthia. But you can get her back if you want to. Do you?"

"I tried . . ."

"Try again! I'll help you. So will Dr. Pickard."

"It's no use . . . it . . ."

"Use? What's no use? Was fighting the war no use? Well, maybe it was, but we fought . . . sometimes we won. We faced the enemy and we fought. You *did* fight, didn't you, Captain? Or did you get that bullet running away? Answer me, you son of a bitch! Were you a coward? Are you a coward now? Or are you willing to fight?"

"I . . ."

"She is! She's willing to fight! I smashed the needle. She watched me do it. I told her that was the first step. Now I'll tell you something! You're the next step. Without you, she's finished! She's nothing but a hollow arm waiting to be pumped full of dope! Waiting to die! Is that what you want? Is it?"

Yuma waited for an answer.

"Johnny . . . Johnny . . . tell me the truth. Did . . . did she say she wanted to . . . to see me . . . to leave . . . there?"

"If you still love her, if you still want her back, if you're willing to fight for her . . . why don't you come with me and find out for yourself, Captain?"

NINETEEN

At ten o'clock the next morning, Yuma and Renfield, in
Renfield's buggy, crossed into the Slot and tied up in front
of the Emporium.

The Emporium still smelled of last night's spilled whiskey and beer. Invisible vapors of exhaled tobacco smoke
clung to the velvet drapes and tabletops. A couple of men
were mopping and cleaning up. The bartender was washing,
wiping, and stacking glasses. A half-dozen customers were
wetting their windpipes and juicing their innards with the
hair of the dog.

There were others there, too. Stella sat at her table. And
at a far table sat Will Cameron and Al Rattigan. Cameron
wore a fresh, crisp, white shirt and was eating a breakfast
steak. Rattigan poured from a fresh bottle of whiskey into
a glass in front of him.

As Yuma and Renfield entered, Rattigan rose and walked
to the foot of the stairway before the two men got there.

"You here to see Needle Nellie?" Rattigan asked.

"We're here to see Cynthia Reese," Yuma replied.

"You are, huh?"

"Is she up there?"

"Far as I know," Rattigan shrugged.

"Then we're going up." Yuma moved past Rattigan and started up the stairway, followed by Renfield, who made his way with the cane.

"Going up's no hard knot," Rattigan said, "getting out's something else."

Yuma paused halfway and looked back.

"You said she was free to go if she pleased."

"I also said you had to get past me and, mister, if you do, I'll quit this place and leave town."

"I'm sure that Natchez'll be sorry to see you go." Yuma continued up the stairway and so did Renfield.

Yuma knocked on the door.

"Come in."

He opened it and stood at the threshold.

"Johnny . . . did . . . is he . . ."

Yuma stepped aside. Hurd Renfield walked into the room. Neither spoke for a moment. She was lovely in the morning light, but the first telltale signs were already there: the need, the craving. By this time any other morning . . . but this was not any other morning. This probably was the most important morning of her life, and Cynthia Reese knew it and was fighting for control. The sight of Hurd Renfield helped her fight, and what he did next helped even more.

He took her in his arms and kissed her tenderly.

Rattigan waited at the bottom of the stairway until Yuma and Renfield had disappeared into the upper hallway. His lower lip rolled across the ridges of his teeth and he cleared his throat. Stella looked at him for a moment, then went back to her solitaire. Will Cameron continued to cut and eat his breakfast steak without any apparent interest in what had happened or what was going to happen.

Rattigan took another look at the empty stairway, then walked past Stella to the table where Cameron ate and where the whiskey bottle waited.

Rattigan poured and drank.

"You're gonna enjoy this, Will."

"Am I?"

"Sure." Rattigan poured another.

"Are *you?*"

"Huh?"

"I wouldn't take on too much of that brave-maker." Cameron pointed to the whiskey bottle with his fork. "It dulls the reflexes."

Rattigan set down the glass.

"I don't need any brave-maker. Not for that squirt."

Sounds came from upstairs. Footsteps. Renfield's cane on the wooden stairway. Yuma came into sight first, then Renfield and Cynthia together.

Rattigan walked toward the center of the room, blocking the way to the batwings. He stroked back the cloth of his coat, revealing the pearl handle resting high in its holster.

"Just a minute," Rattigan said. "I want to talk to you."

"Talk," Yuma replied.

"I mean to *her.*" Rattigan pointed at Cynthia.

"Talk," Yuma repeated.

"Listen, Cynthia, you don't want to leave here. You got everything you want, everything you need. First-class accommodations, first-class customers—not like them in the cribs out back. We're your friends. We take care of you. You need something right now. You're already starting to shake. It's going to get worse. Remember? Go on back upstairs . . ."

"You've talked enough," Yuma said.

"Shut up, Reb! Cyn, you turn around. Go upstairs."

"Yeah, and what's the next stop?" Yuma faced Rattigan. "The cribs out back and then a wooden box!"

"I said shut up, Reb!"

Rattigan went for his gun, barely cleared leather, but Yuma's Colt was already drawn and leveled at Rattigan's midsection.

At the same time, Renfield whipped the stem of his cane across Rattigan's hand, and the gun fell to the floor.

Yuma nodded at Renfield and pointed at the batwings. Renfield and Cynthia moved toward the entrance.

Yuma holstered the Colt and took a step after them, but Rattigan sprang like a tiger, leaping at Yuma, clubbing him hard with both fists, surprisingly quick and agile for a man his size.

But Yuma was quicker and more agile. They were two wildcats. Instead of fang and claw, it was the fury of fists smashing and battering to head and body, and then Rattigan grabbing, trying to gain advantage with size and weight, onto and over tables and chairs, on the floor, twisting and wrestling. Renfield and Cynthia paused at the batwings. Stella sat at her table. Will Cameron watched, impassive.

Yuma prevailed, managing one, two, three clean, sharp blows, snapping Rattigan's head left, right, and left. Rattigan lay limp.

Yuma rose. It was slow and painful, but he rose to his feet. He looked down at Rattigan, who was barely conscious, then glanced at Cameron.

Yuma started to turn, but he knew it wasn't over. He whirled back as Rattigan went for the gun on the floor. He never made it. Yuma drew and hip fired. The gun on the floor sparked and shattered with Rattigan's hand only inches away. Yuma's Colt pointed toward Al Rattigan.

"We'll be leaving now," Yuma said. This time, he

didn't turn his back as he, Renfield, and Cynthia made their way out of the Emporium.

Will Cameron pushed aside the plate, rose, and walked to where Al Rattigan struggled to get to his feet.

"Your resignation is accepted," Cameron said and moved away.

TWENTY

"War is hell," General Sherman said, and he was right. But there are other kinds of hell. Torment, terrifying and unspeakable. Torture of the body and mind . . . a living hell, gripping every vein and fiber, every bone and muscle . . . the hell of withdrawal . . .

They were all there to help, sometimes together, sometimes taking turns: Yuma, Renfield, and Dr. Miles Pickard. A room at Renfield's place had been stripped bare of everything but the brass bed and the straps that held her down when she turned wild and furious.

Dr. Pickard had told them about addicts who nearly went mad with agony and fury when they weren't tied down, who broke chairs and mirrors, smashed windows and tried to kill themselves with shards of broken glass, who beat their fists and even their heads bloody against the walls.

So they had lashed her to the bed, the bed which became a vessel of salvation, but at the same time, of torture, hurtling her distorted mind and aching body deep into a fathomless pit, skewing, twisting, turning, then shooting her upward past unseen stars and suns in another universe, with billowing pain beating a tattoo of torment into her fevered brain.

It had been over a week, but not the kind of time in calendars and clocks.

Time, twisted and stretched, curled and snaked, spiraled and contorted. A clock with no hands.

Time, dripping beads of fire and ice, incessant, ceaseless, burning, freezing, drilling into flesh and soul.

Searing into what remained of Cynthia Reese.

She knew that they were there to help, and at times she thanked them.

But she also knew that they were there to deny her what she craved, and she screamed and cursed at them.

She sweat and shivered and shrieked and burrowed into a venomous garden of living gargoyles, vile serpents and fire breathing dragons.

The chemise she wore clung to her writhing body—her breasts and stomach and thighs. She pulled against the straps that held her legs and arms, sobbing, choking, then cursing again, moaning, sometimes hysterical, sometimes delirious, sometimes begging to die. One night, when it was Yuma's turn to be with her:

"Johnny, I can't."

"Hold on, Cynthia."

"I can't."

"Yes, you can."

"I want to die."

"No!"

"Johnny, give me a gun . . . a knife . . . anything. . . ."

"No."

"Then kill me, Johnny, kill me, please!"

"You're gonna make it."

"I want to die."

"Think of Danny."

"Danny?"

"You saved him."

"Danny . . ."

"Now you've got to save yourself."

"Danny . . ."

She became delirious.

"Danny, Danny, you're going to get well. . . . I'm here with you, Danny . . . holding your hand. . . . You hold on, Danny, hold tight. . . . Danny, don't slip away. . . . Hold on . . . I'm with you. . . . You've got to fight, Danny . . . fight . . . keep fighting. . . ."

"That's right, Cynthia, keep fighting."

"Johnny?"

"Yes?"

"Tell me again about Rock Island."

"Sure."

"You and Danny."

"That's right Danny and me."

"You broke free."

"And you're gonna break free, Cynthia."

"Tell me again Johnny how you did it."

Twice before, Yuma had told Cynthia the story of their escape. It seemed to calm her and please her.

"Tell me, Johnny, about the body bags and you and Danny. How you hid inside with the dead bodies."

"Sure. A friend of ours sewed us in."

"With the dead bodies."

"That's right, a dozen bodies in each bag."

"And you had a knife."

"Danny did . . . a spoon sharpened . . ."

"And they threw you from a cliff."

"Into the water . . . almost frozen."

"And you cut yourselves loose."

"Danny did. He got us out. He saved us . . . like you saved him. That's why I'm alive now, Cynthia, because you saved him and now you're going to save yourself. You're going to fight and save yourself."

She was unconscious. From weakness or pain, it didn't matter. Even in sleep, her body shuddered.

But another day had passed.

"Will, can I talk to you for just a minute?" Al Rattigan had waited outside the Emporium and approached Will Cameron.

"I don't see that we have anything to talk about, Mr. Rattigan."

"Look, Will . . . Mr. Cameron . . ."

"I thought you'd left Natchez; but then, lately, you haven't been doing what you said you'd do."

"All those years we been together . . ."

"Together?"

"What I mean is . . . working for you . . ."

"What about them?"

"I always come through for you, didn't I? Just this once . . ."

"You don't seem to understand the gravity of the situation."

"What do you mean?"

"Just this. First, one girl leaves. Do you know what that does? That gives other girls ideas. Those girls aren't supposed to have those kinds of ideas. If one gets away with it, then maybe another'll try to do the same, and another, and another. Do you know what that amounts to, Mr. Rattigan? Anarchy. And I can't have that, can I?"

"Mr. Cameron, suppose . . ."

"Suppose what?"

"Suppose she comes back? Suppose I bring her back?"

"Then, Mr. Rattigan, we would have something to talk about."

Two more days and nights squeezed by. For Cynthia Reese, they were two days and nights of burning in ice, drowning in desert, and freezing in hell: bones blistering, throat wrenching, mind bending and hallucinating, and the pain, penetrating and eternal, the pain of being turned inside out and wrung dry by steel fingers of an invisible hand.

The hands and voices of Yuma and Renfield and Dr. Pickard did what little anybody could do to assuage the suffering.

Then, Dr. Pickard was called away. Amanda Reese had suffered a stroke. Her life hung in the balance, a delicate balance that could tip either way.

It was Yuma who told Cynthia. He told her in hopes that Cynthia herself would want to get well and go to her mother, but it seemed to have almost the opposite effect.

"She hates me, Johnny."

"That's not true."

"She told me herself."

"People say things."

"Things they mean."

"Cynthia, the worst is over for you. You've almost got it licked. Another day or two, and you'll be clean. It'll be over, and you can start a new life with Hurd and with your mother."

"He's right," Hurd Renfield said. "Johnny's right. After this, there's nothing you can't do, nothing we can't do together. . . ."

"I love you, Hurd," she whispered. "I always have, and I always will. . . . I . . ."

There was a noise outside, and then a knock on the door, loud and persistent.

"I'll get it, Johnny. You stay here."

It was less than a minute when Renfield came back into the room and with him, Miss Morrison, her hair disheveled in wisps across her dirt driven face and her glasses spattered with grime.

"Miss Morrison!" Yuma went to her. "What happened? How'd you get here?"

"How do you think? With Doc's buggy. Just because I'm old and half blind doesn't mean I'm helpless, you young . . . Well, never mind." She walked to the side of the bed. "Cynthia, Dr. Pickard tells me you're going to get well. You do that, child, do you hear me? You do that!"

Cynthia managed to nod.

"Now, Johnny." Miss Morrison turned to Yuma. "You get on your horse and ride like hell back to Amanda. She's been asking for you. Doc said you should hurry."

"Yes, ma'am."

"Johnny . . ." Cynthia tried to rise. "Tell her . . . tell her that . . ."

"I'll tell her."

"Well, get a move on!" Miss Morrison said. "I'll be along as soon as I catch my breath."

"Yes, ma'am." Yuma was on his way out the door.

Miss Morrison took off her glasses and squinted at Hurd Renfield.

"Say," she inquired, "you got any whiskey in this place?"

"Yes, ma'am."

"Well, then, fetch it."

TWENTY-ONE

"Johnny, hold on to my hand. Don't let go."

"I won't Mrs. Reese. I won't let go."

Johnny Yuma had been there for more than an hour. Dr. Pickard had met him in the hallway and told him briefly about her condition. The next forty-eight hours would be critical. Her right side was paralyzed, her speech impaired, but her mind was clear.

At first, in her confusion, she had called for Danny, but finally she realized that he was dead. Then she wanted to see Johnny. Dr. Pickard told her that Yuma was with Cynthia. Mrs. Reese had blanched at the mention of her daughter's name but asked or said nothing about her.

It was Johnny she wanted to see. She needed all the help, attention, and encouragement possible, so Dr. Pickard had sent Miss Morrison. He didn't have to send her, she volunteered, no, not volunteered, insisted, and blazed out like her britches were burning.

Miss Morrison had since returned and sat on an overstuffed chair as Johnny Yuma held the hand of Amanda Reese.

"Johnny . . ." Her words were slow and slurred. "You're my family now. I don't want to die alone."

"You're not going to die, Mrs. Reese, and you're not alone. Dr. Pickard is here and Miss Morrison, but you've got to listen to me. Can you hear me all right?"

She nodded and smiled.

"Good. Mrs. Reese, I want to bring someone to see you . . . someone who *is* your family. Your flesh and blood."

"No."

"Yes. She's been sick, too, but she's going to get well . . . and she needs you."

"No!" Amanda Reese turned her head away.

"Hurd Renfield is with her now. He loves her, and she loves him . . . and you."

"No!"

"Listen to me, Mrs. Reese. Your daughter was a soldier of the South. As much a soldier as Danny, maybe more. She was on the battlefield, a lot of battlefields, with cannon and blood and death all around her. That took courage, more courage than I had, or Danny, or most of us. We had guns and bayonets to defend ourselves. She had nothing but her faith in God, her love of country and family.

"Mrs. Reese, your daughter was wounded in action. A terrible wound. But she didn't retreat. She didn't surrender. She kept fighting, and she's fighting now—for her life and for your love.

"If Danny had come home wounded, with a terrible wound like Cynthia's, would you have turned your back on him? Would you have let him suffer alone, a hero, who fought and fell and tried to rise again?

"Or would you have put your arms around him and helped him to recover? What would you have done for Danny, Mrs. Reese?

"You said you didn't look out the window anymore because your soldier was never coming back. But what about your other soldier? Sick and wounded? The other hero. She can come back. She needs you and loves you, and in your heart you know you love her.

"Mrs. Reese, I'm going to bring your soldier home, so keep looking out that window."

There were tears in her eyes. She nodded and squeezed Johnny Yuma's hand.

TWENTY-TWO

As Yuma held the hand of Amanda Reese, so did Hurd Renfield hold the hand of Cynthia Reese less than two miles away.

Cynthia breathed less heavily now and not as irregularly. There was still an inner churning and craving and cavity, but what had been an internal hurricane was now a rough sea, still with breakers ahead, but navigable, and the horizon was almost in sight.

She smiled at him. "Hurd, I'm going to make it."

"Sure you are, sweetheart. Johnny was right. The worst is over. A few more hours. Just hold on."

"I will."

"I'll be right here."

"I know that. Hurd . . ."

"Yes?"

"I'm sorry . . . so sorry . . ."

"Now stop that."

"Do you . . . do you think that God can forgive me?"

"I think he already has, or you wouldn't be here."

"I'm here because of you."

"And Johnny."

"Yes . . . And you? Hurd, can you forgive me?"

"There's nothing for me to forgive. Johnny said it: That wasn't you out there. That was somebody else . . . and you and I have always been together and we always will be. Now, you rest."

"I'll try."

"Cynthia, I can't stand seeing you tied up like this anymore. I'm going to take off those straps. Do you think you'll be all right?"

"I . . . think so."

"Good. I'll be . . ."

There was a knock at the door.

"That must be Johnny," Hurd said. "I'll be right back."

As Hurd Renfield opened the door, the butt of a pistol sledged across his forehead, knocking him back into the room.

Al Rattigan stepped inside. He viciously kicked Renfield in the back, picked up the fallen cane, and struck him on the side of the head.

"You were pretty handy with that cane, Captain. See how you like it."

But Renfield heard nothing. He was bleeding and unconscious.

"Hurd, what is it? What happened?" It was Cynthia's voice from the other room. "Johnny?"

Rattigan walked to the inner doorway and saw Cynthia Reese strapped to the bed.

"No, it's not your Rebel friend. It's me, your other friend." She struggled against the straps. "Well, ain't this handy. All tied up and ready for pluckin'."

She screamed.

"Go ahead and yell, Cyn. There's nobody to hear but me and them chickens outside."

Cynthia screamed again.

"Go ahead. Get it out of your system. I'll be right back."
He laughed.

Rattigan walked back into the front room, grabbed the
inert man by the collar, and dragged him through the doorway a few feet from the bed.

He ripped a cord off the drapes and tied Renfield's hands
behind his back. Then he stuffed a handkerchief deep into
Renfield's mouth, all the time talking to Cynthia as she
sobbed.

"Now Cyn, we're gonna fix up your boyfriend so he can
watch, just in case he comes to. He's gonna see you in
action, just like at the Emporium. Let's see how he likes
you after that. Let's see how you like yourself."

"No!"

"Oh, yes. But first, Cyn, old girl, I'm gonna give you
something to settle your nerves. Something to make you
feel good. It's something you want . . . something you want
more than anything in the world. I've got it right here."

He removed a black leather case from the inside pocket
of his coat and snapped the case open. He took out the
syringe with the long, shiny needle.

"Look here, Cyn. It's your old friend come to pay you
a visit and take you home."

She turned her head away and squeezed her eyes shut.

"Aww, now don't turn away, Cyn. You know you want
it, and it wants you."

"Please!"

"Oh, it'll please you, all right. It always has . . . and so
will I." He came close and leaned over her straining body.
Then he turned back.

Hurd Renfield had regained consciousness. He was rolling over, trying to pull free from the strong, thin cord that bound his hands.

"Well, well, the captain's come to the party! Good. You watch, Captain. You watch us. It just might be the last thing you ever see!"

"No!" She screamed. "Leave him alone! I'll come with you . . . please!"

"Sure you will. When I'm ready, but first . . ."

Rattigan held the syringe with one hand. The other touched her face with his fingers and palm, then moved down the surface of her throat and body, across her breasts and quivering flesh, and finally came to rest on her arm.

Again she screamed.

"Now, take it easy, Cyn, just relax. You know you want what's coming." He rubbed her arm. "There, right there . . . nice and white and waiting. Just hold still, Cyn. Just hold still and . . ."

Yuma leaped across the room and sprang at Rattigan. They slammed against the wall. The syringe flew onto the bed near Cynthia's arm.

Johnny Yuma held Rattigan by the throat with his left hand, and his right fist crashed again and again into Rattigan's face, battering the back of his head each time against the wall until blood leaked from his mouth and nose and eyes, breaking flesh and bone until it was no longer a face.

"Johnny!" Cynthia shrieked.

Yuma let Rattigan drop. He went to Hurd Renfield, pulled a knife from his pocket, and cut the cord. Renfield took the kerchief out of his mouth.

"Johnny . . ."

"I saw the open door. Heard her scream."

Yuma whirled, drew, and fired. Rattigan fell dead with the gun still in his hand.

"That's just what I wanted him to do," Yuma said.

He walked to the bed and cut the straps. He helped Cynthia Reese to her feet. She reached toward the bed, picked up the syringe and hurled it against the wall. It broke.

The pieces fell where Rattigan lay.

TWENTY-THREE

Amanda Reese and her daughter are together again. The
sheriff said there was no need for a trial after Cynthia and
Hurd Renfield told him about Rattigan. On the way out of
Natchez . . .

Johnny Yuma came across Will Cameron escorting a
beautiful lady. Cameron and the lady were coming out of
an expensive dress shop. The shop was located in an up-
scale section of Natchez.

"Well, Mr. Yuma, I heard you were leaving our fair
city."

"That's right."

"Did you enjoy our hospitality?"

"Some of it."

"We'll have to try harder . . . next time. Oh, this is Miss
Melinda Grahame. Melinda, this is Mr. Yuma."

"Pleased to meet you, Mr. Yuma."

"Thank you, ma'am." Yuma turned to Cameron.
"You're a little out of your territory, aren't you?"

"Oh, you mean the Slot?"

"Yeah, the Slot."

"That's business." Cameron smiled and looked at Melinda Grahame. "This is pleasure. By the way, I understand that Miss Reese and Renfield are getting married."

"That's right."

"I'll have to congratulate the happy couple when I see them."

"You won't be seeing her."

"Never can tell."

"I said, you won't be seeing her, ever again. Miss Grahame, have you ever been to the Slot? To the Emporium?"

"No." She almost seemed amused. "Of course not."

"You will, Miss Grahame. You will."

"Mr. Yuma." Cameron was not smiling. "I believe this conversation is finished."

"So do I. Good-bye, Miss Grahame and . . ."

"Yes?"

"Good luck."

TWENTY-FOUR

Since leaving Natchez just over two weeks ago, I've been riding steadily northwest—toward home—across the Mississippi River into Louisiana, through the southwest border of Arkansas, into Texarkana, and today I am in my native state, having crossed the Red River into Texas . . .

The same Red River that the Austins had crossed, Moses and his son Stephen, and then so many others who were not born in Texas, but who gave birth to what would become, on December 29, 1845, the twenty-eighth state of the United States of America.

The others, men like Sam Houston, Jim Bowie, Davy Crockett, William Travis, Sam Maverick, Henry Kinney, Gail Borden, Robert Hancock Hunter, Ben McCulloch, David Burnet—pioneers, soldiers, newspapermen, physicians, speculators, statesmen—were all born somewhere else, but all died Texans.

For Texas.

Texas, a bountiful land, but since time remembered, a battlefield, and worth fighting for: the rich soil of the central plains, the thick forests of the eastern regions, the deep, natural harbors of the Gulf of Mexico, the flowing rivers penetrating from the interior, a favorable climate and uncounted herds of horses and cattle. Texas was a battlefield, claimed and conquered by Indian tribes who fought each other with arrows and tomahawks: Kiowa, Comanche, Cherokee, and Apache. Then came the conquerors with gunpowder—Spaniards and Mexicans—and then the lusty Americans, the unyielding, unending procession of farmers, cotton growers, cattlemen, entrepreneurs, runaways, outlaws, and lawmen—and with or after them, the women who would bear the firstborn new breed of Texans.

But for Johnny Yuma, it was Sam Houston who most symbolized the spirit, the soul of Texas. Johnny's father, Ned Yuma, not only had known Sam Houston, he had fought alongside Houston at San Jacinto where the Alamo was remembered and avenged. Houston was Ned Yuma's hero, and he made sure that Johnny Yuma grew up listening to the heroic tales about Sam Houston, the Magnificent Barbarian.

Time and again, Johnny Yuma heard how Sam Houston, at age thirty-nine, crossed the Red River in 1832 with written orders issued by the president of the United States, Andrew Jackson, directing him to find, confer with, and make friends of the Comanche chiefs—and make them friends of the United States.

Houston grew up in Tennessee and had lived with and been adopted by a clan of Cherokees when he was seventeen. At twenty, he fought at the side of General Andrew Jackson against the Creeks at Horseshoe Bend, was wounded three times, decorated for bravery, and became a lifelong friend and advocate of the general who later became president.

After soldiering, Houston practiced law back in Tennessee, was elected to Congress, and later became governor of Tennessee until his marriage failed. He resigned and went back to live with the Cherokees until Jackson sent him to Texas.

When Texas declared its independence, Sam Houston was named commander in chief of the revolutionary forces. The fighting Texians.

Houston needed time to gather and organize his army. He ordered Lieutenant Colonel William B. Travis to buy him that time by defending the Alamo against General Antonio López de Santa Anna.

Travis did that with 183 Texans until the final assault by 4,000 Mexican troops on March 6, 1836. All 183 Texans were killed, but so were more than 1,500 of Santa Anna's soldiers.

Santa Anna ordered the bodies of the Texans to be burned. But out of the flames arose the battle cry, "Remember the Alamo!"

Six weeks later, the battle cry echoed and reverberated at San Jacinto, where Sam Houston with 600 Texans, young Ned Yuma among them, crushed Santa Anna's army of 1,250, killing more than 600 and capturing the rest, including General Santa Anna. Nine Texans were killed, 26 wounded. Ned Yuma was one of the 26, carrying a bayonet scar on his left shoulder for the rest of his life.

Ned Yuma went on to become a Texas Ranger. He served for over a dozen years until he met, fell in love with, and married Elizabeth Parker, who was to become Johnny Yuma's mother.

Sam Houston was elected the first president of the new Republic of Texas. He led the movement for Texas to join the United States, and when it did, he was elected to the Senate and later became governor of Texas.

While Houston was governor, in spite of his impassioned

opposition, Texas voted to secede from the Union. At almost seventy Houston stood tall and brave and warned his fellow Texans of what was to come: "Your fathers and husbands, your sons and brothers, will be herded at the point of bayonet . . . while I believe with you in the doctrine of state's rights, the North is determined to preserve this Union. They move with the steady momentum and perseverance of a mighty avalanche: and what I fear is, they will overwhelm the South."

Sam Houston's fear came true.

But he didn't live to see it happen. On July 25, 1863, suffering from pneumonia, he stirred from a deep sleep as his wife Margaret held his hand. He cried out, "Texas! Texas!"

Sam Houston died that day with the sunset. It would be a long, dark night for Texas.

And now, Johnny Yuma, after days and months and years of desperation, desolation, and defeat, had crossed the Red River back into Texas. The most difficult part of his odyssey probably was behind him, but to get back to Mason City there was still a lot of distance and danger ahead. Across the *Llano Estacado*—the Staked Plain. Yuma would still have to travel the length of three ordinary states.

But there was nothing ordinary about Texas: Not the terrain. Not the people. Not the history.

And not Johnny Yuma.

TWENTY-FIVE

I've heard it said, or maybe I read in a book, that somewhere in the world each man or woman has a double—someone who looks the same. I don't know whether that's true, but when I rode into Longview, it appeared that it was true about two places: Longview and Mason City. Even though they were hundreds and hundreds of miles apart, they were pretty much alike, including some of the people in both places—especially the sheriff and the newspaper editor . . .

It was almost like looking at a photograph or painting or into a mirror of the place where Johnny Yuma was born.

The hotel, the bar, the general store, and the sheriff's office, but what caught Johnny Yuma's attention the most was the building that housed the newspaper, the *Longview Chronicle*. It was almost a dead ringer for Elmer Dodson's building and newspaper, the *Mason City Bulletin*.

It had been years since Johnny Yuma had smelled ink, set type, and swept the floor of the *Bulletin* or had even been inside any newspaper office. He tied the sorrel to the hitching post and walked through the open door.

Inside, two men were playing checkers and drinking coffee from tin cups. The coffeepot gurgled atop the potbellied stove. Johnny Yuma took a deep breath and smiled as both men looked up.

"Smells good," Johnny Yuma said.

"Coffee?" The man wearing spectacles asked.

"Ink," Johnny Yuma replied.

The man with the spectacles wore a green eyeshade. The other man wore a badge.

They were both in their fifties. The eyeshade man, bone-thin and pale. The sheriff, big and bronzed, with a pair of crutches leaning against the wall within arm's reach.

"You a newspaperman, son?" The thin one smiled.

"Not exactly, sir. Far from it. But I used to help out in a newspaper before . . ."

"The unpleasantness?"

"Yes, sir."

"I'm Oliver Knight." The man rose and extended his hand. "This would-be checker player here is Pat Conway. Sheriff Pat Conway." Knight pointed to the crutches. "No, he wasn't shot in the line of duty. Got thrown from a horse. Busted his leg . . . and his pride."

Yuma and Knight shook hands.

Sheriff Pat Conway jumped one of Knight's checkers, put it aside, and looked up.

"Your move, Oliver. Howdy, son."

"Would you care for a cup of coffee?" Oliver asked. "Or would you prefer to drink some ink?"

"Neither, thanks." Yuma smiled and looked around. "This sure looks like the *Bulletin*."

"Most small-town newspapers look alike. Where you from?"

"Mason City. My dad's the sheriff there."

"Sheriff of Mason City?" Conway reacted.

"Yes, sir."

"What's your name, son? I didn't catch it."

"Yuma. Johnny Yuma."

"Ned Yuma's boy?"

"Yes, sir. You know my father?"

"Well, I'll be hanged! Know him? Hell, boy, Ned and I fought, drank, trailed, and . . . well, never mind. We was Texas Rangers together! His boots is filled with something special. How is ol' Ned?"

"I haven't seen him in some time, but . . ."

"He's the finest, bravest, most decent man ever to pack a star. Saved my life both sides of the border I don't know how many times! Well I'll be hanged! You hear that, Oliver?"

"I'm standing right here, Pat. Sure, I heard."

"You on your way to Mason City?" Conway asked.

"Yes, sir."

"Gonna be his deputy? He's still sheriff there, isn't he?"

"Yes, sir. But I don't know about being a lawman. I . . ."

"You got ink in your blood, Johnny?" Knight inquired.

"Don't know what I am going to do. But I do like writing about things. When I saw the sign outside, thought I might get a job here for a while, just helping out like I did for Mr. Dodson. He . . ."

"*Elmer* Dodson?" Knight took a step forward.

"Yes, sir. You know him?"

"This isn't a coincidence," Knight proclaimed. "It's a miracle! No, son, I never met him, but he's my hero. He's every newspaperman's newspaperman. Why, when he was the publisher and editor of the *Baltimore Eagle*, Elmer Dodson led more crusades against corruption, wrote more two-fisted editorials, and . . . Hell, do you know that he was first to print the poems and stories of a fellow named Edgar Allen Poe?''

''No, sir, I didn't. He didn't talk much about what he did before Mason City.''

''Well, let me tell you something, Johnny. He did plenty. His stuff was read in every journalism class in the country. The biggest newspapers in New York, Boston, Chicago, and San Francisco followed his lead. Then, all of a sudden, he walked away. Just left everything behind and cleared out. There were rumors that he headed west, maybe Mexico. Some said that he also went to drinking. That true?''

''Not in Mason City. Never knew him to even take one drink.''

''When did he start up the *Bulletin*?''

''Oh, about ten years ago.''

''Well, that leaves a few years blank. You know, I've got a book of poems that he wrote. He called it *Leap upon Mountains*. He ever mention it?''

''No, sir. Like I said, he didn't talk much about the past.''

''Well, I'll be hanged,'' Sheriff Conway said for the third time. ''If this don't beat all. Me knowin' your dad and Oliver here knowin' all about this Dodson fella. I'll be hanged,'' he repeated.

''Johnny,'' Knight said, ''how long you planning on staying in town?''

''Well, Mr. Knight, I haven't been doing much planning, but I'm in no great hurry.'' He looked around the newspaper office. ''Maybe I could stay for a few days and sort of . . . well, help you get out next week's edition of the *Chronicle*.''

''Son, the *Chronicle*'s a weekly all right, but it's been coming out about once a month lately, if that.''

''How come?''

"Oh, I don't know. Just sort of lost my taste for it, I guess. Besides, hardly any advertisers, and now that the war's over, hardly any news. Nothing much's happened in . . ."

Gunshots.

Sheriff Pat Conway went for his crutches. Knight and Yuma moved toward the open door. The gunshots, four of them, had come from the saloon across the street. And hurrying across that street toward the *Chronicle* was a man wearing an apron.

"Sheriff! It's Rooster! He's drunk again and shootin' up the place! Damn fool's gonna kill somebody someday."

Conway, Knight, and Yuma were on the boardwalk as the bartender approached.

"All right, Rafe," Conway responded. "I'll handle it."

On his crutches, the sheriff made his way past the middle of the street and stopped.

"Rooster!" Conway called out. "Rooster! It's the sheriff. Come on out here. You hear me? Come on out!"

A man, hatless and needing a shave, came through the batwings holding a gun in one hand and a whiskey bottle in the other.

"I'm out, Sheriff. What're you gonna do about it?"

"I'm gonna have that gun."

"Oh, no, you're not. Nobody's taking this gun." Rooster slid the gun into its holster and took a swig.

"You're drunk, Rooster."

"You damn betcha!"

"Give me that weapon." The sheriff maneuvered a couple of steps forward on the crutches.

"Sure! You can have part of it!" Rooster drew and fired twice. Dirt spattered close to the tips of Conway's crutches.

Rooster holstered the gun again and laughed.

Johnny Yuma moved away from Knight, walked past the sheriff, and toward Rooster.

"What do you think you're doing, Reb?" Rooster held up the bottle in his left hand, pointing toward Yuma.

Yuma kept walking. Not fast. Not slow. Nearer.

"Come any closer, and I'll shoot you!" Rooster threatened.

Yuma never broke stride.

"I said . . ." Rooster started to draw again.

But Johnny Yuma drew faster and laid the barrel of the Colt across Rooster's skull.

Rooster and the bottle dropped.

There were over a dozen men in the street now, laughing, talking to each other, and one of them clapped Yuma on the shoulder as the Rebel holstered his Colt.

"A couple of you fellas carry this one over to the jail," the sheriff said. "Lock him in till he sobers up. And hand me that gun."

Conway turned to Yuma as he took the weapon from one of the men.

"He's not a bad fella, just a mean drunk."

"I figured that."

"Still, he coulda shot you."

"Not with an empty gun." Yuma pointed to the pistol in Conway's hand. "Counted six shots."

"Pretty smart, too, just like your dad."

"Johnny." Knight smiled. "If you'd like to stick around and help me put out the next edition, well, I could use some help."

"So could I," Conway said. "Till this leg heals. Could use a deputy."

"He asked me first, Pat," Knight said.

"This is pretty good." Yuma smiled.

"What is?" The sheriff asked.

"Well, a few minutes ago, I didn't have a job. Now it looks like I got two."

TWENTY-SIX

Being in Longview is as close to being home as I could feel.
Oliver Knight says that I've lit a fire under him. The *Longview Chronicle* is a weekly again. We've gone to press four
weeks in a row without missing a deadline, and each edition
has more pages and has been sold out.

I've learned a lot from Sheriff Pat Conway—things I never
knew—about being a deputy, about the Texas Rangers, and
even about my father . . .

In the days and weeks that followed Johnny Yuma's ride
into Longview, his hands were stained with ink, and there
was a deputy's badge pinned on his buckskin shirt.

Two different jobs in two different worlds, and he liked
both of them and he was good at both of them.

Oliver Knight almost seemed like a different man. No
longer lethargic, no time for checkers, he found all kinds
of things to write about starting with the encounter between
Yuma and Rooster Trapp. And Knight encouraged Johnny
Yuma to write articles, even editorials, for the *Chronicle*.
By the time the third edition of the *Chronicle* came out,

more than half the copy had been provided by the new-comer.

Yuma wrote a short story entitled "Count Your Bless-ings—and Your Bullets." He wrote obituaries. He wrote about marriages and births, including Mrs. Barker's triplets (three sons).

And at the same time, Johnny Yuma made the morning and evening rounds of the streets, making sure that every-thing and everybody remained secure and peaceful in the town of Longview.

A few days after his arrival, as Yuma sat on a high stool setting type for a story in the *Chronicle*, the door burst open and a familiar figure took up most of the space at the door-way. Both Johnny and Oliver Knight looked up.

"Yuma!" Rooster Trapp barked.

Johnny Yuma stood up. He was calm but ready. There was a moment of strained silence.

"Yuma, you remember me?" Rooster pointed to the bandage still pasted on his forehead.

"I remember."

"You remember doin' this?" With his left hand, Rooster touched the bandage. His right hand hovered near the gun in his holster.

"I do."

"Well, so do I . . . barely. You coulda killed me."

Yuma said nothing.

"Rooster . . ." Knight took a step.

"You stay outta this, Knight. This is between him and me." Rooster never took his eyes off Yuma. "I said you coulda killed me."

Yuma remained silent but still ready.

"But you didn't . . . and I'm here to . . . thank you."

"You're welcome." Johnny smiled.

"For the last couple a days, I been thinkin' that I coulda

been in a box six feet under. Now, I can't say that I'm gonna give up drinkin', no sir. If I did say that, I'd be lyin'. But do you know what I am gonna do?"

"No, sir, can't say I do."

"Well, before I go to drinkin', from now on, I'm gonna make sure I take off this damn iron and hide it someplace so's I don't hurt somebody and in case I meet up with somebody who ain't as, well, as . . . I don't exactly know how to say it, but as . . ."

"Compassionate?" Knight offered.

"If you say so, Oliver. Mr. Yuma, can I shake your hand?"

"It's got some ink on it." Yuma grinned. "But hell, yes!"

They shook.

As they did, with his left hand, Rooster pointed to the star pinned on Johnny's shirt.

"Ol' Pat told me he'd made you a deputy. If ever the time comes you need any backin'—you know, from time to time, there's some hardcases come through—you just holler, Mr. Yuma, and Rooster Trapp'll come a-runnin'."

"I'll just do that, Mr. Trapp, and I thank you kindly."

"You bet." Rooster looked out the door and across the street. "Well, I think I'll go over to the Long Bar and wet my whis . . ." He glanced down at the gun in his holster, then back at Yuma and Knight. "On second thought, I think I'll mosey on home and have a cup of that tar Martha calls coffee."

The three men laughed.

"Oh, by the way," Rooster pointed to the stack of newspapers on a table. "I'd like to buy a copy of the *Chronicle*. Understand my name's in it."

"On the house, Rooster." Oliver Knight picked up a paper and handed it to Trapp. "On the house. Nice little story on page three, written by editor and publisher Oliver Knight himself.''

''Much obliged.''

''Say hello to Martha from the *Chronicle*.''

''I will.''

After Rooster Trapp left, Oliver Knight removed the eyeshade from his head and ran the fingers of his left hand through his hair.

''Johnny, there's a prime example of what might've turned into a tragedy if you hadn't had your wits about you. Some other hothead might've pumped two into Rooster's belly and Martha 'ud be a widow now instead of pouring lampblack into his coffee cup. Well, boy, let me see what you've done with that two-headed goat story.''

It was still early on a Thursday morning. Johnny Yuma had just finished his rounds and was in the sheriff's office with Pat Conway when Agnes Venable raced into Longview on her buckboard. She was in tears as she ran into the office.

''Sheriff! It's Timmy! He's gone. I can't find him! I've looked all over the place. He's gone!''

''All right, Agnes, sit down here, catch your breath, and tell me what happened.''

The woman managed to sit, wiping her fingers across her dry lips and wet eyes.

''Here's some water, ma'am.'' Yuma poured from a pitcher into a glass and handed it to the distraught woman. She nodded, took the glass, and drank. Agnes Venable was in her late twenties but looked older. A lean, angular face with deep creases that bespoke of hard times, narrow, lashless green eyes, and with large, rough hands, she looked like what she was, a pioneer woman.

''Johnny,'' Conway spoke calmly, ''this is Agnes Venable. Her husband Jed got killed at Fredericksburg. She's got a young boy, Timmy. They've got a place a few miles to the north. Now, Agnes, you take a couple deep breaths and tell us what happened.''

"I was up late ... till three or four in the morning ... puttin' up preserves. Fell asleep in the kitchen. When I woke up, he was just ... Timmy was gone. Didn't eat no breakfast ... he just got up and left. I looked everyplace: the barn, the henhouse, even down the well. I heard there was a band of Comanches come through a couple days ago. Sheriff, I'm scared they mighta got him. Timmy's all I got now that Jed ..."

"All right, Agnes. You did right in coming here. We'll find him. I'll call up all the men in town that can ride. You go back to your place. He might even be home by now. I can't set a horse yet, myself, but there'll be a passel of men at your place in just a little while. They'll fan out and ..."

"Sheriff." Johnny Yuma took the empty glass from Agnes Venable. "I'll ride back alongside Mrs. Venable and get a head start. I've done some tracking."

"Sounds good, Johnny. You two go ahead. They'll be right behind you."

"Can you make it back, ma'am?" Yuma asked.

Agnes Venable was already moving toward the door.

Timmy was not at home. He had not come back. Both Yuma and Mrs. Venable made a hurried search and called out the boy's name, but he was not within sight or sound.

"Has he ever gone off like this before, Mrs. Venable?"

"Well, he's a curious little fella, sometimes chases after a butterfly or somethin', but he's never just left the house by himself so early without eatin' or sayin' anythin' to me. Though I'm always up before him. It's all my fault for fallin' asleep like that."

"Now, don't go blaming yourself, ma'am."

"You think them Comanches coulda come in while I was asleep and took him?"

"I think they would've taken you, too, ma'am."

"But if he left, they still coulda found him out there and . . ."

"No sense conjecturing, ma'am. Just wasting time. Now, I've got to ask you just a couple of questions. Was he wearing shoes or are they still here?"

"Timmy's only got one pair. I looked. They're gone."

"Good."

"Why's that?"

"That proves he wasn't taken. He got up, dressed, and left. That's good." Something on the kitchen table caught Yuma's attention, a flutelike piece of wood carved out of a tree branch about seven inches long. "What's that, ma'am? Does that belong to Timmy?"

"Yes. He calls it his tooter. Jed carved that for Timmy just before he joined up. Timmy was too young to play it then, but he plays it all the time now, he . . ."

"I'll just take this along, if you don't mind, Mrs. Venable." Yuma picked up the tooter. "The other men'll be along any time, now. We'll find him."

Yuma began to track as his Kiowa friend had taught him. From the point of origin in an ever widening circle. As a young boy and into his early teens, Johnny Yuma had spent countless hours with Pony That Flies, a Kiowa blood brother to Ned Yuma. Pony That Flies was called that because he left no tracks. He had scouted for the Texas Rangers against the bloody Comanches when Ned Yuma wore a Ranger badge. How the two men became blood brothers, Johnny Yuma was never told, not by Pony That Flies nor by his father. But a few days after Johnny Yuma's mother died, Pony That Flies showed up, stayed until Ned's son was fourteen, then just disappeared again without a word of farewell.

"Will he ever come back?" Johnny had asked his father.

"Can't tell, son. Just be glad that he was here."

Johnny was glad. In some ways, Pony That Flies was just as much a father to him as Ned Yuma. If anybody had bothered to count the hours, the motherless boy spent more time with the Indian than with his father or with his Aunt Emmy, Ned Yuma's sister, who also lived in Mason City.

Pony That Flies had taught Johnny Yuma well: how to track, how to scout. But the Indian had said that part of it was inborn in his pupil. Not everyone could be taught the rudiments of scouting. Not one in ten, or a hundred, or even a thousand. Not if the hunter's instinct was not there to begin with. That instinct seemed to be a part of Johnny Yuma's mind and body. His eyes were made for the unseen trail. But good eyes didn't necessarily make a good scout.

Pony That Flies had honed Johnny Yuma's natural abilities and perceptions. He had taught his eager pupil to accumulate and evaluate what had happened, what was happening, and what to do about it with accuracy and alacrity.

As Yuma widened the circle, the first thing he looked for was tracks of horses' unshod hooves. That would mean Indians. And that would be bad.

But there were none.

Still, Yuma could find no tracks from the boy. The ground was soft and sandy, but it had been a windy day, and the young boy, who couldn't have weighed much, had left faint imprints that were blown away.

But tracks weren't always on the ground, and after circling for nearly five hours, Yuma found a telltale sign in the shape of a wild berry bush. Only a tracker with eagle eyes would have spotted the unspoken story that the bush revealed: a broken stem, and on the ground, three berries that had fallen when the stem had been torn off.

Timmy's breakfast and noon meal.

And near the bush, just to the north, a small footprint. That was enough for Johnny Yuma, more than enough. He would circle to the north. And he did.

The terrain was relatively flat, and Yuma could scan the horizon, but there was no sign of life in sight, not even a snake, horned toad, or jackrabbit.

Yuma called out the boy's name again and again. Then he removed the tooter from his saddlebag and began to play. It wasn't exactly on key, but pretty close to sounding like "Dixie."

He played and circled, circled and played, for almost another hour, still no sign of life, but then something—a sound.

First, it seemed like a faint moan—and then a word—over and over again, until it was clearer and unmistakable.

"Mommy . . . Mommy . . . Mommy . . ."

But the words seemed to come from thin air. There was still nobody in sight.

"Timmy! Timmy! Where are you, boy? Keep talking! I'm here to help you! Timmy, where are you?"

"Down here. I fell . . ." the boy's voice sobbed.

And then, from the sorrel, Johnny Yuma looked down and saw a narrow ravine, no more than two feet across; more like a crevice, but deep, at least ten or twelve feet deep. That's where the voice came from.

Yuma dismounted and looked down into the fissure at the tiny form wedged there at the bottom.

"Timmy. My name's Johnny. I'm a friend of your mom's. Are you all right? Can you move?"

"Not much. Just my arms. I'm stuck. Is Mommy mad at me?"

"Don't you worry about that, boy. First thing we've got to do is get you up here."

"But I can't get out. I tried." The boy began to cry.

"Oh, yes, you can. I'll get you out."

"You can't come down here. It's too tight."

"You just wait a minute, Timmy, and you'll see. You'll come flying out like an eagle."

"I will?"

"Yes, you will."

Yuma walked quickly to the sorrel and took off the rope. He came back and let the loop drop into the crevice.

"Timmy, can you tie the rope under both of your arms? Can you do that?"

"I think so."

"Do it. With the rope in front of you. Let me know when you've done that. Okay, son?"

"Okay, I . . . I'm doin' it."

"Underneath both arms, not too tight . . . not too tight now, nice and easy."

"I did it," the boy called.

"Good. Now, as I pull up, you wiggle both legs, okay?"

"Okay."

"Now, I'm going to start to pull. You just wiggle, nice and easy. I'm pulling, Timmy. Are you coming free?"

"I think so."

"That's it. . . . Up you come . . . up . . . and up . . . Are your legs free?"

"Y . . . yes . . ."

"Great, that's just great. Hey, you're almost halfway here. Just a little more. Hey, this is fun, isn't it?"

"Sort of . . ."

"You bet. Up you come, like an eagle."

And then the boy's head was at the surface. Johnny Yuma reached with both hands and lifted him out of the fissure and onto the level ground. Timmy's face was tear-stained and dirty, his clothes torn, but he was smiling, but not for long. As Yuma freed him from the rope, the boy began to shudder.

"Here, now," Yuma said. "You're safe and sound. What's the matter?"

"Mommy's gonna be mad. I know she is. Probably gonna get a spanking."

"You're too old to spank. You know what she's going to do?"

"What?"

"She's going to put her arms around you and kiss you and fix you supper."

"She is?"

"She is. Now, suppose you tell me what happened."

"From the window, while Mommy was sleeping, I saw a little doggy. I went out to play with him, but he kept running away . . . and then I lost him and then I was lost . . . and hungry. I found some berries."

"You sure did, Timmy, and so did I. Now, how'd you like to get up on that horse behind me and go home and have some real food? Would you like that?"

"You bet!"

"Will you do me a favor?"

"Sure."

"On the way back, will you play something on this tooter?" Johnny Yuma handed Timmy the wooden reed.

"Okay."

Yuma lifted the boy onto the sorrel just behind the saddle, then climbed onto the animal.

"Timmy, do you know how to play 'Dixie'?"

"Sure!"

"Well, then play it."

TWENTY-SEVEN

How Johnny Yuma tracked, found, and rescued Timmy Venable was the main topic of conversation in and around Longview for the next couple of days.

Oliver Knight asked Johnny to write a story about it for next Thursday's edition of the *Chronicle*, but Yuma declined. So Knight interviewed Sheriff Pat Conway, Mrs. Venable, and Timmy, then wrote the piece himself.

That Sunday, after services, there was a marriage at the church. Reverend Thomas performed the ceremony. The bride was Amy Lewis, the groom Jonas Webber. Amy had just turned twenty-one, beautiful, blue eyes, flaxen hair, and just a mite taller than Jonas even as she wore flat shoes under her bridal gown and he wore Justin boots with three-inch heels. But he was shiny faced and shiny haired, the slicked-down hair parted square in the middle of his head, as he beamed and stood as tall as he could next to his Valkyrie bride.

They had been childhood sweethearts in Longview. Their romance had been interrupted, at least geographically, by the cause for secession. Since he came back, Jonas saved every penny he could earn and put a down payment on a spread three miles out of town.

Most of Longview turned out for the ceremony and cider, including Oliver Knight, Johnny Yuma, and Sheriff Pat Conway, who gave the bride away. Both Amy's mother and father were deceased and Conway was a distant cousin of Amy's father, so Amy asked him to do the honors.

By now, Conway had abandoned one of the crutches and managed to hobble down the aisle, almost, but not quite in stride with the long-legged bride.

Two hours later, the happy newlyweds were on a buckboard on their way to their honeymoon shack, and Yuma and Conway were in the sheriff's office.

Johnny had cleaned and reloaded his Henry and was in the process of doing the same with his handgun as the sheriff drank coffee and watched.

"That Henry's a nice piece of equipment," Conway observed.

"Yes, sir." Yuma smiled.

"So's that Colt."

"You bet."

"You know you can thank the Texas Rangers for that handgun."

"How's that?"

"That's a Walker Colt, Johnny."

"Yes, I know."

"Your dad carries one. We all do. Didn't he tell you how it came about?"

"No, but I'd like to hear."

"All right then, you will. You see, the Comanches are the greatest light cavalry in the world. Nobody could match 'em on horseback till the Rangers came along. But the Rangers had single-shot rifles while the Comanches could ride at full speed and shoot arrow after arrow. Then along came Samuel Colt with his invention, the six-shooter. That was a big improvement, but the gun had defects.

"Even the Army wouldn't use it. The Colt was light and flimsy, almost impossible to reload while riding full tilt on account of the whole damned cylinder had to be taken off and replaced. Had to hold on to three parts to do it. No damn good. You follow me?"

"Yep."

"Well, that's where another Sam comes into the picture. Samuel H. Walker, Texas Ranger. By this time, ol' Sam Colt was just about out of business. But Walker goes East and works out some improvements. Sam Colt named the new model the Walker Colt. It was heavier and stronger, .44 caliber, and could be reloaded without taking out the cylinder. That's what beat the Comanches and helped Captain Jack Hays and the Texas Rangers, along with the U.S. Army, win the Mexican Campaign of 1846—that weapon you're holding in your hand right now. And your daddy and me was down there together, from Monterrey to Buena Vista, from Vera Cruz to Mexico City. Yeahbo! You just ask him when you see him!"

"I will. How long were the two of you in the Rangers together?"

"Oh, a long time, Johnny. Until he fell in love with Elizabeth, your mom. That's when he finally quit."

"On account of her?"

"They don't call them Rangers for nothin'. We ranged for hundreds of miles in all directions. That was no life for a married man—or woman. He heard about the sheriff's job in Mason City. That way at least he'd be in one place."

"But he wasn't. Not very much," Johnny said.

"So I heard. Old habits are hard to break."

"Every time he'd get a stack of dodgers, he wasn't sat-

isfied to wait for a wanted man to come to Mason City
he'd . . ."

"Go out lookin' for 'em."

"That's what he'd do. You know he wasn't there when
my mother died."

"He's a lawman, Johnny."

"He's also a husband and father—or was." There was
more than a trace of bitterness in Yuma's voice.

"I know, son. But he'll make it up to you when you get
back. I know he will."

Johnny Yuma did not reply.

A few days later, Amy and Jonas Webber came into Longview to pick up an order from the general store. They were
both radiant and could hardly keep their hands off each
other as they loaded up the buckboard.

That's when three strangers rode into town. They took a
long look at Amy as they went by the buckboard. Too long.
Then they headed toward the Long Bar saloon.

Sheriff Conway and Johnny Yuma also took a long
look—at the three riders: all the same; different ages, but
all pigs with the same face, except for the oldest, who had
a jagged scar across his eye and an ugly, flat face.

Conway was now down to a cane. He followed them
into the Long Bar. So did Johnny Yuma.

The two lawmen approached as the three strangers stood
and drank at the bar.

"I'm Sheriff Conway. This is my deputy."

The men looked at each other, drank, and said nothing.
Conway broke the silence.

"What's your name, boys?"

"Did we break any law, Sheriff?" the man with the scar
sneered.

"No. And you're not going to. Now, what's your name?"

"Benson," said scar. "We're the Benson brothers."

"Where from?"

"Here and there."

"Where mostly?"

"Where the war was. That's where I got this." He traced the scar with a dirty forefinger. "On the same side as him." He pointed to Johnny Yuma.

"What's your business in Longview?" the sheriff asked.

"Just passin' through. Headin' west."

"That's a good direction. You staying in town tonight?"

"Don't think so. We'll find a campsite."

"There's a nice creek to bed down by—just about a mile *west.*"

"Thanks, Sheriff. We just might do that."

When Conway and Yuma were outside, Yuma looked back through the batwings.

"You know, Pat," Johnny said, "I don't think those three were in *any* army."

"Neither do I," the sheriff replied.

Just before sunset and after drinking down a bottle of tequila and buying two more bottles for the trail, the Benson brothers left Longview.

But they weren't the Benson brothers.

They were the Kershaw brothers. Sheriff Pat Conway and Johnny Yuma found that out when the circuit rider dropped off a new batch of wanted posters.

One of the dodgers read:

DEPARTMENT OF INDIAN AFFAIRS
$500 REWARD

THE KERSHAW BROTHERS
RANCE • TRACE • KERN

COMANCHEROS
WANTED FOR
MURDER • KIDNAPPING • HORSE STEALING
ILLEGAL TRADING WITH INDIANS
$500 • DEAD OR ALIVE • $500

ONE OF THE BROTHERS—RANCE—
HAS SCAR ACROSS FACE

"Dammit, Johnny, twenty-four hours earlier, and we woulda had 'em cold." Conway slapped his hand across the dodger.

"Yeah, well, I guess that's why they kept moving. But how far? That's the question."

"Too far for me. I still can't get on a horse."

"I can."

"Oh, no, you don't, Johnny. It's one thing to track a lost boy, but I ain't sending you out against three killers."

"I could round up a posse. Think there's enough men around here who'd be willing to ride?"

"Nope. I won't be responsible for what might happen if I'm not along. If the Kershaws even smell a posse, there'll be ambushin' and back-shootin'. Left alone, the odds are they'll keep on movin'. The pickins are pretty lean around Longview. My notion is they'll head to the south. Bigger spreads, more to steal and trade with the Comanches."

"I hope you're right."

"So do I."

"But there must be something we can do."

"There is. First off, I'll telegraph the authorities and army posts that the Kershaws passed this way."

"What else?"

"We'll have Oliver print up some more of these dodgers
and get 'em posted all over the area—just in case the Kershaws forgot somethin' around here and come back."

A terrible thought occurred to Johnny Yuma, but he
made no mention of it to the sheriff.

"Okay, Pat. But suppose I ride out to that creek you told
them about . . ."

"Johnny . . ."

"I promise I won't do anything except see if I can pick
up their tracks, see which direction they're heading. It'll
help you when you send out those telegraphs."

"You promise you won't try and follow 'em?"

"Hell, yes! I'll just reconnoiter. I've got no intention of
going anywhere near them."

"Well, I guess that *would* help. But you'd better take
my slicker. Looks like we're gonna have some rain."

TWENTY-EIGHT

The rain did not come.

Instead, the dark clouds drifted east, and the searchlight of the sun broke through and by high noon scorched the Texas terrain.

The Kershaws had not camped by the creek. Johnny Yuma didn't think that they would. He had picked up their tracks and was following them. They were easy to follow. If he found the Kershaws, it would not be so easy. Even if he had the advantage of surprise, going up against three killers would not be smart. Yuma did not want to go up against them. Not if he had a choice.

But there was something he had to find out, something he observed about the Kershaws that preyed on his mind.

Johnny Yuma heard the agonizing screams and rode toward them. Then he saw what he didn't want to see:

Jonas Webber spread-eagled and staked out, hand and foot, on the ground near an anthill.

The sun was furnace hot. Yuma dismounted and went to the man writhing on the ground. Webber's face and body were bruised from a vicious beating. Battalions of ants swarmed over every part of him. His face was parched and covered with the crawling creatures.

"Please! Please!" he pleaded. "Get 'em off! For God's sake, get 'em off!"

Yuma's boot kicked apart the anthill. He used his knife to cut free Webber's hands and feet. Webber desperately wiped at his face, smearing it with his own blood from the ants who had fed off him.

Yuma's eyes took in the landscape to make sure that the Comancheros were gone. They were, leaving behind the burned-out remnants of the small cabin and Jonas Webber to die a slow, torturous death.

Thanks to Johnny Yuma, Webber did not die, but he was hysterical and still clawing at the ants.

"There was three of them. They took Amy. One had a scar."

"Comancheros. Been tracking them."

"They told me what they was going to do to her." He shuddered and cried. "Then, if she was still alive, they'd trade her to the Indians. They said . . ."

"Shut up, Jonas. Just shut up! I'll find her. I'll get her back. You get into Longview. Wait there."

Yuma headed toward his horse.

"Kill 'em! You hear me, kill 'em. And if they've done what they said they'd do to Amy . . ." He sobbed. *"Kill her, too!"*

Yuma didn't look back. He mounted the sorrel, went to his spurs, and rode.

The Comanches were angry—and with good reason. They had been content, even eager, to make war with the other Indian tribes that roamed and hunted across what became Texas and south into Mexico.

War was in their nature. They were a violent, merciless

tribe. They were proud of their bloody conflicts with the Cherokees, the Apaches, the Kiowas, and with the Mexicans. The Comanches would hit, steal animals, take captives—mostly women—and ride away with their plunder.

Their anger turned to madness with the coming of the Texans, especially the Texas Rangers.

This enemy was not content just to do battle. This enemy would settle for nothing less than driving the Comanches out of Texas or the extermination of the entire Comanche population. For unremembered years, Comanches were conquerors. They were determined not to be conquered. But the Texans were more determined, and there were more of them.

A prominent Texan had said, "Comanches continue their forays upon the Texas borders, murdering and carrying off defenseless frontier settlers. The Comanches must be pursued, hunted, run down, and killed until they find out we are in earnest."

Most Texans agreed that the Comanches should be killed, and the Rangers were the designated executioners.

In turn, the Comanches redefined the word *savage*. Their prisoners were tortured, mutilated, and skinned. They reserved the most fiendish of their savagery for the Rangers.

For a Texas Ranger, the only thing worse than being killed was being captured by Comanches.

But the Comanches were also practical. They did business with a ruthless breed, dubbed Comancheros, who profited by trading with them. The Comancheros provided Indians with guns, ammunition, whiskey, other provisions, and prisoners. The prisoners mostly were women. The most prized of these women were fair-haired, like Amy.

Johnny Yuma had remembered how the three riders looked at Jonas Webber's bride as they rode into Longview. The look of lust and profit.

The camp was cradled in the high country. The three Kershaws, Rance, Trace, and Kern, had been and still were drinking from the same tequila bottle. As they sat and passed around the bottle, Rance riffled through a deck of cards, laughed, and looked toward the woman.

Amy was next to naked and tied with arms stretched apart to the limb of a scrub oak. She had been abused. There were welts and bruises on her face and body. She knew what had already happened was just the beginning of what the three men had in store for her.

Their dirty hands had stripped off most of her clothes and pinched and probed at her exposed white flesh, her billowing breasts and long lean legs. They had taunted her with words and phrases she had never heard before. They had described in vile detail what each of them was going to do to her, and then they had tied her to a tree to think about what was to come while they laughed and drank and savored the situation.

She knew it would do no good to plead. She had begged them to spare Jonas, but they reveled in her pleading and had gone ahead with what they had intended to do. No cry for mercy would move them. She knew now that nothing would deter them, so she said nothing.

Amy thought of her husband staked out over the anthill. If he weren't dead by now, he soon would be. A slow, painful, crawling death, his flesh deteriorating under the biting blanket of insects.

She remembered how, just a few hours before, she and Jonas were lying in bed making love as the door burst open and the three men stood in the doorway, laughing.

The one with the scar strode to the bed, ripped off the cover, yanked Jonas to the floor, grabbed her arms, and pressed his ugly, smelly face onto her as she screamed.

When Jonas tried to rise and get to the man with the scar, the other two beat him back to the floor and kicked him again and again.

The man with the scar pulled her naked out of bed and forced her outside, while the other two dragged Jonas across the floor and out the door. Through a daze she remembered their rude hands and crude voices.

"Besides her . . . and one horse . . . there's not much here worth takin'."

"Burn it down."

"What about him?"

"Drag him over here. I saw somethin' on the way in."

"You mean that anthill?"

"That's it. And get her some clothes."

"Why cover her up? I like lookin' at her."

"So do I, but it's gonna get Godalmighty hot."

"So what?"

"Don't want that nice white skin burned to a crisp . . . turn red. Comanches like smooth, white skin."

"You right again, Rance."

She had begged and pleaded and cried. The more she did, the more they laughed and taunted her.

When they came to this area, they dismounted and pulled her off the horse they had stolen from the farm.

"This is as good a place as any. Tie her up to that oak."

While two of them bound her, they took off most of her clothes and rubbed their palms and fingers across her body.

"Who's first?"

"Who do you think?"

"Why's it always you?"

" 'Cause I'm the oldest, the smartest . . . and the purtiest."

"Aw, come on, Rance . . . Let's draw for it."

"Why?"

"Tell you what, high card gets her first and half the loot when we sell her, instead of a third."

"Done! And let's have a drink."

Amy waited for what was inevitable and wished that she were dead. Her body sweltered from the heat of the sun, but she shivered.

"Anybody want to cut?" Rance set the deck of cards on a rock.

"Yeah, *her.*" Trace laughed. "I'll draw first." He reached over from where he sat and lifted the top part of the deck. "Ten! Okay brothers, draw . . . and no picture cards."

"Queen!" Kern grinned. "Hallelujah, boys!" He looked toward Amy. "I'm gonna get me a little ol' queen!"

Kern had already started to get up as Rance drew from the deck. An ace.

"Set your ass down, Kern. Ace's high and so am I."

"Lucky bastard!" Trace said.

"I think he cheated!" Kern added.

Rance got to his feet. He unbuckled his gun belt and let it drop to the ground. All three brothers laughed. Rance, carrying the tequila bottle, started toward Amy. He took a knife from his pocket and snapped open the blade.

"Save some for us," Trace hollered.

"Yeah, and the Comanches. They'll pay plenty for the likes of her."

Rance came close to her. She closed her eyes, so as not to see his scarred, ugly face, but she could smell his foul breath as he brushed wet lips across her throat.

He cut both straps of the tattered chemise from her shoulders. It fell to her feet and she stood naked before him. He looked her up and down and grinned. Rance lifted the neck of the bottle close to her.

"Wanna drink, missy?"

Amy turned her head away, but he grabbed her hair, tilted her face up, and poured tequila onto her mouth and eyes and cheeks, then watched as the liquid dripped down across her breasts and below.

Rance cut the ropes that bound her wrists. He grabbed her hair again and pulled, leading her like a dog toward an enclave of boulders.

As they passed into the secluded section, Rance shoved her to the ground. He lifted the tequila bottle to his mouth, and just as he did . . .

Johnny Yuma swung the flat, hard stock of the Henry with all his might, smashing the ugly, scarred, flat face of Rance Kershaw even flatter. Bone, bottle, and gristle broke. Blood, glass, and tequila meshed into what was left of Rance's face. He fell unconscious.

Yuma stepped into the clear as Trace went for his gun. A slug from the Henry tore into Trace's heart, killing him before he met the ground. Kern stood for a split second, undecided whether to make a play.

"Go for it, you son of a bitch," Yuma said.

Kern Kershaw decided not to.

A crowd gathered on the street in Longview as Johnny Yuma led them in. Amy wore the slicker as she rode beside Yuma. Also on horseback were Rance Kershaw, whose battered face was crudely bandaged by two bandannas, and Kern, with his brother's dead body tied to the back of his horse.

Yuma reined in the sorrel in front of the sheriff's office. Conway, Oliver Knight, and Jonas Webber were already standing there, while people from all over town crowded in to get a better view.

Jonas stared at his wife but said nothing, nor did he move toward her.

Yuma dismounted and helped Amy down from her horse.

"All right," Conway commanded, "some of you men get those two inside, and somebody else call the undertaker."

"I'm here," a solemn voice intoned.

"Johnny, you took a hell of a chance," the sheriff said. "You said you weren't going after them."

"Had no choice, Pat."

"I guess not. You're a natural-born lawman."

"No, just a man. Not like those vermin," Johnny said.

Rance and Kern were being led into the jail.

"It was the war," Rance said through bloody bandages. "The war's to blame."

"Yeah." Yuma didn't even look at him. "It's always something."

Rance and Kern were shoved inside. Yuma took a step toward Jonas Webber and just more than whispered, "Go to your wife, Jonas. She needs you."

"Did they . . ."

"Does it make any difference?" There was a hard edge to Johnny Yuma's voice. "She needs you."

Jonas still stood motionless.

"They didn't," Yuma said.

Jonas Webber rushed toward his wife. He put his arms around her. She didn't respond. Not for a moment. First, she looked at Johnny Yuma. There was a faint trace of a smile on her lips . . . and then she circled her arms around her husband.

Johnny Yuma made up his mind. After the next edition of the *Chronicle*, he would leave Longview and head for Mason City. All the reminders here in Longview—the *Chronicle* of the *Bulletin*, Oliver Knight of Elmer Dodson, Pat

Conway of Johnny's father—all drew him toward home. And there was something else not to be found in Longview—*someone else:* Rosemary Cutler.

At first, both Oliver Knight and Pat Conway tried to dissuade him, but they knew it was no use. And in their hearts, they knew it was best. He had been away too long. Both men stood by him as he made ready to mount up.

"Johnny." Oliver Knight handed the Rebel an envelope. "I wrote a note to Elmer Dodson. Would you please see that he gets it?"

"Glad to."

"My boy, I can't thank you enough," Knight went on. "If you hadn't come through, I'd still be playing checkers and making excuses for not going to press. Thanks to you, the *Chronicle* is really a weekly again. Is there a chance you'll pass by Longview again?"

"There's always a chance."

"Well, at the rate we're going, I may be needing a partner pretty soon, so just keep that in mind."

"I will, Mr. Knight, I will." Johnny Yuma took off the deputy badge and handed it to Sheriff Conway.

"I said it, Johnny. You're a natural-born lawman, just like your father. You tell him an old Texas Ranger says hello."

"I'll do that."

"And tell him I think he needs a deputy."

"He's already got one: Jess Evans, a good man."

"So are you, son; and be careful, you've got to cross some pretty dangerous Indian territory."

"I'll keep a lookout."

"So'll the Indians. Just keep that Henry ready."

"I will," Johnny said.

"And don't forget, you've got a five hundred dollar reward coming. I'll see that it gets to Mason City."

"No." Yuma mounted the sorrel.

"What do you mean 'no,' It's yours. You earned it."

"Give it to Amy and her husband. They'll be needing it. So long."

Johnny Yuma wheeled the sorrel and rode west.

TWENTY-NINE

More than halfway across Texas—recalling the events and people encountered the last four years—including the words of Sheriff Pat Conway: "Keep that Henry ready." That was good advice, and prophetic . . .

Sheriff Pat Conway had also said, "You've got to cross some pretty dangerous Indian territory." Johnny Yuma was smack in the middle of the most dangerous part of that territory, because it was the part most in dispute by the Indians themselves. Apaches, Comanches, and Kiowas all claimed title long before the foreigners came—Mexicans, Spaniards, and then Texans.

Hundreds of square miles were claimed by all three tribes and known as Dry Tortuga. It was no different from the territory surrounding it, but Dry Tortuga was soaked in the blood of thousands of Apache, Comanche, and Kiowa men, women, and children.

Since the first light of history, since man came down from the trees and out of the caves and squatting places and formed into tribes, those tribes had traveled in all directions seeking new territory, usually because that territory meant a better existence: a hunting ground where game was more plentiful, a river or port where they could row or sail their ships for trading purposes, fields that were more fertile, or ground that they could more easily defend.

The great conquerors of history from Alexander to Caesar to Hannibal to Ghengis Kahn to Attila to Charlemagne to Napoleon, all sought territory for military, commercial or social advantage.

But why this territory? Dry Tortuga—claimed by all three tribes—and none was exactly sure where it began and where it ended—this worthless span of earth where God had stomped the dirt and dust off his boots, this clump of nothingness, with little or no water to provide nourishment, with no game to provide crops . . . this primitive patch of barren earth soaked with the flesh and bones and blood of Apache, Comanche and Kiowa.

Why?

Nobody really knew—except that their fathers before them and their fathers' fathers since time remembered had claimed Dry Tortuga and had killed and been killed to validate that claim, even until this day as Johnny Yuma rode through it.

The great Apache chiefs, Mangus Colorados, Vittoro, and Cochise; the Comanche chiefs, Isomain, Nokoni, and Tochoway; and the Kiowa chiefs, Kiva, Setangya, and Satanta all laid claim to Dry Tortuga and would fight, kill, and die to preserve that claim, even though none of them or their people lived there.

Still, they sent their warriors sweeping through the desolate landscape, searching for braves from the other tribes to ambush, take prisoner, or kill.

And if the raiders could find no living enemy to encounter, they would let the enemy who would come later know that they had been there and that this was their real estate; that they had passed this way again and renewed their title.

Each tribe would leave its mark, carved or painted or staked on rock or tree or soil.

And when the others came, they would destroy the previous sign and replace it with their own symbol of territorial possession.

There really wasn't much point to it, and it was a dangerous game, but the Apaches, Comanches, and Kiowas thrived on danger, pointless or not.

Johnny Yuma did not thrive on danger. He had his belly full of it. All he wanted was a way to go home, and Dry Tortuga was the way.

When the enemy would attack, it would be from one of three directions: from the rising or setting sun, from higher ground, or from out of some arroyo. This time, the enemy came from all three directions.

Three Indian riders raced in, screaming for the kill. Yuma wheeled and spurred the sorrel in the opposite direction. It would be useless to try to outrace them for a long distance. He knew their ponies were lighter and faster. But there was an outcrop of rocks, an island of stones that would shield him if he could reach it and make use of the Henry.

"Horse, they want your hide and my hair! Let's go!" And go they did, the sorrel and Yuma. The red riders converged, screamed, and gave chase burning the breeze. It seemed that their ponies' hooves hardly touched the earth, gaining ground with every stride, while the attackers fired with their ancient rifles.

Yuma made the rocks, flipped off the sorrel, and drew the Henry from its boot with one motion. In the next instant, the Henry was spewing shot after shot, and an Indian's face tore apart. He fell as one of the other two rode past.

The second Indian leaped off his mount and landed on Johnny Yuma, knocking the Henry to the ground. The red man's knife was in his hand, plunging toward Yuma's heart, but the Rebel grabbed the wrist of the knife hand and smashed his fist into the attacker's face again and again as they whirled into the ground.

Yuma could hear hoofbeats. The third rider was coming back fast. A bullet whizzed by the Rebel's ear. He expected the next shot to kill him, but the shot didn't come. The rider's rifle had jammed, and he galloped past again while the two men fought for their lives.

Yuma's left hand still held the dazed Indian's knife hand, but now, instead of hitting him with his right, Johnny drew the Colt and fired into the man's brain. Yuma spun, ready for the coming charge. From a distance, he could see the face of the mounted Indian. For a beat, they stared at each other, then the rider screamed and rode in the opposite direction.

Yuma knew that the rider was out of range of the Colt, and so did the Indian. He looked back with hate in his eyes and, still screaming, kicked at the flanks of his pony as he made for the horizon.

Johnny Yuma had no intention of going after him. He breathed deeply, grateful that he was still able to breathe.

The Rebel took a couple of steps closer to what was left of the dead Indian. Kiowa. Pony That Flies had taught Yuma how to tell. The red arm band.

Recollection. Other dead men. Enemies and comrades. Those he'd killed and those who had tried to kill him. He wiped the dirt and dust from his face and clothes. He holstered the Colt, walked to the Henry, and picked it up.

Hoofbeats.

Both the Indian ponies were racing away, side by side, riderless, except maybe for ghosts.

Then something caught his eye, something in the sky: birds, huge, black birds of death making anticipatory circles, looping ever closer with each circle.

Johnny Yuma thought of burying the dead and depriving the vultures, but that would take time—too much time— time that might deprive him of his own life. Johnny Yuma remembered the look of hate in the Kiowa's face as he rode away. He decided to move and move fast before he had more Kiowas for company.

That night and the next day, Yuma made dry camp and ate jerked beef and hardtack. He sipped sparingly from his canteen. Even while he slept, his senses were alert for any sound or movement.

The star-sprinkled night was cold blue. Distant hills rimmed the vast, shallow, sandy saucer of desert where nothing moved and it seemed that nothing breathed except Johnny Yuma. By first light, he was moving with his back to the rising sun, pulling the heat up with it.

Still nothing moved but the lone man and horse. A lost, silent land under a cloudless gray sky. Yuma was satisfied with the silence and lack of movement. The quiet and stillness were friendly. Noise and movement might mean danger, even death.

There were no shadows now. The blaze of sun was directly above in the bald, stark sky. Yuma's mouth was cotton dry, his face and body beaded with dripping sweat. He wiped his wet palms across the front of his buckskin shirt and blinked to keep the salty wetness out of his eyes.

He had passed two water holes, both dry. He unleashed the canteen, unscrewed the cap, and brought the container close to his parched lips, but its weight was not much more than the canteen itself. No more than an ounce or two of liquid sloshed within the bottom rim of the container. He barely wet his lips and tongue, then screwed the cap back on.

"Sorry, horse, I know you're thirstier than I am. If the next one's dry . . ."

He spotted it just ahead, in a clump of cottonwood and willow, and from his slight elevation, he could see the sun reflecting in the pool's mirror-blue liquid. A life-saving watery patch in the middle of a no-path expanse of sand.

The sorrel had already caught the scent of it. Nostrils flared and ears pricked forward, the animal humped its back and snorted.

"All right, horse. You'll get your belly full. Let's go have a drink."

And drink they did. Yuma filled his canteen, then lay on his stomach and dipped his face under the surface of the shallow pond. He slapped the water onto his neck and back and ducked his head under again, his cupped hands splattering water over his already dripping face. Then he saw it as droplets of water clung to his brows and lashes.

A blurred, ambiguous, wavering vision.

With a panther-quick movement, his right hand drew and cocked the Colt.

On the other side, a few feet from the pond, a man on a horse. Both the man's and horse's heads were bent. He was a trooper and wore a cap and trousers only, no shirt or boots. From exposure to the sun, and maybe from other things, his skin was peeled and shriveled. He sat in statuary silence, unaware of time and place and person, death's dull expression in his unseeing eyes.

Johnny Yuma holstered his gun as he rose and started wading across the water to the man.

"Trooper . . ."

No response.

Yuma was now little more than an arm's length away. He looked up at the man's sun-boiled face.

"Soldier." The Rebel was almost afraid to touch the inert trooper for fear of hurting him, but he reached out. "Soldier . . ."

Yuma's hand gently tapped the trooper's trouser leg. The man tilted from the horse and crashed onto the ground. Yuma could almost feel the seared skin tearing as the man landed hard.

The trooper lay motionless, his arms and legs awkwardly bent and extended, his face looking straight up with the same vacant expression. Yuma knelt near him, removed his own cap, and held it about a foot from the trooper's face, shading the man's eyes. Yuma slowly passed his free hand in front of the trooper's eyes . . . and then again, closer.

No reaction. Sunblind. But Yuma could tell that the man still breathed and clung to life, but by a thin, brittle thread. A low moan passed from the man's parched lips.

"I'll help you all I can, soldier." Yuma knew it was hopeless.

Another moan from the man, then, barely perceptible, the cracked lips quivered and formed a word . . . two words.

"Concho . . . Fort Concho . . ." He tried, with all the breath and strength that he could muster, but he could say no more.

"Easy, soldier. I'll get you some water." But Yuma realized, even as he spoke, that the man was dead. With thumb and finger, Johnny Yuma pressed the eyes of the dead man closed.

He picked up the trooper's fallen cap and looked at it for a moment, then placed it gently on the soldier's face.

This time, Johnny Yuma would bury the dead, and did, as deep as he could dig, then covered the grave with sand and spread it so it could not be easily discerned. Carefully, he removed the evidence of the resting place and tracks so that the Indians would not find and mutilate what remained. And this time Johnny Yuma spoke a few words.

"We come into this world with nothing. And we take nothing with us. The Lord giveth and the Lord taketh away. Blessed be the name of the Lord. Amen."

Before he left, Johnny Yuma took the time to make an entry into his journal.

THIRTY

Fort Concho can't be too far ahead. On my way to war, I made sure to avoid it. But not this time. This time, whatever I find there will be a welcome sight . . .

But it wasn't.

At the Medicine Lodge council in Kansas, the Kiowa Chief Satanta had said to the commissioners, "I have heard that you intend to settle us on a reservation near the mountains. When we settle down, we grow pale and die. A long time ago, this land belonged to our fathers; but when I go up to the river, I now see camps of soldiers on its banks. These soldiers cut down my timber; they kill my buffalo; and when I see this, my heart is broken. I feel sorry. I have spoken."

There was good reason why Satanta was known as the Great Orator of the Plains.

To protect the settlers, the government had set up army posts throughout the West. The blare of bugles and the hoofbeats of troopers heralded the inevitable change that fell like a dark shadow across the Indian way of life. The

Butterfield stage, covered wagons, steamboats, and the iron horse swept westward across the hunting grounds and with them people from the East and all the nations of Europe: more people than there were buffalo. The gold strike in California had signaled another tidal wave of immigrants.

"Our great mission," said Senator John C. Calhoun, "is to occupy this vast domain."

And as early as 1845, an article appeared in an Eastern newspaper, "Our Manifest Destiny is to over-spread the continent allotted by Providence for the free development of our yearly multiplying millions. We will realize our Manifest Destiny."

Nothing much was said about the destiny of the Indians. But some Indians would have something to say about it. And something to do.

When the war broke out between North and South, the Union Army needed all the manpower that was available, especially if that manpower had already been exposed to the ways of war.

Much of that manpower was in the West.

Some of the forts were abandoned. Others had to make do with reduced ranks. One of the forts that had carried on with fewer troopers was Fort Concho.

Johnny Yuma was now within sight of it. Astride his horse, leading the dead trooper's pony by a rope a few feet behind, Yuma stopped, lifted himself in the saddle, looked around, wiped the sweat away, then urged his horse on.

As he came closer to the wall of Fort Concho, he could sense and then see that there was something wrong.

An unreal quietness.

No guard was posted. No colors flew from the staff. The gates were closed, but nothing stirred. No living sound came from within. When he was close enough to be heard,

Yuma dropped the reins and brought his hands into a circle close to his mouth.

"Hello the fort! Hello! Hello the fort!" The only answer, an echo. No challenge. No living response. Again Yuma called out. Again, the same result: nothing but an echo.

He unsheathed the Henry, pointed it above the wall of Fort Concho, and fired twice. The shots reverberated . . . and then the sound of silence again.

He slipped the Henry back into its boot, unloosed the rope, and flung the loop end high and around a parapet. Off the back of the sorrel, he moved hand over hand up the rope and wall to the top, climbed over, and stood on the catwalk, surveying the innards of Fort Concho.

Empty, silent . . . like a huge, beached, deserted ship anchored in a sea of sand.

He hauled the rope up, looped it into a circle, and started down the stairs from the catapult, still looking about with caution.

He walked across the compound to the main gate, opened it, and let in the two horses. He led the two animals to a large watering trough at the edge of the parade ground. The stagnant water was crusted with a layer of dirt and slime.

With the butt of the Henry, Yuma paddled through the layer of filth, and both horses began to drink. When he thought they'd had enough, the Rebel walked them to the front of a structure marked Headquarters and tied them to a hitching post.

Not fast, not slow, but ready, Yuma opened the door and entered. He walked through the small reception room where the sergeant should have been at his chair behind the desk. The chair and the room were empty. He walked into the inner office, a larger room, also vacant and eerie.

Everything was in its place: desk, chair, the officer's quill and papers. Yuma picked up a sheet of paper and blew at it. Flakes of dust floated off into the room. Yuma set the sheet on the desk and lifted a slim, triangular block of wood about ten inches long with a name painted across it.

Captain Tom Richards.

Yuma wondered about Captain Tom Richards. Had he and his command been ordered out? Was he alive? Was any of them alive? Or were their ghosts all that was left of the entire command at Fort Concho?

Another room in another building. The mess hall. Long tables lined the area. At the head of one of the tables there was a tin plate, a knife, and a fork. They were the only utensils on any of the tables in the entire room. Yuma headed toward them.

A sound: scratching! From the far end of the room, behind him.

Yuma whirled and drew the Colt at three giant rats gnawing and quarreling over a quarter loaf of rock-hard bread near a corner. The Rebel stomped a foot against the wooden floor, and the rats scampered into a hole at the base of the wall.

Then a maniacal laugh swelled through the room as Yuma whirled again, Colt leveled at the sound.

It came from a tall, gaunt, ghostly man clothed in bizarre, tattered, robelike garments. His hair alabaster white, his eyes dark, fallow pits, with deep creases trailing his face and leading to a lipless, laughing mouth.

"Put down that hogleg, boy!" He pointed a long, bony finger at the Colt. The man approached Yuma, half circling and appraising.

Johnny Yuma's eyes followed the man's movements. He lowered the gun but didn't holster it.

"So, somebody got through, huh?" the man cackled. "So, you're the reinforcements? Horses, foot, and dragoons! One schoolboy gonna take back Fort Concho!" He lifted both hands toward the ceiling, then lowered them, still cackling. "That'll take a lot of taking! Who be you, boy?"

"My name's Yuma. Johnny Yuma."

"That don't mean nothin'. You know who I am?"

The Rebel shook his head and holstered the Colt. The man's eyes widened. He stroked at his cadaverous chin, turned, and walked a few steps toward the wall, almost as if he were going to walk into or through it, but then he spun back toward Yuma and roared, "I'm Nebuchadnezzar! Solomon! The Great Jehovah! Big medicine, boy! Powerful medicine! I laugh, and it thunders. I stomp my foot, and it's lightnin'. I wave my arms, and the sea opens wide. Powerful medicine, boy! Now, maybe you ought to kneel. Maybe you ought to curry my favor, cuz I hold the power of livin' and dyin' in these parts." He pointed to the floor. "Now, are you gonna kneel?"

"No, I'm not."

"Well," the man continued, not at all fazed, "maybe it ain't absolutely and positively necessary, so long as you show the proper respect. Mind you do that, boy."

The Rebel said nothing. The man thought a moment and took a step closer.

"Where be you headin'?"

"West. Mason City."

"No, you ain't!"

Yuma didn't argue or contradict. He just stood and waited.

"I said you ain't. You know why? Injuns, that's why! West, East, North, South, and all points o' the compass. Redskins with the smell o' blood in their beaks and murder in their eyeballs."

"I ran into three of them."

"Then how come you're alive?" the old man asked.

"Because two of them aren't."

"But what about the third?"

"What about him?"

"He's still alive, ain't he?"

"Last I saw of him he was."

"But that ain't the last you'll be seein' of him. You can bet your gray hat on that, Johnny Reb." The man laughed again and whooped and stomped both feet in what appeared to be his version of an Indian war dance. Suddenly, he stopped, and a serious, challenging expression crossed his face.

"I can tell what you're thinkin' and wonderin'. What's this coyote's cousin doin' here all alone? You show the proper respect, boy. I'm in command o' the fort now." He tapped his head. "There's powerful medicine in this here skull." He lowered his voice to a harsh whisper. "Injuns! All around. Smell 'em? Injuns hit this fort . . ."

"When?"

"Who knows? A hundred years ago . . . a thousand . . . or maybe it's just been a week."

The Rebel eyed him steadily and thought to himself, *If this man isn't insane, he's skin close to it.*

"Well, anyhow," the man went on, "it was a lot of dead men ago."

"Comanches or Kiowas?"

"Kiowas, boy. They can eat Comanches for breakfast."

Yuma knew the answer even as he had asked the question. The man began to walk around again and wave his arms. "Ol' Satanta's smeared with paint . . . paint and blood, boy . . . and there's nothin' that breathes at Concho . . . 'ceptin' me." He pointed to the rat hole in the wall. "Me and my pets."

"How is it you're still breathing?"

The question stopped the man short. A terrible look flooded his eyes. He didn't answer.

"I said, how come you're the only one alive?"

The man visibly shuddered. He stared down at the floor, then slowly lifted his face and spoke. "Why shouldn't I tell you? I need to tell somebody. It's on account of my superior skull power . . ."

The Rebel waited for him to go on. The man gathered his thoughts and then took gleeful pride in his explanation.

"Injuns is like kids one minute . . . killers the next. Ya gotta outsmart 'em, which is what I done. When they hit the fort, I hid. . . ."

"You what?"

"We didn't have a chance!" the man shouted. "Yer blood would turn green at what I seen while I was hid!"

Johnny Yuma turned away.

"Don't you show your back to me, you Rebel pup!"

Slowly, Yuma turned again and faced the man.

"Don't you see," the man explained, "this way my bones'll still bend. I'd only be dead if I'd fought. What good would that a' done?"

"Your bullet might've killed Satanta."

"The bullet ain't been made that'd kill Satanta."

"Not a coward's bullet," Johnny Yuma said.

"I ain't no coward cuz I hid. I was smart. I saved the fort."

"You saved yourself."

"Cuz I was smart!" He was almost quivering with excitement. "When they was through scalpin' and dancin', I walked out among 'em in these garments . . . big as a buffalo . . . a-babblin', a-laughin' . . . You savvy, boy?"

"Indians won't hurt a crazy man."

"That's it! That's it! You do savvy. I went out among 'em actin' crazy as a red-eyed steer . . . and that took guts

. . . a belly fulla guts . . . you gotta admit to that."

"The soldiers . . . their bodies?"

"I buried what was left of 'em . . . like heroes. The army's got to take care of its own."

"Yeah. After you took care of yourself."

"Huh?" The man's eyes were full of pain and maybe now he *was* mad. "A lot of dead men ago."

"I'm going to get out of here," Yuma said. "You want to come with me?"

"What for? Why would I do that? I'm in command now. Fort Concho stands ready for inspection."

"How long are you planning on staying here?"

"So long as I keep pretendin'. I'm sovereign among 'em. They leave me and this place . . . bring me food and the like . . . Don't you see?"

"I see."

"And I'm in command of the fort . . ."

"And you don't have to face a court martial."

Suddenly there was nothing of insanity in the man's eyes. The Rebel had hit him with the truth and hit him hard. The man was now looking past Johnny Yuma, and in that instant, he erupted into a more passionate burst of maundering than ever before, jig dancing and singing. He jumped into the air, gibbering and laughing.

Even before turning and looking, Johnny Yuma knew why. Keeping his hand away from his Colt, Yuma did turn, not fast, not slow, and looked at the painted Indian standing at the window with a rifle pointed directly at the Rebel.

There were three more Kiowas at the entrance with rifles. They advanced into the room. One of them lifted Yuma's gun from its holster, then pushed him roughly toward the door.

All the while, the other white man continued his jigging and gibbering. As one of the Kiowas walked by, the man cackled and picked up the tin plate from the table and smacked the Indian a resounding whack on the head. The Indian turned in a swift motion but stopped short as the man laughed and hurled the plate against the wall.

He nodded in triumph at Yuma, knowing that he was immune from any retaliation. Johnny Yuma, flanked by Indians, was pushed through the doorway, followed by the crazy man.

Outside in the compound, there were more than a dozen mounted Kiowas and another dozen on foot. The chief was on the biggest horse, a piebald, and closest to Yuma.

Satanta.

His age indeterminable, but he was no longer a young man. His eyes, two hard, narrow streaks. His face worn, dark, and broad, with a strong flat line for a chin. Satanta wore the tunic of a major in the U.S. Cavalry, and around his neck, a leather thong with an eagle claw.

On one side of Satanta was Stumbling Bear, another chief; he was older with a fervid, tragic look. Strapped over his pony was a large burlap sack.

At Satanta's other side on a pinto was a girl, maybe sixteen, in Indian attire, her small features accentuated by her straight, severe, ebony hairdo.

But the one who most caught Johnny Yuma's attention stood off to the left near the Rebel's horse. In his hand he held Yuma's Henry, and that same look of hate still filled his eyes as he stared at Johnny Yuma.

One of the Kiowas pushed Yuma closer to Satanta, who dismounted smartly. As Satanta's feet touched the ground, the crazy man lifted his long, thin arms toward the sky.

"The face a-heaven . . ." the man cried, ". . . the face a-heaven's a-frownin' and a-scowlin' . . . cryin' tears a-vengeance."

Everyone but Yuma looked up at the cloudless sky.

"The face a-heaven cryin' out for vengeance against him who came here to kill my brothers!" He pointed to Yuma and made an all-inclusive gesture as the Indians reacted to the man's words. He turned to Satanta. "The face a-heaven screamin' and a-tellin' you to strike him dead before he brings more like him." Again, he held his hands up to the sky. "The face a-heaven a-hollerin' . . . Kill him! Kill him!"

"All right, fella," Yuma said to the man, "you made your point."

The Indian holding the Henry stepped closer to Satanta and spoke to the chief in their language. When the Indian finished speaking, Yuma grinned at Satanta.

"I killed two of your braves, all right, and they died with honor, but it was this one," Yuma pointed at the Kiowa holding the rifle, "who ran away like a jackal. Not me."

"You understand our words, Yellow Hair." Satanta looked into Yuma's eyes.

"And speak some, too."

"But you are our enemy."

"If you say so."

"It is not what I say. It is what the milk-faces do. They are the ones who broke the treaties."

"Sometimes they did . . . and sometimes you did, Satanta."

"You know my name."

"Everybody does. There was a time they called you the Great Orator of the Plains. Now they call you other things."

"Satanta, why do you listen to the words of this white eyes who fills the air with lies. He . . ." the Kiowa with the rifle said.

"This one knows about lies, Satanta, and about running away from a fight and leaving his brothers to die."

The butt of the Henry slammed against Yuma's head.

The Rebel staggered but didn't fall. The Indian pointed the rifle at Yuma.

"Iron Hand!" Satanta spoke, and Iron Hand froze.

"Iron Hand." There was contempt in the way Yuma said it. "Iron? Ask his dead brothers who spit on him from their souls. The only way he could get my rifle was to steal it."

"What is past between you is past," Satanta said. "But you, Yellow Hair, will die." Yuma looked straight ahead at Satanta without blinking as the chief went on, "Do you know why?"

"I guess," Yuma shrugged, "because you say so."

"A man should know why he dies. That helps him die well."

"If you've got to die," Yuma nodded, "you might as well be good at it."

"We will see, Yellow Hair, if the Kiowa will be proud of your scalp."

"That's it! That's it!" the crazy man yelped. "Got to kill him! Got to kill him dead! I hear the Great Spirit a-tellin' Satanta to kill the white man. He's bad medicine, a-spreadin' disease and destruction. Kill him . . . kill him . . . He! . . . He! He!" The man folded his arms and squatted near the ground, still maundering.

"You will listen, Yellow Hair," Satanta said, "and remember for the time you have left."

"Sure," Yuma grinned. "I'm in no hurry."

"This is Indian land. You will learn that as other milk-faces have."

"Looks like you taught them pretty good." The Rebel glanced around at the fort.

"The long-knives have made my heart a stone, with no soft place in it." Satanta lifted Yuma's cap, looked at it, then let it drop. "You, Yellow Hair, are you a long-knife, too?"

"No. We fought against 'em.''

"Like the Kiowas?''

"Not exactly,'' Johnny answered.

"You were beaten.''

"They licked us.''

"I know. Your chances of winning were not good.''

"They were better than yours.''

"One does not always fight to win. The fight is sometimes to hurt back. Look upon Stumbling Bear.'' Satanta
pointed to the sack slung over the old Indian's horse. "Do
you know what he carries there?''

"No.''

"The bones of his son. Killed by the long-knives.'' Satanta pointed to the land around him. "Look at the earth
about you. Our fathers, our families are buried there. We
will not sell our bones cheaply. That is why we fight. That
is why Yellow Hair will die. Satanta has spoken.''

And while the chief spoke, Iron Hand pulled Johnny
Yuma's journal out of the saddlebag. He looked at it im-
passively and then tore out and crumpled a couple of pages.

Yuma lunged, grabbed the journal, and smashed his fist
into Iron Hand's face. The Indian brought up the butt of
the Henry and crashed it against the Rebel's forehead.
Johnny brought his hand up to the blood leaking from the
open welt near his temple. Iron Hand cocked the rifle and
aimed at the fallen Reb.

"Iron Hand!'' Satanta barked. "Not that way. It is too
quick. He will die as the sun falls, with slow fire.''

Dazed and bleeding, the Rebel was pulled to his unsteady
feet by two of the Kiowas, who started to lead him off.

"Yellow Hair . . .'' The Kiowas spun Yuma around so
he faced Satanta. "What do the milk-faces call me now?''

Johnny Yuma took a quivering breath and looked directly at the chief. "Butcher.''

Satanta motioned, and the two Indians led Yuma away as the others dispersed.

Slowly, the crazy man rose. He nodded to himself and followed after the two Kiowas bracing Johnny Yuma.

A pair of small, dark hands picked up the journal and the loose pages. The young girl looked at them but could not read what was written there.

THIRTY-ONE

The flames of the fire snapped at the extended hand hovering just inches above. Iron Hand turned his palm up. It was blackened from the scorching fire. As he knelt, in his other hand he held the Henry. He rose and faced Satanta, Stumbling Bear, and the other Kiowas who watched.

Johnny Yuma was now stripped to the waist, his hands bound above his head, against an H-beam on the side of the barracks. He was alone and away from the compound . . . alone until the crazy man approached and looked around.

"You know why I had to say all that, boy."

"Sure, I know. This way I never tell anybody about the coward of Fort Concho."

"I got a wife and son. Don't want him to grow up ashamed of my name."

"Oh, they both ought to be proud of you . . ."

"I know you're scornin' me."

"Do you?"

"Sure I do. I ain't . . ."

"Ain't what? Crazy? Well, trooper, I'm not sure about

the crazy part, but there's no doubt about being a coward.''

"Why, they was gonna scorch you anyway, Reb. Now they think I'm loco for certain . . . turnin' on a white man. That's just bein' crafty . . . heh, heh, heh. Well, I'll leave you to your prayers, Reb.''

"Thanks. Say one for yourself.''

From the corner of the barracks, the dark-skinned girl watched the man leave, then came forward a few steps.

"Come ahead,'' said Johnny Yuma, ''I'll take any kind of company I can get.''

After a beat, she walked toward him and stopped, close enough to whisper, but said nothing.

"Can you understand me?'' he asked.

She nodded.

"Can you talk?''

She nodded again.

"Well, what would you prefer? American or Kiowa?''

"I will speak your language.''

"Good. That makes it easier on me. How come you're with them, a raiding party?''

"We are no raiding party,'' she answered.

"No? Well then, what are you?''

"We have buried Satanta's wife . . . my mother.''

Johnny Yuma studied her face and features, her eyes. They were bluish green with the afternoon sun reflecting in them.

"You're not an Indian. Not clear through.''

"My mother and I were the only ones left of a wagon train . . . a long time ago.''

"Kiowas kill the rest of 'em?''

"No. Fever and hunger.''

"Yeah, well, that's not what's going to kill me,'' Johnny said.

"Satanta has been my father. The only father I remember."

"It's good to have a father."

"Do you?"

"I was on my way to see him," Yuma said. "But *your* father's got other ideas."

"Satanta lived in peace until the white man broke his word."

"You heard me say it; that worked both ways."

"Soon Satanta will have to leave the land of his fathers . . ."

"If he lives . . ." Yuma saw the crazy man peering from around the corner. The man caught the Rebel's glimpse and scampered away.

The girl reached up and touched the hair on Johnny Yuma's forehead.

"What's the matter?" he asked.

"My mother . . . her hair was the color of wheat."

"You ever try to escape?"

"No."

"Why not?"

"At first we were too sick."

"And later?"

"Later, there was no place . . . no reason to go." She paused, and then went on, "You, Yellow Hair, have a place . . . a reason to go."

"You bet."

"The papers you carry . . . those that Iron Hand took. Would they harm the Kiowas?"

"Those papers might not do anybody much good." Yuma smiled. "But they mean no hurt to the Kiowas . . . and neither did I."

"They have nothing to do with the military?"

"They're just part of a . . . sort of book I've been writing."

It was apparent that the girl didn't quite understand.

"It's hard to explain," Yuma continued, "but, well, it's not as easy for me to talk to people as it is to put down the things I've felt and found out."

"Your actions put great value on those papers."

"Maybe too much. People got to have something important. Some got mothers and fathers . . . a pet dog . . . a watch fob . . . a special gun. Stumbling Bear's got that sack. You've got Satanta. Me? I got a book I've been writing."

A pause. Then the girl made up her mind.

"Yellow Hair, do you know of the Kiowa challenge?"

"Ta-nee-mara!" It was the voice of Satanta, sharp and hard.

She turned and faced the Kiowa chief, his face a thundercloud. He spoke a few words to her in the Kiowa language.

"She did no wrong, Satanta," Yuma said. "She broke no Kiowa law."

"That is for Kiowa to say, Yellow Hair, not you. That is between Ta-nee-mara and her father."

"I say to her father that his daughter did no wrong to the Kiowas. I swear by the Great Spirit."

"Yellow Hair will be with the Great Spirit before the sun sleeps."

THIRTY-TWO

Johnny Yuma's hands were bound by leather straps. But now he stood in front of the leaping fire. All of the Kiowas, Ta-nee-mara, and the crazy man were watching. The crazy man was ceremoniously waving his hands and still mumbling. He reached to the ground, picked up a stick, broke it over his own head, threw the broken pieces into the air, and started to cackle.

The Indians began their death chant.

Near the blazing fire, the Kiowas had rigged several poles into an apparatus whereby the Rebel would be lifted and hung near the flames until he roasted alive.

The crazy man drifted a few feet away and removed a large, silver pocket watch. He pressed the stem and the lid flipped open, revealing a picture of a woman and a boy pasted onto the lid of the timepiece, which had ceased to tick some time ago.

He glanced at the picture for just a beat, snapped the lid shut, and put the silent watch away. But in his eyes there were tears.

To himself, Johnny Yuma had been rehearsing the ritual

of the Kiowa challenge. Now he shouted, and the chanting ceased.

"Kiowas, brothers of the eagle and the bear, there is something that must be said. A truth that must be told!"

The Indians stood still and silent. He had made the proper start of the ritual.

"What must be said?" Satanta spoke. "What truth must be told?"

"The truth of the searching wind that must be known in daylight and darkness. The truth that will not be hidden."

"And what is that truth?" Satanta looked into the eyes of the Rebel.

"A pig walks among your lodge."

The ritual of the Kiowa challenge had been correctly continued.

"How does Yellow Hair know this?" Satanta asked the penultimate question of the rite. The rest was up to Johnny Yuma.

"By the filth that hangs from his face and the odor of his nearness. A liar. A thief. And a pig . . . the three are one."

"How near is he?" The final question.

"As near as . . . Iron Hand!"

A great squealing howl, like a hundred pigs, came from all the Kiowas. All but Iron Hand.

Still gripping the Henry, Iron Hand took a step forward.

"Yellow Hair lies to save his life."

"The truth is in your hand, pig. Fire at anything you choose, and I'll better your mark. That is a Kiowa challenge!"

"It must be done." Satanta pointed to Yuma's bound wrists. "Cut him loose." The chief moved closer to Yuma. "Where did you learn the Kiowa challenge? Ta-nee-mara . . ."

"Ta-nee-mara didn't tell me. You were there. I was taught the ways of the Kiowa by my father's blood brother, Pony That Flies."

They all reacted to the name, especially Satanta. Yuma knew that he had used big medicine.

"Pony That Flies is my second father!" the Rebel said. "If he was here, he would tell you this."

"Pony That Flies speaks no more. He is with the Great Spirit. You did not know this?"

"No. I have been far away . . . for a long time, fighting the long-knives. When? How did he die?"

"Everybody dies. He knew it was his time. He was ready. He went in peace."

"Enough talk!" Iron Hand barked.

"You're right, Iron Hand. Let the long gun speak." Yuma pointed to the Henry. "The truth will come from there."

The crazy man cackled again and held up a tin drinking cup. He waved it around for all to see. He nodded toward Iron Hand and then banged the cup against his own forehead three times and feigned tossing it into the air.

Iron Hand understood and nodded in return. The Indians moved back to give Iron Hand room. The crazy man flung the cup as far as he could, straight up into the sky.

Three shots rang out from the Henry before the cup hit the ground. The crazy man was already running to retrieve it. He brought it back and handed the cup to Satanta, who examined it and held it up for everybody to see. With his other hand, he held up two fingers.

There were two holes clean through the cup. The crazy man grabbed the cup from Satanta and stood waiting to throw it again.

Satanta took the Henry from Iron Hand and gave it to the Rebel. Yuma cocked the rifle.

"Remember, there are many guns pointed at you, Yellow Hair."

"I'll remember."

As quickly as he could, the crazy man flung the cup again, but this time not straight up. He threw it into the setting sun where it seemed to vanish into the ball of fire.

Yuma cocked and fired four times, faster than most men could think, then he whirled and pointed the barrel into Satanta's face, but only for an instant. That's all it took to make his point. He lowered the Henry and handed it to the chief.

This time, one of the other braves retrieved the cup and brought it to the still startled Satanta.

The chief held up what was left of the bullet-riddled vessel.

Four new holes. The Rebel hadn't missed, not once. A murmur of amazement rippled through the Kiowas as Satanta pointed four fingers into the air.

"He can keep the gun!" Iron Hand exclaimed. "If he lives! We will see who is pig and who will be skinned. We will run for the knife!"

Satanta nodded.

The Kiowas began making preparations for the death contest. Yuma and Iron Hand would be tied left wrist to left wrist by a leather thong six feet long. Satanta would throw a razor-sharp knife with a seven-inch blade into a wall approximately twenty feet away. As soon as the knife stuck, the two warriors would start a no-holds-barred run to get the knife and plunge it into the other's heart.

The crazy man stared silently, bug-eyed; Ta-nee-mara looked toward Satanta, but he did not return her look. Stumbling Bear held the sack containing the bones of his son.

Everything was in readiness.

Satanta held the knife by the tip of its blade. His arm arched back and came forward in a single, swift motion. The knife flew fast and sure, stuck into the wooden wall, and quivered.

Yuma and Iron Hand ran toward the knife, the Rebel a couple of paces ahead until Iron Hand stopped, braced himself and jerked back with all his might against the thong and Yuma, who was halted abruptly. Iron Hand looped the thong. It circled the Rebel's neck.

Iron Hand tugged hard. Yuma spilled to the ground. The brave sprang on top of him, trying to get another loop around Yuma's neck and strangle him.

They twisted over each other's body again and again. Yuma's elbow exploded into the Indian's face, stunning him. The Rebel freed his neck from the encircling thong.

They had rolled just a few feet from the wall. Yuma went for the knife, but Iron Hand leaped after him. He smashed against Yuma, plastering him into the wall. Yuma dropped.

The Indian's right hand freed the knife. Yuma maneuvered to his feet. Iron Hand lunged. Yuma sidestepped and hammered his fist into the side of the brave's face.

Yuma moved back swiftly until the thong stretched taut. While Iron Hand was still off balance, Yuma swung Iron Hand around and around until the Kiowa slammed against the wall.

Yuma crashed on top of him, grabbing the knife hand with his left and slugging the Indian with the other. But Iron Hand spun over and his knees straddled Yuma. He raised the knife and plunged it down.

Yuma moved just in time, and the blade was buried, almost to the hilt, in the ground next to Yuma's ear. In the same instant, Yuma's right fist burst into Iron Hand's nose, splattering bone and gristle. Then over and over they spun, a human whirlwind, enmeshed in the thong that got shorter and shorter, with the knife still stuck in the ground.

Both men were smeared in dust, sweat, and the Indian's blood. Yuma made a final loop around Iron Hand's neck and pulled tight, bringing both their faces close together.

Yuma's arm stretched closer and closer to the knife until his hand gripped the handle and pulled it away from the earthen sheath. Yuma's other hand pulled at the strap that was now strangling Iron Hand. Yuma brought the blade to within an inch of the Indian's throat. The red man's eyes flashed with fear and frenzy. The veins in his neck swelled into thick, throbbing cords as he tried in vain to hold back Yuma's hand inching toward the quivering flesh.

Slowly the blade came ever closer.

Then, Johnny Yuma's hand holding the knife moved in another direction, with one swift stroke, cutting the thong that bound the Rebel's wrist, freeing himself and relieving the pressure from around Iron Hand's throat.

Iron Hand's head fell back against the ground. He was spent, grateful to be alive, and still wary. He did not move.

Yuma rose to his feet. He threw the knife into the ground not far from Iron Hand's face. It was the final gesture of defiance and victory.

Yuma stood, breathing hard breaths, waiting.

The Kiowas waited, too, for Satanta. Never before had the Kiowa challenge ended with both combatants still alive. Always before, victory had meant life and defeat was death.

Satanta, still holding the Henry, moved toward the Rebel. He reached down and pulled the knife out of the ground. For an instant, he held the blade close to Iron Hand, who still had not moved. Then the chief turned toward Yuma. He handed the Henry to a Kiowa brave nearby.

Satanta took hold of Yuma's left arm. The Rebel offered no resistance. Satanta sliced the blade across Yuma's forearm. A thin red line appeared. The chief then cut into his own arm and placed it against Yuma's, letting the blood of both comingle.

And then Satanta removed the thong with the eagle claw from around his neck and placed it around the throat of Johnny Yuma.

"You fight like the eagle. You are free as the eagle. Walk as Satanta's brother among the Kiowa, the Cheyenne, and the Sioux."

Yuma nodded and touched the eagle claw at his breast-bone. He looked square into the eyes of the great Kiowa chief, now and always, his brother.

"Satanta, the troopers will be coming back to take the fort."

"They have taken many things. Our vengeance here is done. If the long-knives follow us, will you . . ."

"I will never ride against my brothers, the Kiowas."

The others nodded and murmured their approval. Yuma stepped close to the brave holding the Henry. He reached out for it. The brave looked to Satanta, who signaled his consent.

Yuma took the Henry and turned to Satanta. He held out the rifle.

"It is not worthy of the gift you have given me. But it is the Kiowa custom that I give you something in return."

"I thank my brother," Satanta took the rifle, "and I make a promise. It will never fire first against the white man, only against our enemy, the Comanche, and to hunt food for our people."

"I know that."

Satanta spoke a command in the Kiowa language. The Indians began dispersing and mounting, all but Ta-nee-mara, who held Yuma's journal in her hands. Satanta motioned for her to come closer.

"You have grown up among us," Satanta said to her.

"But now your mother is dead. Your heart and hand went to him." He motioned toward Yuma. "If the bond is broken, then you can go back to your people."

Ta-nee-mara looked at Satanta, then at the Rebel. Johnny smiled, but said nothing.

"Will I be as the bat . . . not bird . . . not mouse?"

"Some will make you feel like that," Yuma admitted.

"Should . . . should I go?"

"Ta-nee-mara . . ." Yuma was torn by many feelings. "Satanta said it. You've got to decide for yourself."

It was the defining moment.

"I will . . . stay with my father." She looked back to the Rebel. "But I hope we will meet again." She held out the journal.

"So do I."

The crazy man stood not far away, listening. Satanta pointed to him.

"We will take him with us, the white man who sees the face of heaven." Satanta turned and walked toward his horse. Ta-nee-mara followed him without looking back.

Iron Hand approached, leading Yuma's sorrel. The Rebel's buckskin shirt was draped over the saddle. He handed Yuma the Colt that the Kiowas had taken.

"Thanks," Yuma said.

"No. It is Iron Hand who thanks Yellow Hair." He turned and walked away.

As Yuma began to pull on the buckskin shirt, the crazy man came closer.

"Reb . . ."

Yuma looked at him but said nothing.

"You . . . ain't gonna tell nobody . . . what I done . . . are you?" He shook with confusion and shame.

"They're waiting for you."

"You ain't gonna tell nobody, are you?"

"Far as I'm concerned, everybody died at Fort Concho. No use saying anything bad about the dead."

The man knew that he was, indeed, a dead man, maybe worse than dead, having to pretend always, that he was insane. With a slow, deliberate movement, he reached into his pocket, took out the watch, snapped open the lid, and studied the picture. He handed the watch to Yuma.

"My name's on the back. Maybe you can get it to my kin . . . Sandusky, Ohio. Tell 'em you found it on a body."

Yuma nodded.

"Please, one last favor: Say my name just once. It'll be the last time I ever hear it."

Yuma looked at the back of the watch and then at the man.

"Silas. Silas Dirkson."

"Thanks. Thank you, Mister Yuma." Silas Dirkson turned, squared his shoulders, and walked toward the Kiowas and his fate.

Johnny Yuma was the last to leave the fort. The gates were open. He rode through, leaving the open gates of Fort Concho behind him.

THIRTY-THREE

There are those who will swear that they woke up in the middle of the night and saw a ghost. But today, in burning daylight, I saw what appeared to be a battalion of ghosts riding behind . . .

The guidon of the Third Texas . . . and the Stars and Bars of the South. Twin columns of mounted cavalry dressed in the uniforms of the quondam Confederacy were moving across the craggy terrain of the basin just below.

Johnny Yuma squinted his eyes against the sun and through the shimmering heat waves, trying to make sure that what he saw approaching from the distance was not a moving mirage.

It wasn't.

A mirage does not make noise. Johnny Yuma already could hear hoofbeats and the clanking of metal, the scabbards of the swords chinking against stirrups and spurs. The horses snorted and their hooves left behind a wake of dust that evaporated into the beige landscape.

A ghost battalion.

The Third Texas didn't exist. It had ceased to exist years ago. Yuma's comrades were all dead or dispersed into other units. But there were over forty troopers of the Third Texas approaching, and they were led by Johnny Yuma's former commanding officer, Colonel James B. Culver, with the same gray hair, gray eyes, and gray military mustache, just as the Rebel remembered him.

"Company, halt!" Colonel Culver gave the command, and the column obeyed. The colonel reined up his mount and looked at Yuma almost as if he had been expecting him.

"I know you," the colonel said.

"Yes, sir, Colonel Culver. Yuma. Corporal Johnny Yuma. I was with you and the Third Texas from Rose Ridge to the Rappahannock.

"Yes, of course. Good soldier. Thought you were killed, corporal."

"Captured, sir. Sent to Rock Island."

"For the remainder of . . . hostilities?"

"Escaped, sir. I tried to make it back, but they told me that the Third Texas was . . . disbanded."

"We were, temporarily. As you can see." Culver pointed to the troopers. Their eyes were straight ahead in near perfect formation as were their mounts. The troopers ranged in age, a few older than the colonel, others younger than Yuma. The two officers, a captain and a lieutenant, wore cavalry hats. The enlisted men wore kepis.

"I . . ." Yuma looked at the mounted command. "I don't recognize anybody from the outfit, sir, except you."

"No, you wouldn't. These men fought in other brigades. But I've reorganized the Third Texas . . ."

"Reorganized, sir?"

"That's right, Corporal. At my own expense. New mounts, new uniforms, and new weapons. But we're still the Third Texas and always will be. You understand?''

"Yes, sir.'' Johnny Yuma said it, but he didn't under-stand. He had no notion of what the colonel was doing or what he had in mind, but out of deference to his former commander, a good and brave man, a fighting officer who had led them time and again in charges under enemy fire, Yuma was determined to be careful of what he said and how he said it. There was a pause as Colonel Culver ap-praised Johnny Yuma.

"You're not exactly in uniform, Corporal, but we'll take care of that. We'll have a new outfit for you and a new rank. You're promoted to lieutenant.''

"Lieutenant?''

"That's right. Fall in, Lieutenant.''

"May I inquire, sir, where the Third Texas is going?'' Johnny asked.

"Going?''

"Yes, sir.''

"South. We're moving south.''

"How far, sir?''

"Mexico.''

"And, sir, the purpose of the expedition?''

"First, we're joining President Benito Juárez. He's called for volunteers to fight against Maximillian.''

"Maximillian?''

"That's right. Louis-Napoléon's invaded Mexico, haven't you heard?''

"Yes, sir. I heard that some time ago.''

"Juárez needs us, and then we'll need him.''

"To do what, sir?''

"To free Texas.''

Yuma observed the colonel, resplendent in his uniform, sword, and side arm. But it was the officer's face that he studied. Yuma looked for some trace of madness, of frenzy, of fanaticism. But the colonel's features reflected none of this. He appeared calm, reasonable, and rational—except for what he said.

"But, sir," Yuma finally mustered the words, "Texas is a part of the Union."

"Before that, it was a Republic. Joining the Union was a mistake. A mistake I intend to rectify. And when I do, Texas will be a Republic again and forever. And James Culver will be the first President of the New Republic of Texas. I'll need all the help I can get, Lieutenant."

"Yes, sir. Right now it looks to me like you've only got about forty men."

"There'll be more. First hundreds, then by the thousands, coming from all the states of the South, swarming in to join the Third and fight for the New Republic of Texas with the help of President Benito Juárez. Juárez will be obligated to help us . . ."

"Have you talked this over with him, sir?"

"Not yet. But he'll have no choice . . . and neither do we. Join the ranks, Lieutenant. We've got a lot of miles to cover before nightfall."

"But, sir . . ."

"What is it?" the colonel asked.

"The fight's over."

"Who said so?"

"General Lee. I was at Appomattox . . ."

"I wasn't. Lee surrendered the Army of Northern Virginia, but Texas will never surrender. Never." Culver was still calm and convinced of every word he spoke.

"I'm sorry, sir."

"About what?"

"I can't go with you."

"Why not?"

"Because I'm . . . I'm going home," Johnny said.

"Where's that?"

"Mason City."

"Texas?"

"Yes, sir."

"Don't you realize that there is no Texas? At least not at the present time. The Texas we knew was betrayed by traitors and delivered to the enemy to become a part of the enemy's flag. But the lone star of Texas was meant to fly alone, proud and free. Until then, what kind of home can you go back to?"

"That's what I'm going to find out . . . but I wish you luck, sir, and good fortune."

"You'll change your mind, Corporal." Colonel Culver was unfazed. "A lot of people will, and you'll be welcome to join us when we come back."

"Yes, sir." Johnny Yuma saluted the commanding officer of the Third Texas.

"Column, ho!" Colonel James B. Culver waved on the troopers and led them south.

The Rebel watched as they drifted away with the sounds of hoofbeats and the clinking of metal fading into the dust that followed the column south.

In spite of his demeanor, the colonel was mad, but only an infinitesimal speck of the madness that made up the mad spectrum of war. Thousands, hundreds of thousands of men of the North and South, leaders of all the tribes and all the nations of all the world, since the beginning of the history of the world, had yet to devise a viable and conclusive path to peace—other than war.

They would talk, bargain, and negotiate, but more often than not, they would resort to combat. Might did not always make right, but more often than not, it made victory.

Victory and defeat—for too many—meant death. For most of the survivors, it meant peace. But for others, for those like Colonel James B. Culver and the ones who followed him, there was no peace. The war and the madness went on.

Johnny Yuma had left one war at Appomattox when he didn't squeeze the trigger. But he still hadn't found peace.

Maybe he would in Mason City.

THIRTY-FOUR

Nothing or no one stays the same. Not places, not people. Sometimes the change is more noticeable than others. I have changed. So has Texas. I wonder about Mason City and the people there . . .

Two of the most unpredictable times, Johnny Yuma thought to himself, were when you left home and when you went back.

And it was hard to predict which time you expected more: when you left or when you returned. Sooner or later, a man usually comes back to the place of his youth, to the things left behind. And in going back, the last mile was sometimes the hardest: awash with expectation, with trepidation, and too often with regret for things unsaid, undone, and undecided.

And often, those were the reasons why a man went home, to say, and do, and decide. That was the case with the Rebel.

As he started to cover that last mile into Mason City, he

looked at the landscape that had been so familiar those early years of his life.

It had rained the night before, a soft, light midnight rain across the moon afloat in a clouded, purple sky—a rain that at first gently splattered into the barren, thirsty earth and seeped through cracks and slopes filling the hollows of the hills and drifting into rivulets, then streams, and flowing faster, licking at the shallow banks, until they overflowed as the rain drummed hard and steady through the night.

Yuma had spent the night in a cave where he often had played as a child. A cave with Indian markings and carvings on the walls. He had slept less last night than he had during many of the nights when he knew he would be going into battle with the dawn.

Many times during those nights he had thought of death, his own and his comrades' and his enemies'. During those nights, though tired and sometimes wounded, often he did not want to fall asleep. He wanted to be awake and aware of every living and breathing minute. He wanted to feel and hear his heart beat, even to feel the pain of his wounds, to realize that he was hungry and thirsty—and alive. During the war, each new day would mean danger to all and death to some.

But last night, lying in the dankness of the cave, Johnny Yuma did not think of death. He thought of life, his own and the lives of the people he knew. People who were asleep in Mason City. People who didn't know how near to them he was that night—how near in distance—and other things.

His father. His aunt Emmy. Elmer Dodson. Jess Evans, his father's deputy. And most of all, Rosemary—the only girl he ever loved.

It was in that same cave, years ago, on a Sunday afternoon . . . The memories, many of them submerged and faded during the whirlwind of war, now in that last mile to Mason City, surfaced again in Johnny Yuma's mind with sharp and painful imagery.

On that Sunday, years ago, the sudden summer storm had hit with a relentless ferocity. Johnny Yuma and Rosemary Cutler had been on a ride intending to picnic near a stream when, literally out of the blue, the earth rumbled, crooked bolts of lightning punctured the sky, the ground shook, and sheets of rain driven by a north wind slapped into their faces, soaked their clothes, and swashed into the flimsy wicker picnic basket. Thunder bellowed and boomed all around them like cannons. Their startled animals snorted and spun against the deluge. Yuma waved at Rosemary and pointed toward the cave on the higher ground. His horse leaped ahead, and Rosemary followed. Their mounts lunged, with hooves slipping in mud, eyes blinded by the drenching downpour. But they made it to the cave.

Johnny and Rosemary left the animals at the overhang of the mouth of the grotto, affording the horses some protection against the pouring fury, and staggered inside, dripping wet from head to foot.

"I never saw a summer storm come up so fast." Rosemary took off her hat and smiled.

"Neither did I. A real goose-drowner. Rosemary, you're soaked clear through. You . . ."

He had kissed her before. Many times. On picnics near a stream. On the porch before she went inside. Even on horseback, he had leaned across and kissed her. But never before like this, and both of them knew without saying a word.

He kissed her lips, her face, her throat, and they clung to each other, at first through the wetness of their clothes and later against the wetness of their naked young bodies.

Never before had it happened. Many times when they

had been together, they had kissed and held each other close, with tenderness and even passion. They always had torn themselves apart . . . but not that Sunday afternoon.

Not with the dark sky streaked by jagged lances of lightning and with thunder drumming across the sawtooth rims of ragged hills. Not with coursing water washing over glistening rocks and rushing into surging streams . . . not that Sunday afternoon.

Neither of them had tried to tear apart, nor wanted to, nor could have, while nature's tempest pitched and tossed, as beaded droplets filtered through the ceiling and clay walls and trickled down the ancient marks and carvings of the cave while Rosemary trembled in his arms.

And then as suddenly as it had started, the storm was spent and soundless . . . and so were the two of them as they left the cave.

Neither looked at the other while they rode back in silence. There was nothing he could say to express his anguish for what had happened. He could find no words, at least not then. Maybe later the words would come. Maybe tomorrow. Johnny Yuma didn't know as they rode back that that tomorrow *would* tear them apart. That it would be years before he saw her again—if ever.

Late that same Sunday, when Johnny Yuma got back, his father was waiting, with pent-up fury ready to explode.

But it had all started earlier that morning when Johnny Yuma said again he thought that it was time for him to join the Confederacy and fight for the South. Almost all of Johnny's friends had enlisted, and he didn't want to be left behind.

"You're younger than them," his father had said.

"No younger than you were when you went to fight for Texas with Sam Houston at San Jacinto."

"This time, Texas is wrong, and even Sam Houston says

so. We went to fight for freedom. This time, Texas is fighting for slavery.''

"For independence.''

"We're part of the Union now.''

"Not anymore, and I'm going to fight for Texas,'' Johnny said.

"You're not going to do a damn thing but stay here and keep an eye on that prisoner till Jess and I get back . . .''

"Why? Because you say so?''

"That's right. Because I'm your father, and I say so.''

"So you can do your duty again . . .''

"That's right, too.'' Ned Yuma checked the cylinder of his Colt, stuffed it back into his holster, and took the sawed-off scattergun from his desk. "Come on, Jess,'' he said to his deputy, "we'll pick up Morgan's tracks while they're still fresh.''

"It's not your duty to go after Red Morgan,'' Johnny said.

"What did you say, boy?''

"I said it's not your duty to go after him. Morgan didn't commit any crime around here, and he rode out yesterday.''

"Yesterday, I didn't know who he was. Today, I do. He's been identified by . . .''

"He still didn't commit any crime around here and . . .''

"And he's liable to. He's still a killer, and he could be at it right now, and don't you ever be telling me my duty. I'll do it as I see fit,'' Ned Yuma said.

"Like you were doing your duty when my mother died while you went out chasing . . .''

"Shut up! Shut up, boy, or I'll . . .''

"You'll what? And I'm not a boy, I'm . . .''

"You're going to stay here and keep an eye on Goober till Jess and I get back with Morgan! That's what you're going to do! Come on, Jess, we're wasting time.''

Sheriff Ned Yuma went out the door, followed by his deputy, but not before Jess Evans looked back and whispered, "Take it easy, Johnny. He'll cool off. You do the same."

The two lawmen left Johnny Yuma with Goober Brown, who was drunk asleep on the bunk of a cell. Brown had been drunk and disorderly since his wife Sara died over two weeks ago. They had been married for more than forty years. Ned Yuma had locked him up that morning as much for Goober's own protection as for anything else: "So you don't fall off your horse and break your damn neck." But Goober had been in an alcoholic and grief-darkened haze and didn't even hear what the sheriff had said. Now he was snoring and sleeping it off, and Johnny Yuma was pacing up and down the sheriff's office until Rosemary Cutler came in with the picnic basket.

Johnny had promised to take her on a Sunday picnic, and he didn't intend to break that promise, not on account of his father or some drunken fool who was snoring away in jail.

It was the worst decision he had ever made.

Not just because of what happened in the cave during the rainstorm, but because of what was waiting for him when he got back: Sheriff Ned Yuma, Deputy Jess Evans, but not Goober Brown.

"Did you get Red Morgan, Sheriff?" Johnny Yuma asked. "Did you do your duty?"

"No, we lost his tracks in the storm. Had to turn back. No, boy, I didn't do my duty . . . and neither did you." Ned Yuma pointed to the empty cell.

"Where's Goober?" Johnny was startled and upset, first because of what had happened between Rosemary and him and then because he could tell, in spite of his father's outer calm, that something had happened while Johnny had left the prisoner in the cell alone. "He didn't break out, did he?"

"Not exactly."

"What does that mean? Where is he?"

"At the mortician's," his father answered.

"The . . ."

"He hanged himself."

It was as if Johnny Yuma had been hit by a hammer. His brain clouded, his hands trembled, and his body shook. He almost fainted, but he didn't.

"He hanged himself with his belt," Ned Yuma went on, "while I was out doing my duty, and you . . . you had other things on your mind."

Johnny Yuma looked at the empty cell, then at Jess Evans, who gazed at the floor, then at his father who stared at him with cold, hard eyes.

"I'm sorry," Johnny whispered. "I just . . ."

"Just don't say anything. I don't want to look at you, and I don't want to hear the sound of your voice. Just turn around and get the hell out of my sight."

That's what Johnny Yuma did. He turned around and walked out. That was the last time he saw his father.

He rode to Rosemary's cabin where she lived with her widowed mother. He knocked on the door and Rosemary opened it and saw him standing there, still wet in the moonlight.

"I'm leaving, Rosemary. I've got to . . ."

"Because of us?"

"No, but I've got to. You'll hear about it."

"Johnny, I thought you loved me." There were tears in her eyes.

"I do."

"Then I'll wait."

"No! I've got a feeling that I'm not coming back. I'm joining the Third Texas."

"Your father . . ."

"The hell with my father and with Mason City!"

"And with me?" Rosemary whispered.

"No, Rosemary, never with you. I love you, and I always will. I'm sorry for what happened. I'm sorry for a lot of things. I love you, but don't wait for me, I . . ." He touched her hair, her cheek, turned without finishing, mounted his horse, and rode east.

And now, four years later, he was riding west, less than a mile from Mason City.

THIRTY-FIVE

Johnny Yuma was closer than farther now. A lot closer. What had been desert behind him had melded into more fertile ground. The stillborn, ragged brown land had given way to darker, richer soil and green grass that bent with the cordial wind, still damp from the recent rain, and crowned with splashes of wildflowers scattered from the level valley platform upward along the rising flanks of the pitted hills.

A lot had happened—even since Appomattox—since the war ended—since the fighting stopped. But did the war ever end? Did the fighting ever stop? Johnny Yuma thought of what had happened and whom he'd met since Appomattox—of what he had written in his journal.

The last look with his comrade Doug Baines at Robert E. Lee as he bade farewell to his troops and rode south; a campfire and a dirt-spattered stranger with a derringer who turned out to be Lincoln's assassin; the Willows Tavern and a senseless brawl that could have cost him his life or freedom but for a one-armed sheriff who had fought at Gettysburg; a bitter black man and his family with newfound freedom who fought back to back with a Confederate soldier against their common enemies; prejudice, bigotry, injustice—a rifle-shooting contest in St.Louis with a shiny gold brass breech Henry as prize and a card game against a sore loser who tried to rob him and would have except for a saloon girl called Cherry—Danny Reese's mother who grieved and looked out of a window while she waited for a son who would never come home and Danny's sister a different kind of soldier of the South with a different kind of wound, addiction to morphine, a whore disowned by her mother and wasting away but there was a cure and it turned out that killing was a part of it, killing on the part of Johnny Yuma—across the Red River into Texas and Longview, gunplay in the street, an editor with a moribund newspaper and a chance for Johnny Yuma to write, a lawman, former Texas Ranger and friend to Johnny's father, a lost boy and a 'tooter,' and a choice for Johnny Yuma, track and face down killer Comancheros torturing a captive bride—Indian territory, the Kiowa attack, the bark of the Henry and the bite of the Colt, two Kiowas dead, one fleeing—a sunbaked trooper dying with the words "Fort Concho" on his blistered lips—a crafty-crazy trooper at the fort, the great Kiowa Chief Satanta and an Indian daughter who was not an Indian and the Kiowa Challenge to the death, ending in a new life and a blood brother—a Ghost Brigade, the Third Texas—

All this and more had Johnny Yuma faced since Appomattox. Danger. Death. And for the most part he faced it unafraid—since *"death, a necessary end, will come when it will come. Cowards die many times, the valiant never taste of death but once"*—but now Johnny was afraid, not because he was going to face death, that he could handle, but there was something else he had to face. *Someone*—his father. Johnny Yuma never forgot his father's last words to him.

"I don't want to look at you and I don't want to hear the sound of your voice. Just turn around and get the hell out of my sight."

Johnny Yuma had stayed out of his father's sight for years, too many years, and much had changed: the United States, what had been the Confederacy and, of course, Texas; but so had the people, most of all, Johnny Yuma. Who was right or wrong when he left Texas? The father? The son?

Johnny Yuma realized that neither one was all right or all wrong. He was young, hot-blooded, and hot-tempered. What he and Rosemary did was not right, and he had to take almost all of the blame for that. Leaving Goober Brown alone in that cell was wrong. Maybe even going to fight for the Confederacy was a mistake. If it was, that was one mistake Johnny Yuma did not regret. But his father had been wrong about some things, too. A man, even a lawman, should be able to draw the line between love and duty: the love for a wife and son and the obligation and duty of the badge. Ned Yuma had given up something he loved, being a Texas Ranger, for someone he loved more, his wife Elizabeth, Johnny's mother. But he couldn't give up being a lawman, not for his wife and not for his son after his wife died. He was a lawman, first, last, always, and then a husband and father. At least that was the way Johnny Yuma had felt when he left Mason City. Was that just an excuse for leaving? Would he have found another reason? Was he just running away? A confused, rebellious youth who was looking for a cause, a reason to run away?

Whoever was more to blame didn't seem to matter as much anymore. What mattered more was that Johnny knew he loved his father, and he hoped that his father loved him.

He was prepared to say it. But he hoped that words wouldn't have to be said. He hoped that he would just walk into the sheriff's office and stand there and that his father would put his arms around his son and hold him close, even for just a moment. Something that Ned Yuma had never done before.

The sorrel nickered and pulled to a stop without any directive from Yuma. If Johnny's mind had not been on other things, he would have noticed that the animal had been favoring his left foreleg. The Rebel urged the sorrel to move ahead, but after a couple of steps, the horse stopped and pawed at the ground.

Yuma climbed down and inspected the hoof. The shoe was loose, missing a couple of nails. Johnny tore the shoe off the hoof. It would have fallen off anyway, or even if it didn't, the animal couldn't have walked on it and carried a rider. Yuma tossed the shoe away and patted the sorrel's head.

"Well horse, it looks like you and me both are going to have to walk the rest of the way. Not far. Just a good stretch of the legs—the two of mine and the four of yours."

Mason City raddled in an uneven, patternless array of tired buildings, wood and adobe, baking under the sun.

At last Johnny Yuma was in sight of his home—the only home he ever knew.

THIRTY-SIX

Johnny Yuma led the sorrel down the main street of Mason City. For this time of morning, the town seemed quiet—too quiet and too unpopulated. Only a few people made their way on the boardwalks and across the rutted dirt street, and with their heads bent toward the ground as if they didn't want to talk or even look at each other. There were no children playing, no old-timers idling on benches or chairs. Some of the shops were closed, with blinds drawn and doors locked.

Yuma passed in front of the sign across the biggest store in Mason City.

TOMPKINS SUPPLIES
GENERAL STORE . . . MINING EQUIPMENT

Brad Tompkins probably was the richest man in town. His son Gary, a Milquetoast who had no intention of going to war, had always coveted Rosemary Cutler. But Johnny Yuma had always stood in the way, until he joined the Third Texas.

Tompkins General Store was still in business, the front door open, but Yuma didn't look in that direction. He walked on, leading his horse.

The sun at his back cast long shadows ahead on Main Street, which bisected Mason City north to south. Tompkins General Store was at the far east end. Other stores and shops on the same side included the *Mason City Bulletin* on a corner and to the north on a narrow street, the church with a cemetery on the slope of land behind. At the far west end, a squat adobe building housed the sheriff's office with three cells to provide temporary accommodations for misbehavers from minor miscreants to murderers.

Along the south side of Main Street, across from Tompkins General Store, a formidable brick building served as the Mason City Bank. In the middle of the block stood Zecker's Saloon and next to it, a two-story building, Zecker's Hotel, then a barber shop. At the end of the street across from and just beyond the sheriff's office there was a big, red, wooden structure, the barn, stable, and livery owned and operated by the blacksmith, Clem Bevins.

A large circular watering trough reposed, almost like a truncated town monument, in the middle of the street. As Yuma walked toward the tank, two wagons loaded with families and possessions rolled by, leaving Mason City, heading in the direction that the Rebel had come from. By now, people were noticing Yuma's arrival. Some whispered to each other as he passed, but nobody spoke to him.

In front of Zecker's Saloon a half dozen men were watching the wagons' departure—and the Rebel's arrival. Those men did not look or act like the other townspeople. Their guns were slung lower. Their faces dirtier, and there was about them the aura of unquiet arrogance. Of Buscaderos.

One of the men, obviously their leader, was bigger,

cleaner and closer-shaven than the others. He smoked a stogie and surveyed the town as a man looking over his own backyard. Another of the gang, with a dirty, flat face, flat eyes, flat nose, and wearing a flat-crowned hat, had twin gun belts crossed over his waist and a holster in each belt, holding pearl-handled Colts. He looked up at the big man and pointed toward Johnny Yuma.

"Hey, Dow, lookee there. Some stray Reb come here to roost."

Yuma reached the water tank and allowed the sorrel to drink his fill. He took off his Rebel cap and set it on the horn of his saddle. He pulled open the collar of his buckskin shirt and plunged his head into the tank, once, twice, then shook the water from his face, hair, and the eagle claw dangling from a thong at his throat.

"Hey, Dow." The man with the flat face grinned. "See that?"

"Yeah. That boy looks like he really needed that."

A small, gray-haired man wearing an apron over his clothes stepped out of the batwings and took a couple of steps toward the big man.

"Mr. Pierce." The small man's voice and attitude were overly solicitous. "My wife'll have some food for you all in a few minutes. She's . . ."

"Dow," flat-face interrupted, "I think I need to have me some fun with that Reb. Can I have some fun, Dow? Rawhide him?"

"Sure, Bart." Dow nodded. "You go ahead and have some fun."

Bart squared his shoulders, grinned wider, and strutted toward one of the horses hitched to a rail in front of Zecker's Saloon.

"Johnny!" The small man was now staring at the Rebel.

"You know him?" Dow Pierce asked.

"I do, Mr. Pierce, he's . . ."

"Later, Zecker. I want to watch Bart make his acquaintance."

Bart untied one of the horses hitched to the post and began to hum the melody of "Dixie."

Johnny Yuma was still enjoying the luxury of the water, slapping it over his face, then cupping his hands and drinking, as the man, still humming "Dixie," approached with his horse. Yuma ducked his head in again.

A stiff finger poked twice into the Rebel's ribs, then again.

"Hey, you . . . Reb."

Yuma turned and faced the poker.

"You . . . Reb . . . this here water's for horses. It ain't for no jackass." Bart laughed hard at his humor and turned toward the men in front of the saloon. They, too, were laughing.

"I said I need to water my horse."

"Then you do that."

"Not with your face in it. I don't want him to get contaminated." He laughed again, looked toward the saloon, then back to Yuma. "You, Reb . . . you hear what I . . ."

"Don't push."

"Push! Why, Reb, you ought to be used to bein' pushed!" He shoved at Johnny's shoulder. "Why, we pushed you clear from Gettysburg through Georgia . . . from Chickasaw to Appomattox. You been pushed real good."

"Yeah." The Rebel did not flinch. "The war's over."

"So it is. But I'm not. I enjoy pushin' the likes of you." He shoved Yuma again. "I'm gonna push you . . ."

The threat and the shove went unfinished. Yuma's left exploded into Bart's nose, and a right smashed into his gut. Bart charged, grabbing the Rebel around the chest and grappling him to the muddy ground, trying to use his own weight advantage, but Yuma was all elbows, knees, and fists. He cupped the palm of his left hand behind Bart's neck. Yuma's right fist crashed into the man's flat jaw. Yuma sprang to his feet. Bart sprang after him and rammed into the Rebel, forcing him against the water tank.

The townspeople and the men from the saloon had formed a spectator circle and were moving in closer.

He bent Yuma farther and harder. Back . . . back . . . then Yuma's arms burst free from Bart's encircling lock and, using both his fists as a club, he brought them down with a sickening thud between Bart's eyes.

He spun the dazed man, switching positions against the trough, and hammered him with a barrage of lefts and rights. It looked as if the man would crumple, but Yuma grabbed him by the chest and belt and somersaulted him into the tank.

Yuma held Bart's head below the water until it seemed that he would drown; then Yuma's left hand lifted him by the hair. In Yuma's right hand, the Colt was cocked with the barrel an inch from Bart's dripping nose.

"Now you don't." Yuma breathed hard. "You don't push me no more. I'll blow your eyeballs out . . . both of 'em." Yuma holstered the Colt. He took his cap from the horn of the saddle, picked up the reins, and led the animal away as the spectators stepped aside to let him pass. There were smiles on the faces of the townspeople as he made his way past them. Some even murmured approval.

The men from the saloon drew closer to Bart, who staggered and climbed over the side of the tank.

"You had you enough fun for one day, Bart?" Dow Pierce smiled.

"I tried to tell you, Mr. Pierce." Zecker was breathless. "That's Ned Yuma's boy!"

"That a fact, Zecker? Why, that makes him your kin, don't it?"

"Not exactly, Mr. Pierce. He's my wife's nephew, not mine."

"Ned Yuma's boy, huh?" Dow Pierce took a puff from the stogie. He looked toward the Rebel. "Maybe the fun's just startin' . . . all over again."

As Yuma, leading the limping sorrel, neared the sheriff's office, a young boy, maybe seven or eight, but under ten, ran toward him from the direction of Bevin's barn.

"Johnny, hey Johnny!" the boy hollered as he came closer. "You're Johnny Yuma!"

"That's right." Yuma smiled and stopped walking. "How'd you know? Can't say as I remember our ever meeting up before."

"Neither can I. But my dad told me." The boy pointed toward the red barn. "Clem Bevins. I'm Clay, his son."

"Sure, Clay, I remember you. Why you weren't even knee high when I left. How's your pa?"

"He's okay . . . but . . ." The boy appeared uneasy. He cleared his throat.

"But what?"

"Well . . . I, uh . . . Pa sent me over to pick up your horse. Said he'd fix that shoe." Clay pointed to the sorrel's foreleg.

"Well, that's good. I was going to come over there in a few minutes anyhow, soon as I went in and saw my . . ."

"My pa said you'd be needin' that horse," the boy interrupted.

"He did, huh?" The Rebel wasn't sure what the boy, or the boy's father meant. "What else did your pa say?"

"He said not to say anything else . . . that you'd find out soon enough. I . . . I think maybe I already said too much. I . . ."

"Don't you worry about it, Clay. Here, you take care of the horse, and tell your pa I'll be over to see him after awhile." Yuma untied and lifted the saddlebag and set it over his shoulder.

The boy nodded, took the reins, looked at Johnny Yuma, then at the sheriff's office, and led the animal toward the red barn without looking back.

As he opened the door of the sheriff's office and walked through, a mass of memories swept over the Rebel's mind, mostly of his father, Sheriff Ned Yuma. A man of quiet strength, spare of words, and spare of sentiment, not easily moved to laughter and never to tears, not even when his wife died. Case-hardened and single-minded, his mind was on his job, and his job was law. Ned Yuma was good at his job. Maybe too good as far as some people were concerned, especially his son.

Johnny Yuma seldom could remember his father smiling and just about never laughing. He wasn't cold and hard toward Johnny, but he was never warm and tender. He just was.

Yuma tried to recall the touch and feel of his father's hand on him but couldn't. Once in a great while, the lawman would tousle his son's hair or wink or nod in approval of something Johnny had done, but that was about the extent of his father's overt emotion. Even verbally, Ned Yuma was not very chirpy. He expected everybody, including his son, to do what was expected, and he didn't pile on praise when they did it.

On the other hand, Ned Yuma was not one to heap words on Johnny or anybody else who did something wrong. He just pointed out the mistake and expected it to be corrected. He also expected that it wouldn't happen again.

But Johnny remembered his father's hands and fists being laid on those who abused others and who broke the law. And Johnny remembered his father using his gun as a final resort. And sometimes with finality for the offender.

Ned Yuma was a man of even-handed justice and noble heart, if not outward emotion; but whether Ned Yuma liked it or not, Johnny intended to hug and kiss his father just this once in their lives.

He closed the door behind him and looked around at the familiar room. But it was unfamiliar.

The place was sloppy and dirty. Empty and broken whiskey bottles were strewn on the desk and floor. An unconscious figure wearing a badge sprawled on the bunk.

Johnny set the saddlebag over the back of a chair, crossed to the sleeping man, and bent over him.

"Hey . . ."

The man stirred. Johnny's hands shook the man's shoulder, but the man turned, facing the wall. Yuma reached down and turned the man back.

"Hey, come on . . . get up."

The man opened his eyes, blinked, and then wiped his face in blurry disbelief.

"Lemme be . . . I ain't hurtin' nothin' . . . go on and lemme . . . Johnny? Johnny! Oh, no . . ."

"Jess, you better get up."

"Johnny . . ." the deputy said.

"My pa out of town? He comes back and finds you like this, you're going to be in deep trouble."

"Oh, Johnny . . ."

"Jess, I haven't ever seen you drunk before. Now come on, let's get some coffee in you and straighten up the place before pa gets back."

The deputy managed to get both boots onto the floor, but he shuddered. Both shoulders shook, and he rubbed his face with his hands, trying to clear his mind and control his feelings.

"Johnny, you shoulda come back sooner."

"Say, what's the matter with you? What's happened to this town? Jess, where's Pa?" Johnny Yuma looked around at the room. His eyes rested on a hanger in the wall.

Suspended there was a hat, gun, and holster, with a sheriff's badge pinned on the holster. There was no mistaking them. Johnny grabbed Jess Evans and pulled the deputy to his feet.

"Now, you're gonna tell me where my pa is! Jess, where?"

"Oh, Johnny . . ." Jess Evans sobbed, a broken, humiliated relic. Yuma shook him hard.

"Where's my pa?"

THIRTY-SEVEN

NED YUMA
1820–1866

The wooden marker was new. The mound of earth in front
of it was still fresh, next to the time-worn grave of Johnny
Yuma's mother. There were other fresh graves nearby.

The Rebel knelt with his hat in his hand, his eyes wet
with regret for things unsaid . . . and undone.

He wasn't sure what he expected to find when he came
back, but he never expected to find his father's grave.

God, it couldn't be true. But it was. There was no truth
more convincing and final then the truth of a tombstone.
And Ned Yuma didn't even have a tombstone, just a plain
wooden marker next to the faded marker where Johnny
Yuma's mother rested for so many years—and forever.

Sheriff Ned Yuma would never ride away from his wife
again, not to track a lawbreaker, not to bring back a murderer, not for any reason. At last they were together for all
time, to rest in peace. But Johnny Yuma knew that his

father did not rest in peace . . . and neither did the town . . . and neither could he.

A vagrant wind whispered and searched through the cemetery behind the church as the Rebel rose slowly, set the cap on his head, and moved toward the stooped, sunken figure of Deputy Jess Evans.

Yuma came closer. He turned and looked back at the grave, then again at Jess Evans and waited.

"A couple of weeks ago, Johnny," Jess said, "they rode in, took over the mine . . . forced the owners to sell out for practically nothin'. But they done it all legal. Everybody just backed down. Most family people moved away after they killed him." Evans pointed toward the grave. "He wouldn't sing small."

"No, he wouldn't."

"They killed five men already. Always 'self-defense.' " He pointed to the other fresh graves. "It's just not worth it anymore. Take your horse and ride out, Johnny. That's what we're all gonna have to do."

"Did they shoot him in the back?"

"They didn't have to. There was enough of 'em in front of him."

"Was he alone?"

Deputy Sheriff Jess Evans blinked without answering.

"I said, was he alone?"

The deputy nodded and looked at the ground.

"Why was he alone?"

"You don't understand how it happened . . ."

"I understand. Where was the rest of the town? All his friends?"

Evans still stared at the ground.

"Where were you . . . *deputy?*"

It took a while, but the deputy finally looked up and into the eyes of Johnny Yuma.

"Where were *you,* Johnny? The war's been over a long time . . ."

"Has it? Well, there's different kinds of wars. There's wars that don't end just 'cause a white flag goes up . . . or somebody signs a piece of paper. There's wars that go on inside . . ."

"I know, Johnny. I didn't mean to put any blame on you . . . and neither would he. That's not what I meant."

"What do you mean?"

"I don't know. I don't know anything anymore . . . except I know he loved you."

"How do you know?"

"He told me. He did, Johnny. You know that words didn't come easy to him, but he told me after you left, and again after he got that last letter from you. He read it time and again, when you wrote that you were comin' back. He was gonna tell you . . . I know he was."

"Jess . . ."

"Don't blame yourself, son. Even if you was here, it wouldn'a changed the odds . . . not enough. It wouldn't of made the difference."

"It would've changed something. It would've made one difference," Johnny said.

"What?"

"I just would've been here . . . and I'm here now." Yuma started to walk away.

"Johnny, don't do anything crazy. You didn't come back all this way just to die!"

Johnny Yuma stopped when he saw her. Her face was a portrait of sadness.

But Rosemary was still the most beautiful thing he had ever seen on this earth . . . or ever hoped to see.

She stood by the church, the church where they might have been married, and beside her stood a young boy, a tow-head with blue eyes, who held her hand.

It was as if knives had been thrust into both of Johnny Yuma's knees . . . and maybe into his heart. It took all his effort to regain his composure, but he did, as Rosemary and the boy came closer.

"Hello, Johnny." She did her best to smile.

Johnny Yuma managed to nod but didn't speak.

"Johnny, this is my son, Jed . . . Jed Tompkins." She put her hand on the boy's shoulder. "Jed, I want you to shake hands with . . . an old friend of your mother's, Johnny Yuma. Tell Mr. Yuma you're glad to meet him."

The boy obeyed his mother. He put out his little hand and Johnny Yuma took it.

"Hello, Mr. Yuma," the boy said, looking into the Rebel's eyes. "I'm glad to meet you."

"I'm glad to meet you, too, Jed. You're a fine young man, I'm sure of that. And I'm sure your mom . . . and dad are proud of you."

"Thank you, sir."

"Now, Jed, you go over there with your Uncle Jess while I talk to Johnny for just a little while," Rosemary said.

Again, the little boy obeyed his mother. Yuma watched as he walked toward the deputy, who took his hand and led him away from Johnny Yuma and Rosemary Tompkins.

"Johnny . . . I waited for a letter . . ."

"Not very long." He looked at the boy who had to be close to four years old.

"No, but as long as I could . . ."

"Until Gary Tompkins asked you to marry him."

"Yes."

"That jellyback . . . if it was anybody but him . . ."

"Johnny, he . . ."

"I guess I can't blame you, Rosemary, for getting married. I did tell you not to wait, but you sure picked . . ."

"I *couldn't* wait, Johnny, not after what happened in the cave. Our baby had to have a father. I was beginning to show."

"Rosemary . . . oh, Rosemary, I didn't know. If I'd've known, I . . ."

"What could you have done, Johnny, after you left and joined the Third Texas? Could you have taken time out from the war to come home and be a husband and father? Could you?"

He didn't answer.

"Johnny, I loved you, and I still do, but I didn't have any choice and Gary . . ."

"He knew?"

"Yes, he knew . . . and so did some others, including my mother. I think it killed her. Your father and Jess, they knew . . . and, of course, Gary, but he asked me to marry him, and I did, and now you're back and . . ."

"Rosemary, I'm sorry for what I said to you . . . what I said about . . . your husband."

"He's a good man, Johnny. Gary's grown up since you . . . since you left. His father's crippled . . . in a wheelchair . . . and Gary has the responsibility of the store . . . and our family."

"I wrote to Mr. Dodson, and he wrote back. Why didn't he tell me that you . . . that you and Gary . . ."

"I asked him not to."

"Why?"

"You didn't need any more to think about, to take your mind off what you had to do. If you had written me, I would have told you, but I didn't want you hearing it from somebody else. When the war was over, if you were still . . ." She lowered her eyes.

"Still alive?"

"Yes. I knew that someday you'd come back . . . and see your son . . . and me."

"It'd be better if I hadn't."

"No, Johnny. You don't mean that."

"Or if I'd come back sooner . . ." He glanced toward the grave.

"Johnny, don't torture yourself with what ifs. What's done is done. You've got to think about your future."

"I don't care about my future. I don't care about much of anything except . . ."

"What?"

"The Bible says 'an eye for an eye.' "

"Ride out of here, Johnny. I heard what Jess said to you. He was right. You didn't come back all this way just to die."

"There's a lot of us going to die in this town. I'm going to try to be the last."

"Johnny, you can't. If you have any feeling left for me, you . . ."

"Rosemary, I'm going to say this just once, and for the rest of my life, no matter how long or short that'll be . . . I love you, and I'll love you from this world into and through the next . . . and I am glad I came back and saw you . . . and our son. You two are all I've got left and all I really love. But I've got to go up against them for what they did. So, please, take the boy and keep away till it's over. I don't want you or him to see what's going to happen." Yuma glanced at his son in the distance. Jess Evans was talking to the boy and pointing in another direction, diverting the boy's attention away from Johnny Yuma and Rosemary Tompkins.

"Johnny, if you truly loved me, you . . ."

"I do, Rosemary. You've got to believe that just like I

believe it, but somebody once wrote, 'I could not love thee dear so much, loved I not honor more.' I believe that, too.''

"Johnny . . .''

"Now, Jess'll walk you back. Take the boy and go back to your husband.''

"Don't you want to say good-bye to your son?''

"I already did.''

"But not to me . . . not yet.''

She put her arms around him and kissed him. And he kissed her. At first, soft and tender . . . and then it was the same kiss as in the cave. They clung to each other, tangled and fettered together, trembling. It was a kiss infinite and eternal. But this time, they tore themselves apart. They knew they had to, and they did.

"Jess . . .'' Yuma called out.

The deputy had turned himself and the boy in another direction, and now he turned back toward Johnny and Rosemary.

"Jess, would you take Rosemary and the boy back? I'm going to stay here for a little while.''

"Sure, Johnny.''

Rosemary reached out and touched Johnny Yuma's cheek, then walked past him toward the deputy and her son.

THIRTY-EIGHT

There were no cash customers in Zecker's Saloon, and there hadn't been for some time. Not since Dow Pierce and his men took over the bar and the town.

There were six of them, but they constituted an army of occupation. There had been ten in all. Two of them were killed in the confrontation with Ned Yuma. Two more left town on a mission, but were expected back any time.

Pierce was the leader by virtue—if you could call it virtue—of the brains and brawn that thought up the scheme and held the gang together.

Bart was a loudmouth and gun happy. He fancied himself the cock o' the walk, with deference to Dow.

And there was Slim, a lunger who coughed and smiled a lot. It seemed that he had opened death's door a crack and wasn't bothered by what he saw. He wasn't careful about what he said to anybody because he didn't much care whether he died a little sooner than later. But he didn't push Dow Pierce. He wasn't that much in a hurry to die.

Miller wore a patch where his left eye used to be, a memento not from the war but from an irate cuckold husband in Nogales. His head was under a brown, high-crowned hat with dents on the sides. One ear was clipped, branding him a horse thief.

The two others were twin brothers, Tim and Tom. Nobody knew their last name or cared.

Miller stood at the batwings. It was his turn as lookout, and that's what he was doing, with his right profile facing the street. Pierce shuffled a deck of cards, while Slim stood behind the bar with a bottle at the ready.

Bart's clothes hung from a makeshift line, except for his boots and long underdrawers which he wore, along with his gun belts and holsters strapped to his waist. He was checking one of his revolvers after its earlier dunking, fanning the hammer again and again as it clicked on the empty chambers. His face still bore strong evidence of his encounter with Johnny Yuma.

"If the sun hadn't been in my eyes," Bart said as he holstered the gun, "he never woulda got that first one across."

"Well, that accounts for the first one, Bart." Slim smiled. "What about the rest of 'em? They was comin' at you like a Gatlin' gun."

"He got me off balance."

"Is that what happened?"

"Just pour me a drink."

"Sure." Slim coughed and poured.

Bart picked up the glass, drank, and slammed it back on the bar.

"Again!"

Slim looked at Dow Pierce. Pierce nodded. Slim poured.

"You just wait till the next time. Just wait."

"I can wait if you can." Slim poured one for himself and lifted the glass in a toast. "Here's to the next time."

"You bet! I'm gonna put six slugs right through him, belly to brisket!"

"Is that before he gets your eyeballs?" Slim drank.

"What?"

"Sure you will, Bart." He tried to suppress a cough.

"Yeah? Well, you better believe it. He just got lucky. I'm gonna kill him!"

"Bart." Pierce put the deck on the table. "You better wait till your britches dry."

The men all laughed.

"Yeah, well, I killed me plenty of them Rebs."

"From a distance," Pierce said. "But you didn't do so good with this one up close."

"Yeah . . . we'll see. You'll all see . . . and another thing . . . I'm gettin' a little tired of waitin' . . . for a lot of things."

"Is there anything you'd like to do about those other things?" Pierce spoke without looking up or raising his voice.

"Yeah . . . well, when are Lathe and Chet gettin' back with them Mexicans? I'm gettin' sick of this."

"You are, huh?" Dow said.

"Yeah, I am. There's not even any women around here. Not a hog ranch in town. Hell, what kind of a saloon you call this without women?"

"I call it a saloon without women," Pierce said. "Now, are we gonna play some poker?"

"Yeah, sure." Bart took a couple of steps then stopped. "Dow?"

"What?"

"Are Lathe and Chet gonna bring back some women?"

"No, they're not. Just some diggers. Then all we'll have to do is sit back and stack all that gold dust they take outta that mine. But if you can't wait, maybe you'd like to start digging in that hole yourself.''

"Yeah, well . . .''

"Bart, you say 'yeah' like that one more time, and I'm gonna crack your skull. Now shut up! And sit down.''

"Sure, Dow. Sure.''

"What about you, Slim? You want in?''

"I'm in.''

"Bring me over one of Zecker's cigars.'' Pierce pointed to a box on the backbar.

"Mind if I have one too, Dow?'' Slim asked.

"I don't if your lungs don't.''

"Well, I ain't gonna ask 'em—what's left of 'em.'' Slim took a couple cigars from the box, walked across the room, and sat in a chair across from Pierce.

"Five card draw,'' Pierce said. "Jacks or better open. I deal.''

"Mr. Pierce . . .'' Ainsley Zecker came out of the kitchen in the back, followed by his wife Emily.

Emily Zecker, née Yuma, was a tad taller than her husband, a woman in her midforties without a gray hair in her head or a wrinkle on her face, not even when she smiled, which was seldom. She was handsome and rigid, straight as a harpoon and just as hard and cold.

"Mr. Pierce . . .'' Zecker repeated.

"What is it, Zecker?''

"Well, the food's ready anytime you've a mind to eat. Emily here . . .''

"We'll let you know. Right now, we're gonna play us a little poker.'' Pierce lit the cigar, blew out the match, and let the stick drop to the floor.

"Yes, sir.''

Neither Zecker nor his wife moved. She looked at her husband, then nudged him with her elbow.

"Beg pardon, Mr. Pierce, but . . ."

"What now, Zecker?"

"Well, sir, we're about out of provisions . . ."

"So, get some more. Anybody open?"

"Me," said Bart. "One Yankee dollar."

"Well, Mr. Pierce, it's the money . . ."

"What money?"

"Well, you see, that's the point. I'm all out. You promised me money . . . that you'd pay for all this . . ."

"So I did."

"Well, I've spent all I had. If you'd just . . ."

"I just see that Yankee dollar and raise two."

"But Mr. Pierce . . ." Zecker pleaded.

"Your credit's good at the store. Put it on your bill."

"But you promised."

"That's all, Zecker!"

Both Zeckers stood for a moment. Ainsley Zecker finally glanced at his wife, who still stood ramrod straight, looking at her husband, waiting for him to say something more to Dow Pierce. But it was Pierce who spoke.

"Say Mrs. Emmy, you never even went to your brother's funeral, did you?"

She didn't answer.

"Now, Bart there, he says he's liable to have to kill your nephew. Now, I'm not of a mind to let him, but just in case he does, you gonna miss that funeral, too?" The men laughed. Bart laughed the hardest.

Emily Zecker turned and walked back into the kitchen. Zecker wasn't sure what to do, so he just stood there wiping his hands on his apron.

"Dow," Miller called from his post·at the entrance. "It looks like 'ol Dodson's takin' your advice. He's over there loadin' up his buckboard."

"Is that so?"

"Yep. Looks like he's fixin' to leave town."

"He's smarter than I thought. Dealer takes two cards."

The buckboard was pulled up by the side door of the *Mason City Bulletin* on Church Street. Elmer Dodson carried a stack of books and walked toward the wagon.

A man in his sixties, rope-thin, with a long, almost cadaverous face and stringy white hair that spiked down across his narrow brow, he paused as Johnny Yuma approached from the church to the north.

"Mr. Dodson."

"Hello, John."

"You turning out like the rest of them?"

"I'm just a small businessman going out of business." Elmer Dodson attempted an impersonal, guarded tone and attitude. It didn't quite come off.

"You closing down the *Bulletin* on account of them?"

"That's correct."

"Mr. Dodson . . ."

"Oh, yes, I saw what you did to one . . . and as soon as they want to, my innocent lamb, they'll devour you like the ravaging jackals they are."

"If you leave, everybody else will," Johnny said.

"That's up to them."

"No. It's up to you, Mr. Dodson."

"There's just the quick and the dead, and Dow Pierce in between. The jackals'll inherit the earth, at least this part, and they're welcome to it."

"You don't mean that."

"Don't try to fight them, son. You've got about as much chance as a wax cross in hell."

"So long as there's any chance . . ."

"John, the only thing to do is let them take what they want and hope they'll go away. Then, if some of the people want to come back, that's up to them. But me, I'm moving on . . . and not coming back here to live.''

"Neither is my father."

"He wore a badge, John, and he did his duty, at least what he thought was his duty, and he died for it. You're not wearing a badge. Not obliged to anything or anybody in this town. You fought one war and lost. But you lived. Don't die for nothing, John. It doesn't matter what happens here, not anymore."

"How'd they do it, Mr. Dodson? Why haven't you sent for government troops?"

"We did, and we're still waiting. I guess they're too busy tending to the defeated Confederacy and the undefeated Indians. So the town died, and so did your father."

"You and Pa, Mr. Dodson, you were the two people I . . ."

"John, I loved your father like my own brother, but I'm not anxious to join him. I'm sorry if that sounds cruel and cowardly. I don't mean to be the former; I guess I can't deny being the latter."

"The things you wrote, Mr. Dodson, that's what set me off reading and wonderin' . . .''

"Stay ignorant, John. Ignorance is the greatest comforter of all."

"I remember something you printed in your paper, something about . . . 'for everybody there's a time to decide— and that's when the brave man chooses and the coward steps aside.' You remember that, Mr. Dodson?"

"I remember. That was a reprint, like most of my stuff. I finally realize that those kinds of words were a shield to protect me from the fact that I've led a meaningless, unproductive life, which, ironically enough, I am now trying to save."

"It's funny, I thought of asking you for a job."

"John, I read those letters you wrote. The ones you sent me and your father. They were beautifully crude and expressive. You could be a writer."

"I wanted to say things the way you do, Mr. Dodson."

"I suppose after all my brave words, I should be ashamed. But they've smashed my press and promised to smash my head. I don't want my head smashed. Can you understand that?"

"I understand."

"Once before, back East, when I was young and fancied myself a crusader, there was a gang like Pierce's, oh, a bit more subtle but just as deadly. They gave me a choice, stay and die or run away and live. I chose to run away and live. I seem to be making the same choice again. Once again, I looked at death and trembled. So I'm not staying. John, I'm sorry if those brave words confused you."

"Good-bye, Mr. Dodson."

As Johnny Yuma started to walk off, Deputy Jess Evans came up Main Street from the direction of Tompkins General Store and followed behind him. Elmer Dodson watched, the look on his face not quite as decisive as it had been.

Miller, from his post at the batwings of Zecker's Saloon, turned back toward the men playing poker inside.

"Hey Bart, there's your Reb friend now. I think he just come back from visiting his daddy."

"I'm gonna get his nose!" Bart bolted for the entrance.

"Bart!" Pierce commanded. "When I tell you and not before!"

Bart stopped with an obvious look of disappointment on his bruised and swollen face.

"But," Pierce smiled, "you can rile him up some in the meantime."

Jess Evans was still a few paces behind the Rebel when the voice came from the saloon.

"Hey, you, Yuma! You have a nice talk with your daddy? Did you, Reb?"

Yuma's pace slowed. There was something about that voice coming from a distance that pierced his memory, that took him out of the present into the past, the clouded, bloody past.

"How'd he look to you, Reb? A little pale?"

Yuma stopped directly across from the saloon. The one with the flat face leaned out of the partly open batwings, still in his underdrawers with his guns strapped on, leering and taunting.

"Hey, you, Yuma . . . you don't hightail it outta here, I'm gonna get your nose. I'm gonna get you like I got all them other Rebs during the war."

Yuma knew it, even before flat-face said it.

"It's me, Reb . . . Vogan, Bart Vogan. Ohio Volunteers, and I'm gonna get you like I got your yellow-belly, cottontail Confederates . . . like I got your yellow-belly daddy."

Hate. A wild, chaotic hate. A black hate for a man whose face he had never seen during the war, but whose face he was seeing now. A name he knew he would never forget. Vogan. Bart Vogan. Sharpshooter. Killer. Murderer.

"Hey, you little cottontail, you better scat while you can."

The man who, during the war, had killed Danny Reese, the Rebel's best friend. The man who had killed Johnny Yuma's father. Bart Vogan.

"But you can't run far enough, Reb. Not from me. I'm gonna get your nose!"

Yuma's lips were a thin, quivering line. His right hand near his gun. The hand trembling. He would kill this man just as sure as the turning of the earth. But he wanted to kill all of them. All who were responsible for the murder of Ned Yuma. He hesitated, then turned slowly. As he did, there was a burst of derisive mirth from the saloon, topped by that voice, the voice of Bart Vogan.

"Look at that little cottontail get! Big, brave soldier boy backin' down!"

Yuma started to walk, followed by Jess Evans and the mocking voice of Bart Vogan singing to the tune of "Dixie." "Oh, I'm glad I'm not in the land of cotton . . . they lost the war and their bones are rottin' . . . look away, look away, run away . . . Johnny Reb . . ."

From out of a saloon window, among the others watching, were Ainsley Zecker and Johnny Yuma's Aunt Emmy.

THIRTY-NINE

As he walked toward the sheriff's office with Jess Evans beside him, Johnny Yuma said nothing, but he thought of everything, everything that had happened to him during the war and especially before.

He remembered the hundreds of times he had walked beside his father along the same street toward the same office, trying to keep astride the footsteps of the man with the badge and gun, a man who seemed like a giant, strong and skilled and too often solitary . . . private.

How many times since his mother died had Johnny Yuma tried to breach the barrier of that privacy? How many times and in how many ways had the boy tried to get closer? He could not count nor even remember the times and ways, but he could remember that he never really succeeded. Even the few times when the lawman seemed to let down his guard a little, to take Johnny fishing or hunting, even then, it was more like teacher and pupil instead of father and son.

Ned Yuma gave food, clothes, and shelter to his son, but he never really gave himself. He provided all the necessities except for that which was most necessary to a boy without a mother. Johnny Yuma could not even remember his father ever talking about his own mother and father. It was as if Texas was the only family Ned Yuma had ever had. But he did have a sister, and she lived here in Mason City, married to Ainsley Zecker, a musty, mediocre man who cared only for his business, the saloon and hotel, and the help Ned Yuma's sister Emily could and did give him in running his business. The two of them were suited to each other and were both civil if not cordial toward the sheriff and his son.

But Johnny Yuma could count the times on his fingers when the Zeckers invited the Yumas over for Sunday dinner. Aunt Emmy usually did remember Johnny's birthday and gave him a present, always one dollar. Johnny would have traded all of those dollars for just one cake, but she never got around to baking one for him, only pies for the customers at the saloon and hotel.

Johnny could never remember his father walking with, talking to, or being with another woman after his mother died, except in the line of duty.

Two men close to Ned Yuma were Jess Evans, his deputy, and, even closer, much closer, Pony That Flies, his blood brother. But even between the three of them there were not many words. Johnny had asked both his father and the Indian how the two of them came to be blood brothers. But neither would tell the boy more than it happened when Pony That Flies was a scout and Ned Yuma a Texas Ranger. Then they would either change the subject, fall silent, or walk away.

The other man close to Ned Yuma was Elmer Dodson. Often, to Sheriff Yuma's embarrassment, the newspaperman wrote about the lawman's courage and accomplishments, and it was Elmer Dodson who set fire to young

Johnny's imagination with tales of King Arthur, Robin Hood and the American heroes from George Washington to Andy 'By God' Jackson.

As the Rebel and Jess Evans entered the sheriff's office and closed the door behind them, Johnny's eyes fell on the badge pinned to his father's holster. He remembered coming into this same room when he was a young boy years ago and finding his father sitting at the desk holding the badge in his hand and silently staring at it.

That was the closest Johnny Yuma had ever come to seeing tears in the eyes of his father. For just that unguarded moment there was an aching, melancholy, almost tormented look on the face of Ned Yuma, a look that his son had never seen before or since.

Johnny Yuma often wondered what his father was thinking as he stared at that badge in his hand. Of the law he upheld? Of the sacrifices he had made and had imposed on his dead wife in pursuit of upholding that law?

Of what?

Johnny Yuma would never know because as soon as his father realized that the boy was in the room, he shook off the mood, pinned on the badge, and walked toward the coffeepot on the stove.

And now Johnny Yuma wondered what his father's last thoughts were when he, alone, went up against Pierce and Vogan and the rest of them with all their guns ready to cut him down. Were his thoughts of his wife, long dead? Or of his badge and duty? Or were they of his son who hadn't come home when the war ended?

Johnny Yuma would never know that, either. But one thing he did know. He knew that he had to kill Bart Vogan. For killing Danny Reese and for killing his father.

But killing Bart Vogan was not enough. He had to kill Dow Pierce and as many of the rest of them as he could.

Enough to finish what his father started. To rid Mason City of them, whether Mason City deserved to be rid of them or not.

That's what his father had intended to do, and now, so did he. The words that he had spoken to Rosemary in the cemetery came back to him.

"There's a lot of us going to die in this town. I'm going to try to be the last."

The man in the wheelchair had been listening to the slavering voice of Ainsley Zecker since the little man had come practically stumbling into the place a few minutes ago. Finally, Brad Tompkins managed to interrupt.

"You might as well save your breath, Zecker. You're talkin' to the wrong man. I told you before; I signed the store over to my son. It's up to him."

"Sure, sure, Brad. But you and me, we're old-timers. I just thought you'd understand the situation . . ."

"See if Gary does. He's the owner now."

"Sure, sure. I'll do that."

Gary Tompkins stood in front of the counter near the cash register. He was tall, thin, and pale, with a slanting brow and brittle, brown hair, not an imposing man in spite of his height. He was narrow of shoulder and lantern-jawed but not homely. The sum of his features was somehow not as skewed as the parts. Rosemary and her son stood nearby.

"Gary, please, you've got to let me have them provisions." Zecker's voice was as unctuous as ever. "You heard what I said to your pa."

"I heard."

"They promised me a share of the mine. I'll have lots of money . . ."

"Like you had before, Zecker. Always paid cash and always demanded a discount, a big discount."

"Well, that was business."

"So's this."

"No, it ain't; this is survival, Gary, survival for all of us. For all of us that help 'em."

"You only ever wanted to help yourself, Zecker. Never wanted to do anything that'd help this town. Not once if it would cost you a dime."

"All that's past. Don't be a damn fool, Gary. I already put in a good word for you. They've left you alone so far, you and your . . . family, haven't they? Well that's on account of me. They listen to me. They like me."

"You ought to be proud of that."

"I am . . . in a way. It don't pay to get 'em mad at you . . ."

"And you always do what pays."

"And what do you do, Gary? I didn't see you goin' off to war."

"No, I didn't, and I'm not proud of that. But that don't mean I have to be like you."

"This is crazy. You're crazy, plum crazy!" Zecker yelled.

"Maybe I am. But for you, it's cash and carry. Why don't you walk across the street to the bank and get a loan?"

"The bank's closed. You know that."

"That's right, and I know why. So do you, and it's going to stay closed till that gang leaves town. You picked your side Zecker, right from the start, as soon as that bunch rode in. You couldn't wait to fall all over 'em. We had a chance at the beginning if we'd backed the sheriff, but we didn't . . ."

"Including you."

"That's right, including me."

"Gary, you've got to do this. Everything I got left's at stake."

"Just what *have* you got left, Zecker?"

"But what'll I tell 'em?"

"Tell 'em cash and carry, just like always. They got money. Get a loan from them."

"You're a damn fool. You'll regret this!" Zecker turned in a fury, stormed out, and slammed the door behind him.

"He's right, son," Brad Tompkins said. "You will regret it. I'm afraid we all will."

"Maybe so. But I'm not helping Zecker. At least not yet. Let him sweat. Rosemary, you stay here. Lock that door. I'm going out the back."

"Where are you going?" she asked.

"I'm going to do my best to stop some killing."

"Please Gary, be careful."

"I've always been careful."

FORTY

There was a knock outside of the side door of the sheriff's office.

Yuma and Jess Evans looked at each other. The deputy's hand trembled a little as he wiped his dry lips.

"Go ahead and answer it, Jess. I don't think Dow Pierce or any of the rest of them are going to waste time knocking."

The deputy nodded, tried to smile, walked to the door, and opened it.

"Come in, Clay," Evans said. "Come on in."

The boy stepped into the room and cleared his throat as if getting ready to deliver a prepared speech.

"My dad . . . my dad, he . . . he . . ."

"Take it easy, Clay." Johnny Yuma took a couple of steps closer to the boy. "Just take your time and tell us. Is your dad all right?"

"Yes, sir, but . . ."

"But what?"

"Well, first off, he asked me to give you this." The boy fished into his shirt pocket and pulled out a folded piece of paper. "Ma wrote it for him on account of Pa can't read much or write any." Clay Bevins still held a tight grip on the paper.

"Okay." Yuma smiled. "You want to give it to me now?"

"Sure." He lifted the paper up toward the Rebel.

Johnny took it, smiled at the boy, looked at Jess Evans, and started to unfold the note.

"Thanks," Yuma said and read the note to himself.

Johnny—your horse is shoed, rested, and fit to ride. I told Clay to tie him out back of the sheriff's office. For everybody's sake, including yourself, get out of town right now before bullets start flying like hornets and more people get killed, including you.

Good Luck,
Clem

PS—Sorry about your dad. He was a good man.

Johnny Yuma handed the note to the deputy.

"Okay, Clay. Thanks for bringing it over. Did your dad say how much I owe him for taking care of the horse?"

"He said to tell you, if you asked, that there was no charge. He was glad to do it for you."

"I see. Well, all right son, thanks."

"It's out back . . ."

"What?"

"Your horse. It's out back. Pa told me to put it there so those men in the saloon won't see it."

"That's fine," Johnny said.

"Are you?"

"Am I what?"

"Are you gonna leave?"

Yuma looked again at Jess Evans, who had finished reading the note and was watching Johnny.

"We'll see. But I'm going to ask you to do me a favor, okay?"

"I don't know . . . could I get . . . get . . ."

"Hurt?"

The boy nodded.

"No. Nobody's going to hurt you." Yuma walked to his saddlebag slung over the straight-backed chair, flipped the bag open, and took out the envelope with the letter Oliver Knight had written to Elmer Dodson. And he took out a coin from his pocket.

"Clay, you go out the back and take this over to Mr. Dodson at the *Bulletin*, and here's a hard dollar for you."

"A whole dollar?"

"Will you do it?"

"You bet I will," the boy answered.

"And tell your father I said thanks."

"Sure . . . but . . . are you?"

"Get going, son."

The boy nodded, put the dollar in his pocket, and ran out of the open door as fast as he could.

Yuma walked over to the deputy, took the note from him, tore it to pieces, and let the pieces flutter to the floor.

"Clem Bevins is the biggest, strongest man in this town. I remember seeing him crack walnuts between his thumb and forefinger. And now he's afraid to show his face," Yuma said.

"They all are, Johnny. I guess I should say *we* all are. Ever since . . ." Evans stopped in the middle of the sentence. Both he and Yuma saw him in the open doorway at the same time.

Gary Tompkins.

"Can I talk to you, Johnny?"

"Aren't you taking a risk coming over here?"

"Not as big a risk as you are. Not nearly."

"Johnny," Jess Evans said, "I'll be right back. There's somethin' I got to tend to." The deputy walked through the open doorway past Gary Tompkins.

Tompkins stepped into the room and closed the door behind him. The two men stood for a moment in silence.

"I see that your horse is out back." Gary Tompkins broke the silence.

"Shoed, rested, and fit to ride, according to Clem Bevins. He sent his boy over with a note. Seems that nobody in town is anxious to be seen with me."

"It seems that way."

"Then what're you doing here?"

"I know that Rosemary talked to you at the cemetery. She and the boy."

"Spying on her, were you?" Johnny asked.

"She told me . . . afterward."

"Yeah." Yuma nodded. "I'm sorry I said that. She would tell you. I should've known that."

"She's always told me everything, Johnny. I always knew where I stood—and still do."

"Yeah, I guess it hasn't been easy for you, at that."

"Easier than it's been for you. I didn't go to war. I didn't lose my father . . . and all the time, I've been able to be with her."

"And the boy."

"Yes. That part wasn't so easy. A lot of people knew, and they know now, that Jed's not my son. We were going to tell him as soon as he got old enough to understand."

"Tell him what?"

"Well, it depended on how things turned out. Maybe we

would tell him that his father was a soldier and that he died in the war."

"Too bad he didn't die. But he didn't. So then what were you going to tell him?"

"We just weren't quite sure. But for sure we were going to tell him someday that I'm not his father—and that's pretty plain just looking at him—and looking at you."

"All right," Johnny Yuma said. "So I'm alive, and now I'm back, and what're you going to do about it? You still haven't told me why you're here."

Silence.

"Well, why?" This time, Yuma broke the silence. "Tompkins, you've been pretty damn noble about this whole thing. Are you being noble now?"

"No."

"Then, what?"

"Johnny," Gary Tompkins spoke slowly and the words were painful, "I know you never liked me. I never was a very likable fella. I was spoiled rotten and always got what I wanted and mostly without having to work for it or earn it. I took everything any way I could—including Rosemary."

"You don't have to justify anything to me. I'm not . . ."

"Maybe I don't. But some things I got to justify to myself."

"And that's why you're here?" Johnny asked.

"No."

"Then why?"

"To ask you to leave."

"That figures."

"Not for the reason you think."

"No? Then suppose you go ahead and explain it."

"If you go up against them, they'll kill you."

"Then your troubles'll be over," Johnny said.

"Not if she watches it and watches you die. Then I'll have to live with your ghost for the rest of our lives. I've got a chance against a human being. I don't know how much of a chance . . . but I can't fight a ghost."

"There's not much I can do about it."

"Yes, there is."

"What?"

"Like I said, leave now. Sooner or later, Pierce and his gang'll take what they came for and go away. Then, if you want to come back, what happens'll be up to her and you . . . and maybe me." Gary Tompkins looked away from Yuma and toward the floor.

"You know something, Gary?"

"What?"

"You're pretty damn noble, after all. But there's only one thing you forgot. The most important thing."

"What's that?"

"You forgot that those bastards killed my father . . . and some other people. You forgot that in order to get what they want, they're liable to kill some more people, maybe even you and Rosemary and Jed. You forgot that, didn't you?"

"I guess I did. But aren't you forgetting something, too?" Gary asked. "What're the odds? You against all of them? What chance have you got?"

"Not much, I suppose, if any. But if during the war there were times we stopped to think about that when we had to take a hill or a barn or a bridge, we would've turned tail and run. If I do that now, then I'll have to live with that for the rest of my life. And you know something, Gary? It wouldn't be worth it, and I just plain can't do it."

"Well, what are you going to do? And how're you going to do it?"

"I'm not sure, yet. But I know one thing; I can't do it

just waiting here for them to come after me. We had a captain in the Third who used to say, 'Always ride into the sound of the guns.' "

"Johnny . . ."

"Look, you tried. And no matter what happens, I'll remember that, and I'll know that you'll take care of Rosemary and the boy just like you've been doing. So, thanks for coming over here, and thanks for trying. Now, go back the way you came . . . and tell Rosemary . . ."

"Yes?"

"Nothing. Just take care of them and yourself. They need you."

Tompkins nodded. He walked to the side door and opened it. Standing there were Jess Evans and Emily Zecker.

"Well, hello, Gary!" Emily said.

"Mrs. Zecker."

"I'm . . . well, I . . ."

"What is it, Mrs. Zecker?"

"It's just that I . . . well, I must say that I'm surprised to see you here with . . ."

"Yeah," Gary Tompkins said in a not polite tone, "I guess you would be."

"My husband was going over to the store to talk to you. Did he?"

"He came over," Gary answered.

"Did everything work out?"

"You better talk to him about that."

"Well, I'm sure it did. You always were a sensible young man," Emily said.

"Yes ma'am, I always have been. But that's not what you told people when I married Rosemary." Gary Tompkins brushed by her and walked out the door.

"Johnny!" Emily Zecker turned and faced Yuma.

"Well, Johnny," Jess Evans said, "I guess I better go out for another walk. I ran into your aunt just as I was coming back and . . ."

"No, Jess," Yuma said. "You stay here."

Elmer Dodson was reading the letter that young Clay Bevins had delivered.

Dear Mr. Dodson,

Although we've never met, you have been mentor, model, and inspiration to me and hundreds of others in the field of journalism and the cause of justice. Your wisdom and courage have been a flaming sword that has lighted the way for the rest of us to follow in your footsteps, however feebly, in pursuit of truth and honor.

Johnny Yuma told me that you never had sons of your own, but please rest assured, sir, that we—the hundreds of newspapermen whom you have inspired through the years— we all of us consider you the teacher and father of our great family.

Johnny is a fine young man, and you must be very proud of him, as he is of you.

Milton said, "They also serve who only stand and wait"— he could have added those who write—who illuminate and lead the way as you have done and, I know, will continue to do.

We who write, and who have read and pursued the principles of Elmer Dodson, will hold your banner high as long as we live and guard it with our sacred honor.

Gratefully,
Oliver Knight

Elmer Dodson set the letter on his desk. He looked across the room at the broken press. He rose and walked to the filing cabinet where he kept copies of the editorials he had written through the years.

At Zecker's Saloon, Pierce and his men were playing poker, all but one of the twins, Tom, who stood at the batwings looking onto the deserted street. Bart Vogan was wearing his clothes again—wrinkled, but dry—and his guns, loaded.

"Three aces!" Dow Pierce exclaimed. "And it's about time I won me a pot!"

"Not yet." Slim smiled. "All blue." He raked in the money from the center of the table and added it to the pile already in front of him.

"Son of a bitch!" Pierce exploded. "You're either the luckiest bastard I ever come across or . . ."

"Or what, Dow?" Slim was still smiling. "You dealt 'em. I just played 'em. Ain't that right?"

"Yeah! Yeah! Hey Tim, come over here and get in this game. Might change my luck . . . and his." Pierce pointed to Slim.

"I'm Tom," the twin said. "Tim's already sittin' in."

"Well, Tim or Tom, whichever one you are, get your ass over here, too."

"Don't you want me to look out?"

"I want you to come over here and get in this damn game."

"But . . ."

"But do what I tell you. There's nothin' gonna happen out there till I make it happen. Now, you come over here and sit between me and him." Again he pointed to Slim, who covered his mouth as he coughed.

"Mr. Pierce . . ." Ainsley Zecker stood just inside the

open kitchen door. He had come in the back way and had been standing out of sight until he worked up enough nerve to speak.

"What is it, Zecker? Can't you see I'm busy?"

"Yes, sir, I see that."

"Did you get them provisions?"

"Well, that's what I want to talk to you about, Mr. Pierce."

"Johnny!" Emily Zecker repeated. She went to her nephew and kissed him on the cheek as he stood rigid, tolerating it. "You've gotten to be a strapping young man, haven't you?"

Yuma said nothing. Jess Evans walked toward the front window and looked out onto the street.

"Well, now," Emily Zecker continued as she realized that nobody was going to speak. "How does your Aunt Emmy look to you?"

"You look the same," Yuma replied. "Just the same."

"Well, why haven't you come by to see me?"

"I thought you were too busy catering to your brother's killers."

"Johnny, that's not fair!" An expression of hurt, of reason, and then almost, but not quite, of indignation came across her face and into her voice. "We're tryin' to keep things goin' . . . tryin' to keep the town together. That's what we're doin', Johnny."

"Is it?"

"Somebody around here has to show some sense," she said.

"You trying to make sense with the ones who killed your brother?"

"Johnny . . ."

"Is that it?"

"Just cause your pa was a fool doesn't mean the rest of us don't have to go on livin'."

"Oh, you'll go on living all right, any way you . . ."

"He let himself be goaded into bein' shot dead. He was a fool, Johnny . . ."

"What about the other ones they killed?"

"It was all on account of him. He . . ."

"Don't you talk that way about my father."

"What did he ever do for you, Johnny? He thought more about law and duty and honor and a bunch of words than he did about his own family."

"And you never thought about anything but your own skin."

"Why'd you run away a dozen times before you was fifteen? Why'd you go to war? To fight for a cause? You didn't know about any cause! It was just another kind of running away. Well, why don't you keep on running? All you can do around here is cause trouble for the rest of the town."

"You don't care about the rest of the town."

"I came here to help you. To get you to leave before it was too late."

"You, too, huh? First, everybody wanted me to come back; now, everybody wants me to get out. Well, I'll get out when I'm damn ready."

"You don't go now, you'll never get out. You'll be buried back there with your . . . listen to me, you young fool!"

"You're just thinking about yourself and your bootlicking husband."

Emily Zecker walked toward the side door, opened it, then looked back. Her voice was bitter and her lips tight as she looked across the room at her nephew, her brother's son.

"Oh, all you Yumas hold your nose when Zecker walks

by 'cause you can't stand the scent of good sense. Well, Zecker knows what he wants. He wants to take care of what's his! He's smart! He's what a husband should be. Smart and sensible!''

She walked out and slammed the door.

Dow Pierce slapped Zecker's face, hard.

"You had no cause to do that, Mr. Pierce." Ainsley Zecker cowed and trembled. "I've tried to help you right from the start . . . to cooperate. All I'm askin' for is part of what you owe me . . . just so I can get provisions for you.''

"And that's just what you're gonna do, Zecker.''

"It's that damn Tompkins kid. Like I told you, he's stubborn.''

"So am I . . . and the sight of you makes me puke.''

"Why do you talk like that, Mr. Pierce? I've been the only one to help you." Zecker reached into his back pocket. "I've got bills here . . .''

Dow Pierce's fist smashed into Zecker's face before he could finish. Zecker fell into Bart Vogan's arms. Vogan spun him around and, laughing, pounded his fist into Zecker's rib cage, then pushed him back toward Pierce.

Pierce's hawser hands grabbed hold of the dazed man and dragged him toward the batwings.

"If the provisions aren't here in an hour, I'm comin' after them and Tompkins . . . and you!" Pierce hit Zecker again, sending him reeling through the swinging doors.

Jess Evans, looking out the front window from the sheriff's office, saw Zecker pitch through the batwings, spin across the boardwalk, and tumble onto the dirt of Main Street.

"Johnny!"

The deputy pointed, and Yuma walked to the window in time to see Emily Zecker and a couple of other citizens, an older man and woman, helping Zecker to his feet. As he struggled to maintain his balance and wipe the blood from his mouth, two other men appeared and steered Zecker toward Tompkins General Store.

"That's the way it is, Johnny," Deputy Jess Evans said. "You can't fight 'em, and you can't even do business with 'em."

"Well, I've got no notion of doing business with them."

"We're all of us changed, Johnny, mostly me." He removed the hat from his head and wiped the sweat off the headband with his hand. "They shamed me. They called me down, and I ran. I ran straight for a bottle."

"Jess . . ."

"I got no right wearin' this badge. It's just got too heavy for me since they killed your Pa."

At the saloon, Pierce, Vogan, and the other men were near the entrance, watching, all but Slim who still sat at the poker table with almost all of everybody's money stacked in front of him. Slim poured himself another shot from the bottle. All afternoon he had been winning and drinking— and coughing.

Dow Pierce turned from the street and started to walk toward the kitchen in the back of the saloon.

"Slim, you come with me. I want to talk to you." Pierce reached into the cigar box on the bar, took out a stogie, and moved to the room in the rear.

"Close the door," Pierce said as he lit the cigar after Slim followed him in.

"What's this about?" Slim asked as he closed the kitchen door.

"It's about me wantin' to talk to you."

"What for?"

"You sober?" Pierce asked.

"Sober enough."

"Good. Slim, you know who was the smartest man in the war those idiots fought?"

"No. Who?"

"Quantrill. Colonel William Clarke Quantrill. That's who."

"What's that got to do with us here?"

"Just listen. He was the smartest 'cause he didn't give a damn who won, just so he got his share of the loot and more. That's what it's got to do with us. You and me."

"What the hell are you talking about?"

"Just this." Pierce took a long draw from the cigar and let the smoke drift from between his teeth as he talked. "Once we get that gold outta that mine, we don't have no use for the rest of 'em out there. Now, I got me an idea in mind so just the two of us end up with the whole caboodle. Enough to last us for the . . ."

"For the rest of our lives?" Slim finished.

"Yeah, that's it."

"Only you know that I don't have much time left, don't you. So that'd leave just you with the whole caboodle. That's it, too, isn't it?"

"Slim . . ."

"And maybe you wouldn't even wait that long," Slim said.

"Slim . . ."

"If you'd double-cross them, why wouldn't you do the same to . . ."

"Hell no, Slim, you and me'd be partners."

"So are they. I think your partners ought to know what kind of son of a bitch . . ."

This time Slim didn't finish. Pierce drew and fired twice into Slim's chest. Slim coughed one last time and was dead before his head hit the chopping block. His body slumped to the kitchen floor.

When Dow Pierce walked back into the saloon, all of the men were on their feet, facing the back room. Bart Vogan had drawn both his guns.

"Put them irons away," Pierce said as he entered, still puffing on the cigar.

"What the hell happened?" Miller asked.

"I had to drill him. That son of a bitch was aiming to double-cross us."

"I thought *you're* the one who wanted to talk to him," Miller said.

"I did, 'cause I had my suspicions." Pierce walked across to the poker table and sat down. "And I was right." He raked the pile of money from where Slim had sat to his side of the table. "Now, let's play poker. Bart, you keep an eye on the street for a while in case anybody gets nervous on account of them gunshots."

Yuma and Jess Evans both had heard the shots. So did most everybody else in town.

"Johnny, what do you think happened?" Evans asked.

"I don't know, but it's about time I made something happen."

Yuma started to take off the gun belt he had been wearing as he walked to the belt, badge, gun, and hat that hung on the wall peg. He placed his own gun and holster on the desk and strapped on his father's. He unpinned the star that had been attached to the holster, held it in his palm for just a beat, then put it on the desk. He drew his father's gun out of its holster and started to check the chambers.

"It's loaded, Johnny," the deputy said. "I loaded it myself after . . . I don't know why, I just did."

Yuma nodded and holstered the Colt.

"Johnny, you can't face 'em down all alone, you . . ."

"Jess, I'm getting awful sick of you whimpering and bellyaching." He walked toward the front door, opened it, then looked back. "And another thing. Quit following me around like some puppy dog. You're supposed to be a man." Johnny Yuma walked out and closed the door behind him.

Deputy Jess Evans watched Yuma cross in front of the window and head up Main Street; then Evans looked back at the nearly empty whiskey bottle still on the desk.

He licked his lips and walked toward it. He lifted the bottle and moved it close to his mouth.

Holding the bottle, the deputy looked out at the street again.

FORTY-ONE

Johnny Yuma walked, not fast not slow, east on Main Street, his eyes straight ahead. There was nobody on the boardwalk on either side or on the road. No people in sight. Not any horses hitched to the rails in front of the buildings. Not even a dog foraging for food or company. Just a cat sitting on a crate in front of a closed shop.

At least the cat's not black, Johnny thought to himself, *it's gray* . . . and he kept on walking.

"John."

It was the voice of Elmer Dodson. He stood just inside the open door of the *Bulletin*. He held an ancient pistol in his hand, hidden from view of the street. Yuma stepped into the doorway.

"John," he repeated.

"What is it, Mr. Dodson? What're you doing with that gun?"

"I thought about what you said, and I read that letter from Oliver Knight. Then I reread some of my old editorials. It may be that a man who listens to himself is twice a fool. John, I realize that my life wasn't all that it could've been, but I also realize that I've got to stay, maybe just long enough to write my own obituary. But I can still pull a trigger." He held up the old revolver, then nodded toward the room. "And I think I can fix that press."

"That's fine, Mr. Dodson, but there's more around here needs fixing than that press."

"What should we do, John?"

"You already did. Now, please, just stay inside . . . and thanks, Mr. Dodson." Yuma stepped outside and walked on.

"Hey, boys, lookee!" Bart Vogan's voice called out from the batwings at the saloon across the street. "Here comes the soljerboy again! And he's got his daddy's gun on! He wants to die the way his daddy did!"

Yuma did not slow down or react.

"You gonna be by your daddy's side, sonny. I'm gonna put you there when the time comes. I'm gonna stand on your face, Reb, and it'll six feet down! Me! Bart Vogan! Remember that, Reb!"

Yuma knew that Vogan would not face him alone, any more than any of them would have faced his father alone. Their kind always played the odds. It was up to Johnny Yuma to reduce those odds. The Rebel moved on. He walked until he came to the supply store, then turned and walked in under the sign.

TOMPKINS SUPPLIES
GENERAL STORE—MINING EQUIPMENT

"He went into the supply store." Bart Vogan reported to the men playing cards. "The Reb."

"So?" Dow Pierce said. "I got a full house."

"So nothin'! I just thought I'd tell you."

"So, you told me. Miller, how much time Zecker got left?"

Miller lifted a watch from his vest pocket and peered at it with his seeing eye.

" 'Bout a half hour, Dow."

"Well, then, let's play some more poker. Bart, you want in, this hand?"

"Sure." Vogan took another look toward the supply store and walked to the table as Pierce shuffled the deck.

Inside the store, Rosemary was cleaning Zecker's battered face and dabbing it with iodine while his wife held his hand. Brad Tompkins sat in his wheelchair. Gary stood behind the counter. Jed watched from a distance. The people who had helped bring Zecker from the street waited in silence.

They all turned and looked at Johnny Yuma as he approached the man at the counter.

"Gary, I'm going to ask you to do something. I need your help."

"You want me to get my rifle?"

Rosemary took a step forward before Yuma answered.

"No. The truth is, you'd just be in the way out there. But there is something else."

"Tell me."

"I want you to give me the key to the room back there."

Gary Tompkins hesitated. Rosemary watched and waited to see what he would do. So did everybody else in the room. But it was Brad Tompkins who spoke as he wheeled the chair toward his son.

"Gary, you better wait and think this . . ."

"Dad, we've all done too much waiting. Now, this is my store, and for once in my life . . ." Gary Tompkins didn't finish. He reached out near the cash register for the key on a large brass ring, picked it up, and handed it to Yuma.

Johnny Yuma took it and walked toward the door. He unlocked it, went inside, and closed the door behind him.

"What's he gonna do in there?" Emily Zecker asked.

Nobody answered. Nobody knew. But they all looked toward the sign on the door of the room.

DANGER

DO NOT ENTER

Inside Zecker's Saloon, Pierce, Vogan, Miller, and the twins, Tim and Tom, were still playing poker. Bart Vogan was seated next to Pierce.

"Dow."

"What?"

"What're you doin'? I mean with that Johnny Reb out there? Ain't we gonna . . ."

"Sure we're 'gonna'. When I say so. Bart, you ever see a cat play with a mouse? Sometimes the mouse goes plum crazy without the cat's ever really hurtin' him."

"Huh?"

"You had your fun with him; now I'm havin' mine. Only this time, it's gonna turn out different. We're playin' draw, jacks or better to open, deuces wild. . . ."

They all stared in fascination, fear, and awe as Johnny Yuma stepped through the doorway of the back room . . . his Aunt Emmy, Zecker, Brad and Gary Tompkins, and everybody else in the store. Rosemary, with her hand on the young boy's shoulder, cried out, "Johnny!"

But Yuma kept moving past all of them without looking at any of them. He moved through the store and out the door onto the street, past another, smaller sign.

MINING EQUIPMENT
DYNAMITE

He turned and walked west toward the saloon. His right
hand hovered near his father's gun. The Rebel's left hand
held a homemade bomb with a lighted wick that hissed and
steadily burned down toward the payload.

Yuma's pace was unhurried, as if he had calculated with
military precision the distance to his destination against the
disappearing wick.

With each advancing step there was less of the wick left
... less ... and less ... and less.

The Rebel stopped in the middle of the street, directly in
front of the saloon. He looked down at the bomb with the
flickering wick, switched the bomb into his right hand, and
screamed the Rebel yell ... as he hurled the missile like a
grenade over the batwings and onto the floor of the building.

The explosion rocked the building, blasted off the batwings, splintered the doorway, and shattered the windows
into countless shards of jagged glass scattering onto the
street.

Black smoke billowed out of the ruptures, then white and
yellow flames flared up the front of the wrecked structure
as the charred men coughed and staggered out. Miller led
the way, wiping at his good eye, followed by Tim, then
Pierce and Bart Vogan. Tom was dead, his body burning
inside the ruins of the saloon.

Miller managed to pull his gun out of its holster. In a
smooth hook and draw, Yuma's father's gun was leveled,
and the Rebel started to cock the hammer and he squeezed
the trigger.

But the hammer stuck. He tried to fan it with his left
palm. Still stuck.

As Miller fired, so did someone else: Deputy Jess Evans from beside a wagon on the street. Miller took the shot between his good eye and blind eye and dropped.

"Johnny!" Evans hollered.

Yuma spun as Jess Evans stepped out and tossed him the sawed-off shotgun.

"Scattergun, Johnny!"

Yuma dropped the Colt and caught the shotgun. He rolled onto the ground, cocking one of the hammers of the double-barreled scattergun.

Tim fired at Yuma but missed. Jess Evans didn't. Tim shrieked and fell.

Dow Pierce shambled through the smoke and aimed, but Yuma squeezed off a blast that tore into Pierce and pitched him back through the broken window.

"Vogan! Bart Vogan!" Yuma yelled.

Vogan's answer from out of the smoke was two fast shots that winged past the Rebel. The second shot seared his shoulder, but Yuma blasted off the other shotgun barrel through the smoke and haze at the sound of the gunfire.

Bart Vogan caught the load in his chest and face. He lurched backward and fell on the boardwalk, twitching.

Yuma looked at Jess Evans and nodded. Still holding the scattergun, the Rebel moved closer to where Vogan lay.

He leaned down. Vogan was still breathing, barely.

"Vogan. Bart Vogan. Can you hear me?"

Vogan's eyes blinked.

"It's Yuma. Third Texas. Lee's Army of Northern Virginia. I was on that bridge at Appomattox. *Johnny Yuma. Remember it . . . in hell.*"

FORTY-TWO

Through a Chinook wind, gentle and warm from the north-west, the morning sun caught the curvature of the thick, gleaming white tombstone between the two graves on the slanting green mantle of ground. The inscription, recently carved, was chiseled deep—deep enough to be there through the end of the century and long beyond.

YUMA

ELIZABETH YUMA   NED YUMA
1824–1850   1820–1866

LOVING
WIFE AND HUSBAND

BELOVED
MOTHER AND FATHER

Johnny Yuma knelt near the flowers he had placed at the base of the tombstone. A mother long dead, a mother he barely remembered. A father murdered just days ago, a father he should have known better. The sadness of a lone son kneeling near the graves of his mother and father.

A slender shadow appeared on the tombstone. The Rebel knew without looking.

"Johnny," Rosemary said. "Jed and I picked some wild-flowers. Would it be all right if I put them next to yours?"

Yuma nodded.

She placed the flowers beside the ones already at the tombstone. Johnny rose.

In the distance, Gary Tompkins stood next to the boy near the church, close enough to watch but not to listen.

"Mr. Dodson said you were leaving this morning."

"In just a few minutes."

"Johnny, will you ever come back? Will you ever settle down?"

"Maybe I'll come back someday . . . and I suppose I'll settle down sometime, someplace . . . but not here. I couldn't do that, Rosemary. I couldn't look at you every day and not touch you or hold you . . . or him. I couldn't even try."

"I know."

"Do you, Rosemary? Do you?"

"I read in a poem, just a short time ago: 'Of all sad words of tongue or pen, the saddest are these—it might have been.' "

"Not always. Things usually work out for the best. We've got to keep thinking that, both of us. Promise you will."

"I will, Johnny." She kissed him gently on the side of his face. "But I'll always remember."

"So will I, Rosemary."

They walked toward the church where Gary Tompkins and the boy waited.

"Jed." Rosemary tried hard to compose herself. "You say so long to . . . Mr. Yuma."

"So long, Mr. Yuma. Why do you have to go?"

"I just do, son." Yuma didn't mean to call him that, but it was too late.

"Why?" the boy repeated.

"Someday you'll understand." He turned to Rosemary. "Mrs. Tompkins, you've got two good men here."

"Three," said Gary Tompkins and put out his hand.

Johnny Yuma and Gary Tompkins shook hands.

"So long." The Rebel turned and started to walk.

"Johnny," Rosemary called. Yuma looked back. "We'll put fresh flowers on the graves."

"Thanks."

Johnny Yuma turned from Church Street onto Main Street. Ainsley and Emily Zecker were crossing toward him, away from the ruins of the saloon.

"Johnny!" Emily Zecker said. "We don't want you to go . . ."

"Don't you?" Yuma didn't even slow down.

"Why, no. Zecker and me, we'd like you to stay and help us build up the business."

"You'll get your fair share," Zecker added.

"And so will you," Yuma said and kept walking as they stood and watched.

Clem Bevins and his son Clay were on the street not far from where the sorrel was tied.

"Johnny . . ." The huge man took a step forward, away from the boy. Since Yuma rode into town, this was the first time he had seen the blacksmith.

"Hello, Clem."

"We, all of us, everybody here, well . . . we owe you a lot for what you did for us."

"No, you don't, Clem. I'm glad I could help, but I didn't do it for you."

"But you . . ."

"I did it for . . ." Yuma didn't finish. "I appreciate you taking care of the horse."

Johnny Yuma moved toward the rail in front of the *Bulletin*, where the sorrel was tied and where Elmer Dodson and Deputy Jess Evans waited. Evans held the scattergun in his left hand. Yuma loosened the reins from the post and turned to the two men and smiled.

"Well, like Clem Bevins said, he's shoed, rested, and fit to ride . . . and so am I."

"Johnny." The deputy held out the scattergun. "I know your pa would want you to have it."

Yuma nodded and took the gun.

"John." Dodson put his hand on the Rebel's shoulder for just a moment. "Thanks for helping me fix that press, and for . . . other things."

"I thank you, Mr. Dodson, for everything."

"You sure you don't want to stay and . . ."

"No, sir. The things I got to find aren't here. This was just another stopping off place."

"I know that. Keep writing, John."

"I intend to. And I'd like to send you what I put down from time to time. Maybe you can keep it and help me fix it up later."

"I'd like to do that, son. You've got a lot to see, and I think one day you'll have a lot to say. But you can't write about it unless you've lived it."

Johnny Yuma put his boot into the stirrup and swung onto the saddle.

"Where'll you go?" Evans asked.

"Here and there." Yuma looked down from the sorrel. "And Jess, I don't think that badge is a bit heavy for you."

As he started to ride out, Gary Tompkins, Jed, and Rosemary turned off Church Street. They waved when he went by. Rosemary took a step forward from the others.

Johnny Yuma didn't look back as he rode along the street—the street where he had ridden in, just a short time ago, when he thought he had come home.

This morning I left Mason City. I stopped for a few minutes outside of town and looked up at the cave.

But that was part of the past. I thought about it for just a little while and about the war. Then I thought about the future. I heard General Grant say that we are all brothers again. And President Lincoln said that we must bind up the nation's wounds.

There's a lot to be done: railroads to be built and bridges— land west of the 100th Meridian to be surveyed and settled. And a lot of people still have to settle their differences and build bridges of brotherhood. I am a blood brother to the Kiowas, but the Kiowas and the Comanches hate each other and are at war, as was our country.

There never was a good war—except for what we learn from it. I'm still learning. And there never was a time and place like the American West. But much of the West still has to be fought for and won.

A lot of that will happen in the next few years. I want to write about it, but, as Mr. Dodson said, you can't write about it unless you've lived it.

I intend to do that—and now I'm turning west . . .